LITTER

A FIRST NOVEL
by
LES ROSS

Published by

Malvern Publishing Company Limited
PO Box 16
Malvern
Worcestershire
WR14 1UH
England

ISBN - 0-947993-04-5

Printed and bound in Great Britain by
Sharp Bros. (Printers) Ltd., Evesham, Worcs.

DEDICATION

To my wife and daughter with thanks for their
patience and forebearance.

CHAPTER ONE

"As veritable seats of learning. Ve-ri-tab-le." Dryden paused.

"Leave it out, Sir. We can't spell that."

"It's up on the board, Bryce."

"What's it mean?"

Dryden sighed: "It means 'real', 'proper'."

"I'll write proper then."

"Suit yourself."

He glanced at his notes.

"As veritable seats of learning . . . the monastic foundations of the Baroque . . ."

Pens clattered angrily on desk tops. There was a mutinous scraping of chairs. Dryden sat down. The class looked at one another expectantly. He cupped his hands above his eyes and waited. There was still a full half hour of the lesson to go.

"Can I go to the toilet, Sir?" He looked up. Laura was already making for the door.

"Laura, can't you wait?"

"Nah. Need to go."

"I think, Laura, that at your age we should really wait for the bell." The class tittered at his use of the word 'we'. Dryden ignored it.

"Look, Sir," Laura said crossly, "I need to go."

Bryce, a minute youth with short cropped hair and little gold earrings leaned back in his chair and grinned at her.

"What you grinnin' at?" She dealt him a stinging blow across the cheek. Bryce's grin vanished. He sat bolt upright. Dryden closed his eyes. When he opened them again Laura had left the room. He looked around the class wearily.

"Shall we continue?"

"We can't, Sir," came a chorus of voices. "Laura's gone to the toilet.

Dryden shrugged. Of course, it wasn't fair. Laura had gone to the toilet. If he continued with his notes while she was occupied elsewhere she would miss them. And if she missed them she couldn't learn them. And if she couldn't learn them, she wouldn't get the mark in the European Studies Test she felt she deserved. This, in time, would bring Laura's large and formidable mother along to the school to interview Dryden. Wrapped in the polite middle-class conventions of the interview would be an unmistakable threat. It was not for nothing that Laura's mother cultivated friends who were on the Board of Governors.

Glumly, he gazed out of the window at the spire of Great Battley Church. The class had now resumed general conversation. A hum of teenage voices discussed the topics of current interest: violent race riots in Birmingham and a gruesome murder in North London.

Strategy, Dryden thought, mustering his years of experience negotiating with the younger generation. But this was beyond strategy. Monastic foundations of the Baroque? It was ghastly, irretrievably ghastly. He had sunk deeper and deeper into the quagmire of European Studies. He was beyond rescue.

Laura re-entered the classroom, delighted to find that general conversation prevailed. On the race riots in Birmingham opinions were divided. There were those who thought that Blacks and Asians should be shot and those who thought they should all be sent back to where they came from in the first place (the more Liberal view). There had been a time when Dryden would have intervened in the discussion, horrified at such reactionary views in adolescent minds. He would have gone on at great length about civil rights in the United States, about the fact that West Indians were actively recruited to come to Britain in the nineteen-fifties, about black identity, black unemployment, black this and black that. He would have packed them off with a large liberal flea in the ear. Now he was too tired. He glanced at his watch. Ten minutes to the bell. He gathered up his notes, resisted a sudden, almost overpowering urge to hurl them into the waste-paper bin and set about re-organising his briefcase. This was something he did when he didn't know what else to do. Oblivious to him now, his class chatted on happily, as he fished out bundles of unmarked essays, a shrivelled apple-core, a broken ruler, several paper clips and a white board marker that had gone hard. Finally, he turned his briefcase upside down over the waste-paper bin and shook it. After that operation he felt decidedly better. There were only two minutes of the lesson left.

Four minutes later the bell rang. For the third time that morning Dryden altered his watch to coincide with school time. Still, he thought, with luck the next lesson would finish eight minutes early. There was a deafening scrape of chairs. Heavy teenage bodies lurched tiredly towards the door.

"See ya, Sir," Laura called back to him cheerfully. He grimaced. With a sigh of relief he picked up his briefcase, glanced at the board on which the words 'veritable' and 'Baroque' were scrawled in letters two inches high, decided to leave them there to impress whoever was teaching in the room next and made for the door. He almost collided with a figure standing just inside the room.

"Sir?" From beneath a thatch of red hair an earnest spotty face peered up at him.

"Yes, Ian, got a problem?" Ian always had problems. Dryden silently ground his teeth. God, he was desperate for a fag!

"Well—it's just that—I looked over my notes last night, like you told us, Sir, for homework and—well—I don't understand them."

"Oh, really?" Dryden smiled unctuously. "I thought they were perfectly clear." He shot a wistful glance at the door.

"Not to me, Sir. My dad couldn't understand them either. And he's got four 'A' levels."

"I see." Dryden put down his satchel. The boy's light blue eyes watched him like those of a cat.

"What is it exactly that you don't understand, Ian?" Dryden's voice was soft, earnest, caring.

"It's all of it, Sir. I don't understand any of it." Dryden took the proffered notes and frowned at the lines of neat, legible handwriting.

'The rich profusion of theological and historical themes,' he read, 'in the Church painting of the Baroque period testifies to the scholarly collaboration of the Church dignitaries who awarded the commissions. The iconography of the many libraries illustrates perfectly how interrelating ideas have become an integral part of the decorative function . . .' His eyes glazed over. God, what a hell of a lesson that had been! Amidst cries of outrage he had doggedly written the notes up on the board. 'Leave it out. Not more bloody notes,' they had shouted. And it was only yesterday, too. It seemed more like ten years ago, for until this precise moment he had successfully blotted it out of his mind altogether. Wearily, he pulled up a chair and sat down. Four 'A' levels indeed, he thought venomously. The boy's father, a production controller at Fords, was a menace to the whole teaching profession. He was the sort that came along to parents' evenings to give teacher hell. On his son's last report he had penned insulting comments such as 'This mark is hardly surprising considering the incompetence of the Maths Staff' or 'I'm sure my son's sound examination mark in History was due in large measure to the help I gave him with his revision, in the course of which I discovered to my consternation and, I might add, to that of my wife, Susan . . .'

"Well, Ian," Dryden glanced at the youth wearily. "I realise that some of the words are quite difficult. Have you by any chance got a dictionary at home?"

"Yes, Sir. My dad bought me the new Webster's for my last birthday."

Dad would, Dryden thought grimly. He smiled sweetly at the lad. "I suggest, Ian, that you sit down with these notes when you've got a bit of

3

spare time and look up all the words you don't know in that new dictionary of yours. Then, write them out carefully. That will help you to spell them won't it?" He watched the boy's face closely, trying to gauge whether he had swallowed it. He had.

"Then," Dryden went on triumphantly, "if you're still having trouble with them in a day—week or two—then come back to me and we'll go through it together. Okay?" This was a particulary cunning move on his part, Dryden thought to himself. With luck the boy would get tired of it all and forget about it. Ian gave him a glum look. Dryden frowned at him.

"Of course," he added hastily, "I could sit down with you now, Ian, but . . ." He glanced ostentatiously at his watch, "I've got a very urgent meeting in a few minutes and . . . uh . . . I can't spare the time at the moment." To underline this urgency Dryden picked up his briefcase. The red haired youth sighed, replaced the notes in his bag and followed Dryden out of the room.

There were always a few, he thought, as he hurried along the corridor. What with video nasties and electronic games one would have thought kids like Blotchy Face were extinct long ago. But no, there were still those thirsting for an education, those who still refused to believe it was a complete waste of time.

He opened the door of the Resources Room.

"Dryden" A nasal, drawling voice penetrated his consciousness as he leaned against the door for a second or two, his eyes closed. "I don't know whether you remember collecting in those Third Year textbooks last summer but according to my records there are still six outstanding." Dryden opened his eyes. Stephen Mott was sitting at the table, in front of him a sheaf of immaculate textbook lists.

"Oh," Dryden said. "Oh yes. Come to think of it, there probably are. I'd forgotten actually."

"I thought you probably had," Mott drawled triumphantly. "It was lucky I didn't. I'll show you the list if you like."

"No, don't bother," Dryden waved his hand tiredly. "I'll take your word for it. Six, did you say?"

"That's right. I've written all the names on a memo. It's in your pigeon-hole in the staff common room."

"Thanks." Dryden turned to open the door.

"Just before you go. Could you see to it that they bring them in tomorrow? If possible, I'd like to get the lists up to date by Friday. Maurice says we'll have to know exactly how many new books are needed so that capitation estimates are as accurate as possible."

"Sure." Dryden opened the door.

"Just one more thing, Dryden. You know we all agreed at the last meeting about locking the resources cupboard after school. I'll get the minutes if you like."

4

"No, I remember," Dryden said wearily.

"Well, I think you were supposed to do it last evening. When I arrived this morning the cupboard was still open."

"Christ, was it?" Dryden feigned horror.

"Yes it was. I've put a memo in your pigeon hole, just a reminder not to forget it again tonight."

"Okay, fine. That's two memos then."

"Three actually." The voice trilled in triumph. "One from Maurice. He wants that UCCA form by this afternoon. Funny thing was, he thought you might have given it back to him. He even asked me if I had it? I told him you probably still had it, so he's put a memo in your pigeon-hole about it."

He hurried downstairs to the common room, Mott's triumphant reminders still ringing in his ears. The common room was empty, save for a large pregnant P.E. woman hanging on to the receiver of the staff telephone in one corner. He extracted the three memos from his pigeon-hole, all three addressed to DKP and beginning re . . .', crumpled them up and hurled them into the waste paper basket. Seizing the Times Educational Supplement he collapsed into an armchair and leafed through it angrily to the last few pages. Botswana was in again, he saw. So was Burundi. He tried to visualise himself standing in front of a class of black giants with quivering head-dresses. Or should it be pygmies? Bermuda? Palm trees and long white beaches? The P.E. woman gazed at him, a vacant smile on her face. Her pregnancy seemed to have captured the imagination of the whole school. Day after day it had been the focus of intense speculation. At some time or other almost everyone in the staff common room had listened to her stomach. Dryden and one or two other relics of a bygone age had naturally refused. It seemed to him almost that, if she suddenly gave birth on the premises, the whole school might indeed be summoned to watch. There was no doubting that the Head of Things Domestic, a power-crazed woman by the name of Nerys Hughes, would use this satisfying event to promote her new pedagogical passion, a subject of her own devising called Life Studies.

He tossed the Times Educational Supplement aside and set about making himself a cup of coffee. Over in the corner the P.E. woman shouted something about the Isle of Wight into the receiver. Was she informing the island's population of her pregnancy, Dryden wondered maliciously. He was at once overcome with shame. He was always malicious after one of his classes in European Studies. Like a threatening cloud his incompetence was hanging over him. He was failing on all fronts.

"Hello? Auntie?" The woman suddenly bellowed into the receiver. "It's George. I'm fine. How's uncle? He's out? Is Roger there? He's out too? Oh, what a pity. What's that? Oh, he's fine." Dryden poured hot water onto his coffee granules and retreated round the corner to the staff notice board. The woman's voice grew louder as she launched into the lurid details of the foetus. Dryden's eyes strayed to the headmaster's notice board. It was still there, he thought. Good old Basil! The notice concerned the Headmaster's prime obsession—litter.

'It has hardly escaped my notice,' Dryden read, 'that the litter situation in the below-mentioned areas has contributed immeasurably to the general non-compliance of a considerable minority of pupils to the specific regulations regarding the maintenance of school premises.' Perfect, Dryden chuckled. He warmed to Basil through the walls that at that moment separated them. At his best Basil was brilliant. By the judicious use of negatives he could expand the simplest verbal communication into a jungle of impenetrable contradictions. Elsewhere the English language might be collapsing into volleys of guttural monosyllables but in Basil's hands it was entering into new, undreamed of realms of Byzantine floridity.

'Notwithstanding this widespread dereliction,' he read further, 'of what is, after all, a principal objective of both pastoral and administrative criteria, the following proposals have been adopted . . .'

"Hullo there." The P.E. woman had rung off, sailed round the corner and dropped anchor next to Dryden. "You on lunch?"

"Yes. I hope I didn't disturb you . . ."

"Nah. Course not. That was my Auntie Tessa on the isle of Wight. She's got a new phone, you see, one of those new fangled push-button ones. She wrote me a letter to tell me to ring her up on it. Says it's fabulous. Much easier than dialling. She's got a bit of arthritis in her fingers, you see, and the push-buttons are just the thing." "I can imagine," Dryden blinked at her pleasantly. "I've only ever seen pictures of them, of course, but I believe they're fantastic to use." He let his eyes rove idly over the staff notice board. "I must say I get fed up with the dial phones sometimes." He looked round. The woman had vanished. Baffled, he stared at the space beside him where she had stood but a moment before. She must have moved at the speed of light, stomach and all. He shook his head and sighed. he had only wanted to appear interested out of politeness. People were peculiar, he reflected, the way they would suddenly come at you and deliver long speeches on odd topics like carburettors or paint thinner. His own good manners invariably obliged him to match their enthusiasm for these things. he would respond with some appropriately lengthy statement only to find they had disappeared. Or else they were suddenly indulging in violent fits of yawning. he had concluded there was definitely something missing in his make-up. Some normal sense for the appropriate.

He dithered about in front of the notice board and sipped his coffee. Then he heard the door open. For a moment he thought it was Rosie Kennedy, the Senior Mistress, clumping through the common room, checking up on layabouts. He peeped round the corner. A sallow, beaky face grinned back at him.

"How's my Rosie walk coming along?" Nathan Goldway clumped up to the notice board.

"It's chillingly authentic," Dryden said grimly. "I thought you were on lunch now?"

"And so I am. How long have you been skulking round here?"

"Since twelve." Dryden scowled at the dark little man who was Head of History.

"You look terrible. European Studies?"

"Yes, and there's nothing in Botswana, Burundi or Bermuda." Goldway grinned. "You'd hate it, mate. Shall we go?" Goldway asked.

The saloon bar of the Spotted dog had not yet filled with the usual crowd of lunchtime drinkers. Dryden and Goldway settled themselves in a corner with their pints of bitter and bags of crisps.

"Had a chat with your fancy this morning," Goldway grinned.

"She's got a lovely arse, hasn't she?"

"Yes. What pretext were you using to get that close?"

"It may not have escaped your notice that I am her Head of Department. As such it's my responsibility to ensure that she's coping. Besides, I didn't actually touch her arse—I only looked at it."

"I'm glad to hear it. Is she coping?"

"Brilliantly," Goldway said through a mouthful of crisps. "A comitted teacher, I'd say."

"Committed to what?"

"Teaching. Unlike you, dear boy, she didn't just answer an advert. in the Sits. Vac. column of an evening newspaper."

"She'll no doubt go far," Dryden murmured, suddenly taken aback at the hostile looks he was getting from a dangerous looking youth in an overall.

"By the way," Goldway leaned over the table, "Devereaux's noticed her too."

"Has he?" Any woman Dryden was interested in was usually the one that at least half a dozen others had their beady little eyes on. Devereaux sized up every new woman teacher as soon as she set foot on the premises. The man was married, for God's sake. Not that this was a question of morality, purely a question of consideration. There was nothing worse than a married man patrolling what should rightly be considered the preserve of the unmarried. The youth in the overall was now beginning to alarm Dryden with his murderous looks. He had never clapped eyes on him before in his life.

"I'm not surprised," Goldway observed. "Taken over all, she's not bad."

The youth had now put down his glass and was making his way towards them.

"Hullo, Sir?" He grinned down at Dryden manically. "Out for a drink are we?"

"Yes?" Dryden stared up at him, uncomprehending.

"I'd buy you one, Sir—'cept I ain't got no money." The tone was defiant.

"I'm unemployed see."

Dryden smiled and shook his head. "I'm sorry but I don't remember you."

"Lacey, Sir. I was in your tutor group." The youth's voice was loud now. "Don't you remember?"

Around them the conversation had stopped. Curious faces idly contemplated the scene.

"I don't. I think you must have made a mistake."

"Oh no, Sir! I never forget a face. That bloody school did for me. An' so did you."

"Look whoever you are," Goldway leaned back in his chair, "we're having a quiet drink here. You've obviously got the wrong person . . ."

"Shut it," the youth scowled. "I ain't got the wrong person. Nor the wrong school, my friend. An' I never forget a face."

"Look," Dryden shifted into what he deemed was a superior and threatening sitting position. "I've never seen you before in my life."

"Don't worry—Sir," the youth sneered. "I ain't gonna do anything. Just thought I'd say hello. Tell you I'm grateful for all you and that lot of middle class berks did for me up there. They got me diggin' ditches out at Farnton. Youth Opportunities they call it. Opportunities, my arse. Workin' for the dole's what it really is." With that, the youth gave Dryden one last long stare, turned on his heel and shouldered his way out of the bar.

"I've never seen him before in my life." Dryden grinned sheepishly round the circle of faces in the bar. For a moment or two they stared at him, curious, then resumed their conversations.

"I've never seen him either." Goldway shrugged. "He certainly looked a nasty piece of work."

"Oh well, good luck to him," Dryden murmured, still in a state of mild shock. The worst thing was, though he had never seen the youth before, he was now feeling distinctly guilty. They finished their beer and got up. As they stepped out of the door, Dryden hastily scanned the car park. It would not have surprised him if the youth had been lying in wait among the cars, a meat axe clasped in his grubby paw. A month or two earlier Dryden had read of a teacher being stabbed to death by an eight year old outside an inner city Junior School.

CHAPTER TWO

For eight long years Dryden Pollock had fought a losing battle with an increasingly recalcitrant younger generation. After graduating with an undistinguished degree from an undistinguished University, he had drifted about for a year or two, totally at a loss as to what he could possibly contribute by way of anything useful to society, surviving on hand-outs and poorly paid jobs, teaching English to unsuspecting foreigners, until in a state of near desperation he had applied for a post at a grammar school. The grammar school, it turned out, had been equally desperate for a set of initials to match the timetable of a certain mademoiselle. Her untimely departure from England had left an embarrasing gap in the school's staff/pupil ratio. Dryden's fate had been sealed. He had had to become a grammar school teacher.

Lacking ambition and saleable talents he had stayed at the grammar school rather a long time without giving any indication of wanting to further his career. Only gradually did it dawn on him that teaching was a career. He had thought of it as a job, a job to be taken seriously to some extent or one would never survive but a job nevertheless. Politicians and general managers of vast corporations had 'careers'. They rose like stars in the night sky, shone brilliantly for a moment or two and either plummeted rapidly towards the horizon with the onset of age or burst in a shower of sparks as the result of scandal or fraud. But teachers? Teachers simply wore out, like coalminers, only instead of contracting lung disease, they were slowly reduced to doddering simpletons, ranting on to an ever dwindling audience. That was hardly a career. Thus he had trotted into school at the beginning of each day and trotted home again at the end, totally oblivious to the fact that around him the staff room was seething with ambition and double-dealing. He had, of course, grasped the idea that there was something called 'promotion' but it didn't tempt him. Being promoted to master-in-charge of lunches or master-in-charge of exits and entrances struck him as the height of whimsicality. Yet men promoted to these responsibilities changed. They began to stride about arrogantly, dishing out orders to 'junior colleagues', complaining about 'endless paperwork' and indulging in ferocious character assassinations. It was all extremely puzzling.

In the fifth year of his supposed 'career' at the grammar school, however, things had begun to change rather rapidly. It all began when the Headmaster seemed to forget who Dryden was and started referring to him by the name of Binney. This had gone on for a while, to his colleagues a huge joke, to Dryden a source of increasing anxiety. This anxiety was confirmed in a most painfully humiliating way. All at once he began to receive clippings of jobs from the Times Educational Supplement in his staff common room pigeon-hole. Attached to these were various exhortations in the headmasterly hand such as 'This looks a good one, Binney' (who Binney was Dryden never found out!) or 'Why don't you try this one, Binney? You told me once you liked the West Country.'

As if this wasn't enough, Dryden had also started receiving sinister letters from the County Council on the subject of his tenancy of the small cottage he rented from them. Apparently, the cottage was due to be demolished in order to make way for a new ring road. Fortunately, this disturbing prospect was postponed for several months, since the County soon fell foul of its own labyrinthine bureaucracy. An internal wrangle developed between the county Agricultural Authority, who were laying claim to Dryden's rented cottage on behalf of one of their pig farmers, and the County Highways Authority, who, of course, wanted to demolish it for their ring road. Very sensibly, however, Dryden had concluded that in the long term view he did not figure prominently in the schemes of either.

After an agony of indecision and under and increasingly violent barrage of curt notes from his headmaster, he had finally sent off a dozen or more applications for various teaching posts around the country. From eleven schools he received no answer. From the twelfth, Great Battley International School, he received a letter summoning him for an interview.

* * * * *

"Welcome to Great Battley. I'm Arnold Scoresby, Deputy head here. You must be Randolph White?"

"No, I'm Dryden Pollock."

"Ah yes, of course. From Dorset."

"No. From Cambridgeshire. Bartonfield."

"Bartonfield?" The Deputy Head, a small wiry man, had looked alarmed. He had consulted what seemed to be a hastily scribbled list in his hand. Then his face had relaxed.

"Of course," he had smiled. "How silly of me. I'd put you down as coming from Dorset. Bartonfield, eh? I'd forgotten we had one coming from there."

Dryden had been instantly impressed by the appearance of Great Battley International School and more especially by an imposing billboard at the school gates. Boldly emblazoned upon it was a bow and arrow rampant in a circle of gold stars. Beneath this emblem were the words: 'One World.'

How he had thrilled with excitement when the Deputy Head had out-lined the school's unique mission. The brainchild of a certain Mr. Cyril Bennett, O.B.E., a late lamented chairman of the County Education Committee, Great Battley had been conceived as an institution that would bear the torch of a new internationalism, occasioned by Great Britain's entry into all sorts of internationally minded organisations. Mr. Bennett, the Deputy Head explained, had witnessed the futility and horror of war at first hand, first as a despatch rider in London during the blitz and later as a clerk in the British zone of occupied Germany. Fired with zeal for the elimination of ignorance and hostility that had hitherto blighted international relations, Mr. Bennett had con-cluded that in education lay the final victory over insularity and petty nationalism. His first scheme, a grand international academy costing millions in taxpayers' money, had been shot down in flames by a par-simonious Government. Undeterred, Mr. Bennett had continued to work for the realisation of his vision until in the late nineteen seventies a battle had erupted between the County Education Committee and the villagers of Great Battley over the proposed closure of the village's sec-ondary modern school. Letters had been despatched to Government Ministers, petitions had been drawn up and pamphlets distributed to bewildered commuters on the trains that halted for a moment or two at Great Battley station. On the very day the county bulldozers had moved into the village to demolish the school buildings, Mr. Bennett had had his way with the Educational Finance Committee. The county bulldozers withdrew, the villagers of Great Battley dismantled their barricades and phoenix-like the Great Battley International School had risen from the ashes or, more precisely, the derelict secondary modern school. Mr. Bennett had lived just long enough to receive the O.B.E. and attend a garden party at Buckingham Palace before he had keeled over with a massive coronary.

The post at Great Battley which Dryden had applied for was that of 'Assistant Co-ordinator of European Studies.' Quite what European Studies entailed was a matter of some confusion in Dryden's mind. From Maurice Talbot, the Senior Co-ordinator of International Studies, he had received a long, rambling letter which had given him the impression that it was all something to do with art, architecture, cuisine, geography, history and traffic signs. This last had filled him with anxiety. Never having driven a car abroad, he could not remember ever having seen any traffic signs, let alone tried to decipher them. Talbot, a tall, spare, earnest man, had explained to the several candidates on interview that European Studies had no counterpart in any other school in Britain. Ranging as it did from the mountain fastnesses of Norway to the plains of Rumania, it was a subject designed to enhance the rising generation's awareness of their place as Europeans in a Europe increas-ingly united by common bonds of culture and outlook. A chill of fear had passed through Dryden as it had suddenly occurred to him he was totally unable to cope with traffic signs in either Norwegian or Ruma-nian. This would be his undoing, he felt, visualising himself at a com-plete loss when confronted in his interview with a Rumanian traffic sign. It was then that he had turned to a fellow candidate and asked him, partly in jest, to be sure, if he knew what the Rumanian was for 'Get in lane'. The answer had come back without a moment's hesitation.

Dryden had entered the Headmaster's study in a cold sweat. A formidably large vicar in a cassock, the Chairman of the Board of Governors, had studied him through half-closed eyes. The Senior Mistress, a determined looking woman by the name of Rosie Kennedy, had frowned at him suspiciously. Basil Woodbine, the Headmaster, had looked surprised as if he had been expecting someone quite different. For a moment Dryden had wondered, panic-stricken, if the Headmaster of Bartonfield Grammar might not have written a reference for someone called Binney. The interrogation had begun.

The first part of the interview had been designed to ascertain his overall commitment to the profession of teacher. 'Commitment' was a word that never failed to bring beads of perspiration onto his brow. 'Commitment', it had always seemed to Dryden, was ultimately the expectation that the teacher was prepared to lay down his life for his school. Needless to say, this was rarely demanded of him but a twenty-four hour devotion to children was. That is until one became sufficiently powerful and influential enough to delegate everything to underlings which then allowed one time to read the morning paper at one's leisure and terrorise junior staff. Deputy Heads and Senior Mistresses were experts on commitment. They were able to tell by the bat of an eyelash or the twitch of sweaty palm whether this or that person showed true 'commitment'. Painfully aware of the Senior Mistress's eyes examining every detail of his appearance, Dryden had burbled on manically, trying to dream up new and original formulations of the concept 'commitment'. At that point the vicar had seemed to be dozing. Dryden, however, had fancied he detected a pair of malevolent blue eyes flickering back and forth beneath their heavily wrinkled lids.

Finally, the interviewing panel had broached the question of Dryden's competence in the field of European Studies. Fearfully, he had glanced at each face, ordinary English faces, to be sure, yet behind them ticked the brains of dedicated internationalists, cosmopolitans, citizens of the 'One World' on the school crest, people who were equally at home in Paris, Berlin, London, New York or Katmandu. In a sudden surge of near panic he had let rip.

European Studies, he had begun, was a subject of vital, nay, crucial significance for the future. Centuries of senseless rivalry and cruel strife had sundered the nations of the continent where so much culture, thought and art had for so long striven to bring them to an understanding of all they had in common. At once a deathly hush had settled over the interviewing panel. His face flushed, his eyes firmly fixed on the map of the E.E.C. on the wall above the Headmaster's desk, he had rambled on hysterically, unable to halt the tide of lyrical observations on the legacy of Ancient Greece, the Pax Romana, the Holy Roman Empire and the E.E.C. Be it now, be it twenty years, fifty years or even a hundred years hence, he had intoned, a spark of common feeling was

12

being kindled in the hearts of a new generation, a spark that carefully nurtured would ignite a fire of such magnitude as would sweep away all barriers, all prejudices, all the history of turmoil and strife to unite all Europeans at last in a community of mutual respect and understanding.

There had been several minutes of utter silence. Dryden had stared hard at his shoes. "Thank you, Mr. Pollock. Thank you." The Headmaster had said in a voice husky with emotion. Maurice Talbot had then risen and ushered Dryden quietly out of the door.

An hour later they offered him the job.

Dryden was unaware, however, that the fellow candidate who had spoken fluent Rumanian, though the interviewing panel had apparently found him wanting in the qualities Dryden had so admirably displayed, had been offered another post, one of lesser importance, namely that of Co-ordinator of Linguistic Resources. This individual, equipped with a droning public school voice, was none other than the fanatical Stephen Mott, whose spouse, Christine, was the Co-ordinator of French and German Studies.

Thus it transpired that on the very first day of his new job, Dryden discovered that his immediate superior in the International Studies Faculty was the bedmate of his immediate subordinate.

A few weeks later the Motts invited him to dinner one evening in their splendid neo-Georgian semi-detached house. Feeling distinctly apprehensive Dryden stood at the front door listening to the musical chimes sounding somewhere inside the house. The estate where the Motts lived had been very carefully laid out in a complicated pattern of curving streets, to create the impression of random development, he supposed, with sharply defined footpaths, closely cropped lawns and road verges and carefully spaced trees. In short, a world of order and precision in which Dryden felt immediately he had very little part to play. As the door opened, he was assailed by the scent of an expensive air-freshener. He felt dirty and unkempt as he stepped into the hallway. One quick glance in the Motts' hall mirror confirmed it. He was dirty and unkempt. The Talbots were already in place, Maurice Talbot greeting him cordially, Maurice Talbot's wife gazing at him with a look of vague contempt.

The evening's social intercourse commenced with a long tour of the Mott's house. They inspected every room, discussing furnishings at length, while Dryden trailed round unhappily, listening to Christine extolling the virtues of her husband, Stephen. She assured the Talbots that he was the most painstaking man she had ever met. Why, he had gone so far as to tear down a whole week's work of laborious wallpapering when he had suddenly discovered that his careful calculations were out by several centimetres. In the Motts' household there was no shoddy overlapping, no 'let's get it over with and be damned.' That sort of thinking was far too prevalent in today's world, Christine had thought.

"Quite," Mrs. Talbot had agreed, baring her huge teeth. "And not least in the teaching profession. Thank Heaven, the younger generation of teachers is actually dedicated to its job. I went to a grammar school, you know. My teachers couldn't have cared less. They wouldn't have known the meaning of the word 'commitment'. The teaching profession has been blighted by slovenliness, disorganisation and general incompetence for far too long."

Dryden had nodded sagely at this. How right she was, he thought, grimly determined to make a fresh start in life there and then. He hadn't dared glance at himself in the hall mirror on their way back to the dining-room for fear that his own reflection would induce such self-loathing, as to render the prospect of turning over a new leaf a pathetically hopeless delusion.

He had sat sandwiched between the Motts on one side of the dining-table while the Talbots had occupied the other side. Slovenliness and lack of commitment had continued to be the general theme of the dinner converstion. Terrified lest he inadvertently dribble gravy on the snow white tablecloth or spill his wine, Dryden had concentrated on every movement of his own limbs, acting in slow motion while everyone else seemed perfectly at ease with themselves and their pristine surroundings. In the Mott's spotless toilet he had scowled with disgust at his own urine sullying the shine on the bowl. Washing his hands, he had been horrified to see a grey river of dirt besmirching the highly polished basin. He hadn't dared use the towel marked 'Guests'. He had had the feeling that his grubby paw marks would have been instantly noticed downstairs, for where dirt and degeneracy were concerned these people had X-ray vision.

As the evening had progressed he had become more and more nervous. Why hadn't he left? Somehow he had become mesmerised by the immaculate world of his hosts. How did they do it, he wondered repeatedly. Did they walk about on air? Had they been born without sweat glands? He began to wonder if he had flushed the toilet properly. Had he left greasy marks on the basin, dirty footprints on the floor? Was his own body exuding an unpleasant odour at this very minute? His neck felt grubby, his ears full of wax, even his decrepit Vauxhall Viva parked outside was doubtlessly being inspected from behind a dozen windows. It would be the talk of the whole estate for a week.

He had begun to drink then. Slowly his words had become more and more slurred, his eyes misted over, his mouth set in a foolish grin, he had begun to nod somewhat too emphatically at everything everyone was saying. For God's sake, Pollock, a voice had kept pleading with him from inside his head. Get a grip on yourself. But it had been too late. Four pairs of eyes in the Motts' living-room were watching him slowly degenerating into a disgusting lush. The wine had run out, it was after ten o'clock and he had had an overpowering desire to stand up and suggest he nip into town to the nearest off-licence to procure another litre or two—his shout, of course. He had wanted to wrap the Motts and the Talbots in a smog of vinous breath and cigarette smoke, not because he disliked them but because they were right, so right, unquestionably right about everything and everyone and he wanted to show his appreciation of their wisdom.

At eleven o'clock the Talbots had graciously excused themselves. By now, suffering an attack of violent hiccoughs, Dryden had abandoned all caution and was suggesting all manner of outrageous schemes, coffee and cigars at his place (though where he thought he was going to conjure up cigars from at that time of night was anybody's guess!), a visit to a Club in London, for God's sake, even dancing. You can't go now, Maurice, Val, he heard himself protesting to the Talbots in a loud, vulgar, alcoholic tone, the night is young. The Talbots had slipped hastily out of the door. At five past eleven Dryden had plumped himself cheerfully back down on the Motts' elegant sofa and rambled on drunkenly about this and that, losing the thread of his sentences, hiccoughing and laughing inanely. Meanwhile, the Motts had been tidying up with military precision, attempting to bring their unfortunate guest to his senses by means of their dishwasher which made a loud, relentless noise. Christine had disappeared then re-appeared in a dressing-gown, Stephen had disappeared altogether, but the sounds of dishwashing, cleaning teeth, flushing the toilet, had barely penetrated Dryden's consciousness if indeed his mental state at this point could have been called 'consciousness'. At midnight Christine finally persuaded him to get to his feet. She offered to call him a taxi. No, no, he didn't need any taxi. He had bowed, kissed her on the neck and tottered backwards out of the front door, rambling on and on about how grateful he was and weren't the Talbots a super couple and wasn't the Motts' house a dream and what a culinary masterpiece dinner had been and oh what a lovely evening, look at all the stars and wasn't the moon bright tonight though there was definitely a nip in the air and no, not to worry, he'd be fine, he'd driven home once so thoroughly neutered he'd been astounded to find himself in his own bed the next morning, God knows how many innocent pedestrains he might have knocked for six, careering round the streets, pissed out of his brains . . . The door had closed firmly in front of his eyes.

The next morning he had seriously considered committing suicide. Standing in front of his bathroom mirror, tears of shame had welled out of his eyes and poured down his unshaven cheeks. Running a bath, then lying in it, he had been sorely tempted to leave his head under water for as long as it took. Later, he had thought about ringing the Motts and the Talbots or writing them long, cravenly apologetic letters, sending them beautiful gifts, still later running away across the Channel to France, then on to India, or pretending serious illness, madness even, hiding in his house acting out a charade of a highly-strung, gibbering hysteric whose outrageous behaviour at the Motts, far from arousing disgust, would instead arouse the most intense sympathy for his plight. Gradually these more extreme forms of atonement for his ghastly behaviour gave way to a dull, anxious determination to brazen it all out.

And on the following Monday morning he had crept into the staff room, discovered in the course of the morning that his performance the previous Saturday evening was not the general topic of conversation and had later even ventured to within a few yards of Christine and Stephen Mott. Nothing had been said, of course, but he had noticed them regarding him with a look of faint amusement.

CHAPTER THREE

Basil Woodbine, Headmaster of Great Battley, was a thick-set man with dark jowls and an expression of continual wonder on his face. For a minute he seemed to hesitate as if not quite sure where he was before he continued resolutely towards the canteen servery.

"Poor old Basil," Goldway observed. "He hates meeting the staff."

They had gathered to drink tea and welcome new colleagues. It was the sort of occasion Dryden preferred not to attend, were it not for the fact that Wendy Bashford was there. He kept stealing glances at her. She was standing a few yards away, deep in discussion with Reg Devereaux, the Head of P.E.

Rosie Kennedy, the Senior Mistress, entered. She was an unusual looking woman. Beneath a shock of fiery red hair, her face was large and square with bushy eyebrows. She had a very determined jaw. As she walked she held her arms akimbo as if she was about to suddenly seize anything or anybody that stood in her way and fling them aside.

Goldway grinned at the sight of her. "There's Rosie. Looks as if her corns are playing her up a bit." Devereaux, Dryden had noticed, had moved much closer to Wendy. He fancied himself irresistible. He was admittedly good looking, possessed a healthy physique and addressed himself to people, especially women, with a confidence that Dryden envied. He scowled at him, then suddenly saw that Wendy was glancing up at Devereaux's hair. Aha, he thought, she had seen he was going bald. In a vain attempt to conceal his baldness, Devereaux had trained long wisps of hair over his skull.

"Nathan? A word, please, if I may." David Hepworth was at Goldway's elbow. Goldway flashed a glance of amused horror at Dryden before turning to Hepworth with a look of earnest attention. Wendy had now moved back from Devereaux. Not far, of course, but far enough to evoke a silent cheer from Dryden.

His interest in Miss Wendy Bashford had begun on the second day of the new term. By chance, following her up the stairs, the movements of her well-proportioned body beneath its tight-fitting dress occasioned in him a violent sensation of lust. He had arrived at the top of the stairs feeling quite dizzy. Throughout that morning he had been plagued by recurring visions of her ascending the stairs, until, come the lunch-hour, he knew he was on yet another of his silent, aching quests.

Lust was the bane of Dryden Pollock's life and it was as capricious as it was all-consuming. There were by now hundreds of women walking around England who at some time had been the altars of his desire. There were fat women, lean women, small women, tall women, blondes, redheads, brunettes, all of whom, with a few exceptions, had lived for a time in his life, totally oblivious of the influence they exerted over him. How often had his daily routine been radically altered for the sake of a chance encounter with the adored one? How many times had he missed appointments, forgotten important messages, spent enormous sums of money, endured cold, drizzle, fog and snow, all for the sake of pursuing the object of his desire. Then, at the end of it all, those frequent, shattering moments of loss when the loved one, with a cheery wave and a smile, trotted out of his life for ever. For days he brooded in loneliness, despising himself for his weakness, hating them for their indifference. In a few cases, to be sure, they had noticed his doggy-like pursuit and either gently intimated that he wasn't really their type or bluntly told him to piss off. But why, oh why, wasn't he their type for God's sake? They were his.

Wendy Bashford was. He was convinced of it. She wasn't beautiful and, to be truthful, she wasn't even particularly pretty. She had an ordinary, earnest English face with a pleasant smile. She dressed well and she had nice hair. Yet in her movements there was an almost over-powering sensuality. She gave him an instant erection. He had begun to dream of conquest.

Now he saw Devereaux hanging over her like a vulture, itching to get his hands on her body. At that moment Rosie Kennedy approached. She cast a disdainful glance at Wendy who promptly retreated into the crowd. Dryden chuckled. Rosie was tugging the leash. So much for Devereaux's shameless crawling.

"Now's your chance, mate," Goldway murmured in Dryden's ear. Dryden reddened. Goldway didn't miss a thing. Wendy looked round vaguely. Dryden rocked back and forth on his heels. He was on the verge of panic. Days of stalking her in silence had left him totally unprepared to talk to her. It was too soon. The first phase of his passion had hardly got under way. There were still weeks of silent yearning to be lived through.

"Go on, mate. Don't be such a wanker," Goldway hissed. The word 'wanker' stung Dryden into action. Above all else, he hated being called that. Deep down, in moments of extreme self-disgust he had sometimes thought he was one. Blindly, he marched over to Wendy. He arrived just as Ken Tyler, the arch bore of the Science Department was about to move in.

"I saw you there with no-one to talk to," he said. She cocked her head on one side.

"Sorry? I didn't hear what you said." Dryden cursed himself. He always did this. Jabbered incomprehensibly to the women he loved.

18

"I saw you here with no-one to talk to. I'm Dryden Pollock. European Studies."

"Oh. I haven't seen you around," she smiled. "I teach European Studies, too. Norway."

"Norway's indented coastline?" he grinned.

"Pardon?

"Nothing. How do you like it here Wendy?"

"It's wonderful, she said. "The kids are so well behaved, aren't they? So willing to learn.

"Are they? Yes, I suppose they are," Dryden said hastily. "Where were you before?"

"The Charles Darwin School in London. I was there two years. It was ghastly. The children were out of control. They never listened to anything anyone ever said."

"That's unusual."

"In any case, no-one could make themselves heard above the din," she signed. "Still, I tried. I did my best. All they ever wanted to talk about was sex. With me mostly."

"How awful," Dryden said solemnly. "I mean I suppose it's very upsetting when you're trying to teach them something useful, isn't it?"

"It was frightening. Once, they threw my overhead projector out of the window. And all my books. Theirs had gone out of the window long before."

"Good Lord. How did you handle that?"

"I shut myself in a cupboard and locked the door from the inside. After a while they gave up and went home. It was then I knew that Charles Darwin wasn't the place for me. I had to get another job."

"I saw you talking to Reg Devereaux before," he ventured, surprised at his own boldness.

"Yes. He's nice, isn't he? He wanted to know if I was interested in netball after school. Aerobics, too. He's very interested in that. Anyway, we're going out for a drink this evening to talk about it."

Dryden stared at the floor. Hell's bells, Devereaux wasn't wasting any time was he? The man was married, for Heaven's sake. There were two young children.

"His wife's very nice too," Dryden smiled. "And they've got two lovely kids. A very happy couple, so I'm told."

"Yes. She's a singer, isn't she? He told me that."

Dryden was stumped. Devereaux was a lot more cunning than he thought.

"What's this aerobics?"

"Aerobics? Oh, it's the latest thing. Movement to music. It's quite strenuous. We never dared do anything like that at Charles Darwin, of course. Staying alive was our main aim there, I'm afraid.

"Look." Dryden suddenly had an inspiration. "I'm the Assistant Co-ordinator of European Studies, Wendy. I do Baroque art and culture with the Fifth Year. I'd like to have a chat with you about Norway sometime if that's okay. How about over a drink in the Spotted Dog tomorrow lunch-time?"

"Well . . ." she looked flustered. "Actually, I don't know the first thing about Norway. We've spent the last two lessons finding out where it is." Dryden smiled sympathetically. "Sure, it's always difficult for a start. But we'll talk about it, shall we? One o'clock in the staff common room?"

"Yes, all right." She suddenly stood on tip-toes and waved across the room. "Reg Devereaux's giving me a lift home," she smiled. "Got to go." Dryden had a momentary vision of Devereaux's slow and painful castration at the hands of a group of Fifth Year hooligans.

"Well, hello Dryden. Nice to see you back this term. Did you have a good holiday?" The Headmaster glanced round furtively as if he had just said something he shouldn't.

"Yes, thanks, Head. And you?"

Basil took a deep breath. "I was in France, actually. That's a part of the world you're familiar with, I take it?" He blinked at Dryden. "Yes, we were in France, that is my wife and I, down in the Auvergne. Seeing my son Nigel. Very agreeable it was, too, I mean, not seeing Nigel in particular, though of course that was agreeable in itself, but being, as it were, in the Auvergne. Nigel was already in the Auvergne, you see, so we thought, that is my wife thought, that it would be a good idea to motor down to the Auvergne to see Nigel. Since he was there. He was there too, of course. He's been there for—oh let me see—six months is it?—when was it he went down there?—no eight months, it must be eight months. Heavens, doesn't time fly?—anyway that's where we were, in the Auvergne. Very agreeable it was too. Whereabouts in France were you again, Dryden? The Dordogne was it I thought you said you were going to? Ah yes." The Headmaster's eyes lit up. "Of course, I remember. You were going ballooning in the Loire Valley, weren't you? My goodness me, yes. I thought it was you but I couldn't be sure it was. How did that go, by the way?"

Dryden thought frantically for a second or two. Should he admit he hadn't left Blighty's shores or should he simply pretend he had been ballooning in the Loire Valley. Basil could get very annoyed if he thought he had made a mistake. He prided himself on his memory.

"It was wonderful, Headmaster. I'd never been ballooning before. Certainly not in the Loire Valley. It was very panoramic."

"Quite. It must have been. Panoramic. I like that. Of course, France is a beautiful country isn't it? I mean, there's so much of it. Nigel's been on the move a great deal there these past ten months or so. It was his idea we should meet him down there in the Auvergne and do a tour.

Extraordinary. Yes, well, nice to chat, Dryden. All the best for next year. Where is it you're going?" Basil eyed him expectantly. Dryden had gone cold. He wasn't going anywhere that he knew of.

"Sorry to interrupt, Head. Can I pop in for a quick chat tomorrow morning?" Goldway had come to his rescue. Dryden heaved a sigh of relief.

"Oh, hello, Nathan," Basil smiled. "Yes, of course, that is . . ." And he drew Goldway aside into a huddle. Dryden beat a hasty retreat.

"Fancy your form winning the International Quiz," Rosie Kennedy's voice said behind him. "They must have been cheating. Or else you told 'em all the answers mate," she chuckled.

"They're very internationally minded, Rosie," Dryden grinned. "Like their form tutor."

"That's what you think, mate," Rosie narrowed her eyes at him. "The only internationally minded people in this school are the Head and Maurice Talbot. The rest of you are all frauds."

"I'm not a fraud, Rosie," Dryden protested. "I believe passionately in European Studies. You know that."

Rosie's arms moved back and forth in front of her plump body as she laughed.

"I'll never forget that blimmin' speech of yours at your interview, mate. The Head was almost in tears. You got it all from Cyril Bennett, of course, didn't you? Swotted it all up the night before. They all do it. There's people queueing up to work here you know. Old Goldway there, I remember, was terribly lyrical about Europe. I thought at the time, I thought, you blimmin' con man, Goldway. There you are, sitting there holding forth about Europe and your grandparents were probably gassed at Auschwitz. And I thought Jews had long memories." She roared with laughter and moved away into the crowd. Rosie was unashamedly gruesome. As Senior Mistress of Great Batley she had reigned supreme since the school's foundation. She was the single most xenophobic person Dryden had ever encountered. She was an invetarate globetrotter and, given the opportunity, she would hold forth for hours on her experiences abroad. Her favourite anecdote concerned the night she had spent in an hotel in the Andes under siege from a horde of sexually deprived Inca Indians.

"Saved you there, mate," Goldway murmured. "What was Basil on about?"

"Ballooning in the Loire Valley," Dryden said. He was convinced that was what I was doing over summer." Goldway laughed. "He also thinks I'm leaving," Dryden murmured. That wasn't funny. Memories of his former Headmaster rose up to haunt him. 'This looks a good one, Binney' scrawled across an advertisement for a Scale Two post in the depths of Lincolnshire.

21

CHAPTER FOUR

"Delightful place, isn't it?" Dryden grinned. "We could go somewhere else."

"No, this is fine," Wendy said. "I haven't much time you see. I've got things to mark for this afternoon."

His heart sank. He had been hoping they might spend the whole lunch-hour together in the Spotted Dog, even if it was crowded.

"Did you enjoy the tea yesterday?"

"Yes, I did. It was so civilised, wasn't it? Just to be able to stand round drinking tea and chatting without wondering if they haven't set the school building alight."

"That was Charles Darwin, I take it?"

She nodded. "They burnt down Home Economics the year I arrived. Technology went up in flames the year after."

"There can't have been much left."

"There wasn't. The main block was solid brick. They would have had to dynamite it." He smiled at the solemnity of her last statement. She was talking like a war correspondent in the last days of Saigon.

"Here they just switch off," he said. "It's called passive resistance."

"Everyone's so committed though," Wendy said. "It's another world altogether. The way Reg and the others talk. They really believe in education." Her eyes were shining. Dryden stared gloomily out of the window. She had used that terrible word 'committed.'

"Yes, there's a great deal of commitment at Great Battley," he said slowly. "Though commitment to what, I'm not quite sure."

Wendy glanced at him nervously and frowned. He had been too cynical.

"Well, let's talk about Norway, shall we?" he said hastily. "How are you getting on with it?"

"Well—we know where it is. And we know it's mountainous and that it has a severely indented coastline."

He smiled. "That's pretty good going for four lessons. Better than average."

22

"What puzzles me though," Wendy leaned earnestly towards him over the table. "Why Norway? Why not Sweden or Denmark or Holland? Holland's a bit closer, isn't it? Besides, Norway isn't even in the Common Market apparently. They chose to stay out of it, didn't they?"

"Why Norway?" He pretended to reflect on this question at length. Oh, how he longed to reach out and touch her body, whisper sweet nothings in her ear. "I think," he said solemnly, lowering his gaze, "Norway is studied because of its severely indented coastline. Nowhere else in Europe has such a coastline, Wendy. It's unique.'

"You've been there, have you?"

"No, not exactly. I've been to Copenhagen but not to Norway."

"Has anyone been there? I mean it would help if I could get a first-hand report of it."

"As far as I know, no-one's been there, Wendy. Unless Rosie perhaps. No, she tends to go for places where there might be a bit of action. She's been to Alaska."

"Has she?" Wendy raised her eyebrows. "That might help, mightn't it? It's sort of similar, isn't it?"

Dryden nodded. "I hadn't thought of that. She might have photos or slides too."

"But that wouldn't help." Wendy shook her head. "I mean, I couldn't show the kids slides of Alaska and pretend they were pictures of Norway, could I?"

"Why not?" He kept a straight face. "They probably wouldn't realise." She could get away with showing them pictures of the Taj Mahal and tell them it was Norway. She looked at him in alarm.

"Surely that would be unethical? I mean, what was it the spiral curiculum man said? 'You can teach children of any ability anything at an intellectually honest level' or something to that effect. Showing them pictures of Alaska and pretending it was Norway wouldn't be intellectually honest, would it? In fact, it would be terribly dishonest."

He said nothing. Was it worth flying his true colours now? European Studies was anything but intellectually honest. And that was just the tip of the iceberg. No, it wasn't worth saying anything now.

"No, of course not, Wendy. I was just joking. No, that wouldn't do at all. Norway must be Norway."

Norway must be Norway. He liked it. It said something about the subject he was condemned to teach. After all was said and done, education was largely a process of learning things that were not of immediate practical use. It was a truism. Hadn't Dryden spent six years studying Latin? And he could still conjugate the verb 'moneo' in all its tenses, though, if he was honest about it, he was a bit ropey on the Future Perfect. Still, it mattered little that he had forgotten almost all the Latin he had ever known. The important thing was that he knew there was a

Future Perfect of Second Conjugation Latin verbs. It was that sort of knowledge that had got him a University educaion. It was that sort of knowledge that had raised him above the common herd. He was an educated person.

"Another drink?"

"No thanks. I think I ought to be getting back. I've got the Crusades," she smiled.

"The Crusades." He raised his glass in a toast.

Driving back to school in Dryden's decrepit Viva, they suddenly found themselves the focus of attention of a number of spotty youths. Old Bollocks out to pull the new bit of fluff, eh? Dryden glared back at them. His mental machine-gun raked the roadway.

In the staff common room Rosie Kennedy was holding court. Given its dedication to the ideals of Internationalism, her presence in Great Battley was something of a mystery. In Rosie's frank opinion (and she prided herself on her 'frankness'), foreigners were lazy, slovenly and untrustworthy. The Germans were fanatical, the French deceitful and the Italians—well—her experience of the ticket counters at Fiumicino Airport (an absolute disgrace in itself) had stopped her setting foot beyond the air terminal. And if Italian currency was anything to go by, then the Italian world outside must be in a state of unbelievable disorder.

It was Nathan Goldway's theory that Rosie's presence in the school served as a brake on a too hasty dash into Internationalism. She was the devil's advocate in the process of Cyril Bennett's (O.B.E.) canonisation. Cyril's love of foreigners had been forged at a time when the British could afford to be magnanimous towards the Hun, the Frog and the Dago. Things were different now. Former enemies and other foreign riff-raff were clamouring to run the show. Rosie was, nevertheless, careful not to go too far with her xenophobic outpourings, otherwise doubts might have arisen as to her position in an institution devoted to international understanding. It was a position she blatantly enjoyed, not just by virtue of its financial reward but also by virtue of the power it gave her to compel large numbers of people to listen to her endless globetrotting anecdotes.

"There I was," she bellowed, "with nothing but my suitcase and my ticket surrounded by all those men with nothing more than a nappy to hide their privates, all shouting and yelling at this little conductor to let them onto the train. I was the only woman on the whole platform and the only white woman for hundreds of miles. You could see it written all over their dark little faces. I was hanging onto my suitcase for dear life, just waiting for the first hands to start touching me . . ." She glanced up at Wendy and Dryden as they crossed the staff common room. "Anyway, I finally managed to fight my way through to the little conductor, thinking, of course, that he would come to my rescue, what with his uniform and so on, and just as I was about to hoist myself up into the carriage, do you know what he said to me?" Her audience raised their eyebrows a fraction to show their continuing interest in the story (which they had all heard many times before), though beneath their brows their eyes had a distinctly glazed look.

"You sleep with me, missy, I get you seat."

"Good Heavens!"

Rosie looked round triumphantly.

"I'll never forget that as long as I live."

"What on earth did you do?" One of the audience had seized the opportunity offered by Rosie's survey of the general level of interest in her anecdote to yawn mightily.

"Well, I certainly didn't do what he asked me to do, mate."

She swung round. The yawner's jaws snapped shut.

"I told him if that was his idea of running a rail service, I was going to hire a donkey to get me there." She chuckled at this, in her mind's eye seeing the look of stupefaction on the little conductor's face. Dryden was fishing idly in his pigeon-hole, pretending he had something to do.

"I've never been back there, of course," Rosie declared. "Filthy country it was. Utterly filthy. Just imagine all those men touching me. They could have had anything on those fingers of theirs. Anything!"

"You'd never get me out to a place like that," Bernard McGraw, the Head of Musical Studies said in his 'hee-haw' voice. "I know where I'm well off. Right here in Winkworth. Born and bred Winkworth, that's me. I can't imagine why people bother going to all these places abroad. It's a waste of time and money."

"You're such an old stick-in-the-mud, Bernard," Rosie twinkled. "Do you good to get out and about a bit, mate."

"What's the point? Winkworth's where I belong. I shall be here for the rest of my days. All this travelling about and what happens? You all end up back here. If I'd known you years ago, Rosie, I could have told you what Winkworth was like. Saved you all that trouble."

Rosie threw back her head and roared with laughter. "If I'd known you all those years ago, Bernard, I'd have taken you with me. Then I wouldn't have had all those men after me, would I?"

"They might have been after me, too, Rosie." McGraw's high-pitched laugh was eerie in contrast to Rosie's deep-throated guffaw. "You just don't know in some of these places, do you? You hear some terrible stories."

The bell for afternoon registration rang and Dryden reluctantly left the staff common room and made his way slowly upstairs to his form room. His tutor group, Five Grigorescu (named for an obscure Ruma-nian painter) lay round the room like a collection of beefy nudes waiting to be captured on canvas. Under Dryden's tutelage they had quickly degenerated into a collection of sullen, ill-mannered, unco-operative teenage layabouts. At times their behaviour could be truly barbaric. Today, fortunately, they were still comatose after a pre-lunch dose of

European Studies combined with the unseasonably sultry September weather. Registration proceeded without incident. They answered their names with a curt 'yeah' that not long ago would have sent Dryden into a long reverie in which he, a Commandant in the S.S. was supervising their march to a short but bloody death. As they lined up below him in the trench they had just dug, he called their names out, softly, savouring the muted, terrified, 'Yes Sir' from each one of them before the machine-gun beside him rattled into action. This horrible fantasy had led Dryden to question seriously his whole position as a form tutor. After all, it hardly accorded with generally accepted notions of pastoral concern. He had considered talking to the Head of Fifth Year about it but as yet had not succeeded in finding her. She was known for her strict adherence to times, namely the school's time and her time. She seldom arrived before nine o'clock sharp in the mornings just as Fifth Year tutors were struggling to quell the anarchy in their 'tutor bases', while lunchtimes she regarded as a convenient gap in the day to go home and walk her dog.

Registration came to an untidy end. Five Grigorescu ambled away sullenly. Dryden sat contemplating the two remaining periods of the day. During the first he would have to investigate a long and tedious passage about a visit to a French post office, in the second he would be embarking on an endlessly boring train journey through Germany. The perpetrators of these horrors, he was sure, had long since retired to cool villas on the Mediterranean coast to count their royalties over a gin and tonic in the sun.

CHAPTER FIVE

A gruelling one and a half hours later the classroom and corridors of Great Battley International School rapidly emptied. Wearily, Dryden climbed the stairs to the Resources Room, grimacing as he glimpsed the Motts and Maurice Talbot through the narrow window in the door. They were deep in conversation. He pushed open the door and beamed.

"Hello, Dryden." Maurice Talbot slammed shut the drawer of the enormous filing cabinet behind his back. Christine and Stephen Mott glanced up from their work at the table. Ever since his terrible behaviour that evening eighteen months ago the first sight of them always filled him with dread. The proprietary air with which they settled themselves down at the table in the Resources Room after school invariably made him feel like an intruder. Indeed, the Motts, man and wife, had made this room their home from home. They arranged the books on the shelves, pinned the notices to the notice-board, they tidied Maurice Talbot's desk for him, they labelled everything in sight with little colour-coded stickers, rang their bank manager, their building society, their travel agent, the Gas Board, the Electricity Board, the garage that serviced their gleaming yellow Volkswagen Polo with its immaculate tartan upholstery, all from the telephone in the Resources Room. It was the Mott's room, as ordered and as pristine as their splendid neo-Georgian semi twelve miles away in Winkworth. Dryden was admitted to this room with the same cold graciousness they had shown him that ghastly evening when they had invited him for dinner. He nodded at the three of them and looked round for his satchel.

"It's in the corner," Stephen Mott said without taking his eyes off the exercise book he was marking with straight neat ticks. Even their pupils adhered to the Motts' unswerving crusade against slovenliness and disorder. The Mott's pupils all covered their books and wrote neatly on every page, ruled lines beneath the dates, crossed their 't's and dotted their 'i's.

"Thanks," Dryden murmured. He bent down beneath the shelves to reached his battered briefcase.

"I put your books on top of the lockers." Christine gave him a chilling smile. "We decided we were going to put them there, didn't we?"

"We need to keep the table free for people to work on, don't we?" her husband added, without looking up.

"Yes, of course," Dryden murmured.

"By the way, Dryden," Maurice Talbot was studying a thin sheet of crisp white paper he had withdrawn from a file, "I still haven't had that UCCA form. You did get my note, I presume?"

"Oh, Hell!" Dryden clutched his head. He had completely forgotten all about it.

"I thought you'd probably forgotten." This was punctuated by Maurice Talbot's short, dry laugh. "No matter. It's just that it's due in tomorrow morning."

"I'll do it right now." There was a trace of defiance in Dryden's voice. Wasn't there anything he could do properly, for God's sake?

"If you like." Talbot sat down at his desk. Dryden rooted through his briefcase, feeling himself growing hot at the thought that he might have lost the bloody thing altogether. He found it eventually, wedged between a sheaf of essays on Baroque something or other that he had no intention of marking and a dog-eared mark register in which he recorded the marks of fictitious tests in European Studies.

"Found it?" Christine Mott smiled at his audible sigh of relief. "I'll move round a bit. There."

He sat down at the table, sandwiched between the Motts and their neat piles of exercise books. His ballpoint scratched uselessly on the paper.

"Use mine, Dryden. Lucky I've got a spare one." He accepted the pen Christine offered him and began to write. He was relieved to discover that his excellent training in the production of densely worded, learned nonsense had not deserted him in this moment of dire peril. He finished the report with a flourish and returned the pen.

"Excellent." Maurice Talbot glanced at the UCCA form Dryden laid on his table. "Off now, are you?" He laughed his short, dry laugh.

"Don't forget the cupboard, will you, Dryden?" Christine smiled. He didn't. After locking the cupboard he hurried downstairs and out of the building. By now, he thought, they would have begun dissecting him, their small, shiny surgeon's knives making clean, straight incisions in his body. Each segment would then be carefully labelled and colour-coded.

"Oh look, Maurice, I've found that report we thought we'd lost,"—in one rubber-gloved hand Christine held up a blood soaked sheet of paper. "Oh, that's where the plug for the speaker got to," Stephen exclaimed, burrowing deep into Dryden's exposed innards, removing the fatty tissue from the small plastic plug and popping the object into a self-sealing plastic bag. "Better sew him up now," Maurice Talbot laughed his short, dry laugh. "Want him back on his feet for tomorrow, don't we?"

That evening was bright and clear, the sort of evening that was utterly

28

wasted on a town like Winkworth. Dryden turned the corner into the High Street and muttered imprecations at the tall, square Police building that dominated the town's skyline. Why on earth the local constabulary needed such an eyesore he had never been able to fathom, unless at some future date they were planning to lock up the entire population of the town. The building blazed light, like a huge hotel, dwarfing the dark spire of the Cathedral next to it. From behind the Victorian façades that had been conserved along the High Street came the low rumble of traffic from the by-pass that actually cut the town in two. The locals seemed to find it perfectly normal to have to wander about in a maze of subterranean passages to get from one side of their town to the other. By the time he had reached the first of a long line of pubs in the High Street, he felt a lot calmer. He entered the saloon bar, noted with satisfaction that his usual table was free, bought himself a pint and a packet of crisps and sat down. Though this was by no means his favourite saloon bar, the table he usually occupied was in an excellent position for viewing the goings-on in the whole bar.

The bar was not crowded but he quickly sorted out the few young women whose movements would keep him pleasantly occupied for a while. There was also a mirror opposite his table, expertly lit for the purpose of admiring one's own reflection. It was just far enough from his table to blur his rather irregular features into the appearance of a dark and mysterious stranger. It was as re-assuring as his Rock Hudson photograph, as he called it, the only permissible photograph of himself, taken by mistake at a friend's wedding. The unique light on that occasion (Indian summer) had turned his profile into a close resemblance of the famous Hollywood star. And by God, he needed re-assurance. The trouble was, no matter how hard he tried to persuade himself that Wendy Bashford was just not his type, he had spent the whole afternoon dreaming about her. About her body in partricular. As he drank he brooded darkly on the subject of Reg Devereaux. The man was ruthless, as only P.E. teachers could be. Why couldn't Devereaux have been gay like the sports teacher at the grammar school? But he wasn't and it was no use wishing he was. If only Wendy could see him now, he thought. He flashed a couple of glances at himself in the mirror, singeing, dark-eyed glances, the look of a brooding, refined type.

The young women in the bar were suddenly enchanted by the entrance of a trio of huge, hairy, sporty types. They lumbered up to the bar counter, patting one another in comradely fashion as they basked in the glow of female admiration. Dryden slipped several notches down towards depression. He thought of Devereaux lolling about in just that attitude, basking in the admiration of Wendy Bashford. He decided to practise his dark-eyed look on the nearest young woman. You never knew if you might not arouse the tiniest spark of excitement in her soul, drawing her attention away from the hairy hams as it dawned on her that there could be more to a man than a bull neck and bulging thighs. Alas, this had never happened with any of the hundreds of women he had flashed dark-eyed looks at over the years. How many times had he been left gazing forlornly at the back of yet another woman with whom he had imagined he had been conducting a daring and subtle ocular exchange? He had then realised that she had simply been wondering who the hell the pervy creep was up in the corner.

He drank his pint slowly, dwelling on morbid visions of Reg Devereaux and Wendy Bashford sharing a joke at his expense in some other pub somewhere. Down in the bar the young women were growing more and more excited at the behaviour of the lolling oafs, squealing at them and at one another. As if any of these women were waiting for her soul to be touched by the look of a dark-eyed stranger, he thought disdainfully. This wasn't Petersburg or Baden Baden . . . this was Winkworth. Still what comfort was there in that, for God's sake?

At that moment the bar door opened and a figure he vaguely recognised waddled in. He froze at the sight. It was Bloxham, the Head of English Studies. Bloxham hadn't seen him. Maybe he could just about slip round the wall of the bar and make it to the door while Bloxham was buying himself a drink. What the hell was he doing in here anyway? If there was one place Dryden thought himself safe from Great Battley International School it was the saloon bars of Winkworth High Street. Just as he began to make his way stealthily round the edge of the bar, Bloxham's dumpy body swung round.

"Pollock?"

Dryden stopped and smiled, raising his eyebrows in pleasurable surprise at discovering Bloxham in the bar.

"Hullo, Nigel," he called back cheerfully. "Fancy seeing you here."

"I might as well pose the same question." Bloxham's face met his pint of beer at tie-knot level.

"You got a drink?"

"No, I haven't . . . I was . . . uh . . ."

"Get you one." Bloxham reurned to the bar. "What is it?"

"Just a pint." Dryden raised his hand in a gesture of surrender. He led the way back up to his table.

"Come in here after my evening group," Bloxham explained as they sat down. "Institute, you know?" Dryden nodded.

"Wednesdays," Bloxham muttered. "Need a drink usually."

"I didn't know you took evening classes."

"Five years now." Bloxham wiped his hairy chin on the sleeve of a faded corduroy jacket.

"Not too bad. Beats teaching at that place though."

Dryden smiled and wiggled his head. He didn't really know Bloxham but on the occasions he had heard him speak he had been repelled by his pretentious public school accent. Bloxham he had categorised as that other sort of public school boy, the shambling, artistic poseur as compared with the frozen and fanatical Stephen Mott.

"You come here often?" Bloxham's eyes were large and watery beneath his mop of black, though prematurely greying hair.

"It's my local," Dryden said. "Or one of them."

"Winkworth is ghastly, isn't it?" Bloxham wrinkled up his nose in disgust. "Utterly soulless place. I live in Thetterington. Come down here once a week. Find it quite enough."

"That's quite a drive, isn't it? From Thetterington to Great Battley I mean," Dryden remarked pleasantly, faintly annoyed at Bloxham's round condemnation of Winkworth. It was ghastly, of course, but it didn't help being told how ghastly it was if one was doomed to live in it for the foreseeable future.

"Bloody awful," Bloxham suddenly shouted. "Hate it." There was a slight lull in the conversation down in the bar. Seldom in fact did this bar ring to the rounded tones of a plummy public school voice. Dryden shifted in mild embarrassment.

"The trip's bad enough from here," he commented, suddenly aware of a nascent boredom with Bloxham.

"Rather live up there in Thetterington than in this ghastly tip," Bloxham bellowed. There was a longer lull in the conversation down in the bar.

"How long have you been at Great Battley?" Dryden veered hastily onto another track.

"Too damn long. Ludicrous place. Three years, Pollock. Three grisly years. Can't wait to get out of it." Bloxham certainly didn't beat about the bush. "An appalling place. Lunatic asylum if you want my frank opinion. Woodbine is mad. That monstrous woman, Rosie Kennedy, is irredeemably vulgar and as for that pipsqueak of a deputy head, Arnold Scoresby, he is the epitome of north country chapel smugness."

"I see." Dryden stared into his drink.

"But the creature I feel moved to vilify in the most extreme terms is that whey-faced, holy fool who runs your Department. Talbot. A pratt of the first order," Bloxham fulminated, beer running out of the corners of his mouth and into his beard. "And what do you think, Pollock?"

Dryden experienced a sudden strange urge to declare his unqualified admiration for Great Battley International School and all who sailed in her but, sensing that Bloxham's humour did not run to that, he murmured his agreement.

"Mediocrity rules," Bloxham shouted. "If there's one thing I can't stand it's mediocrity marching beneath the banner of high-mindedness. Not that I believe for one minute that that gibbering crank, Bennett, had anything to offer in the way of an original idea in the first place. Man was a pious idiot, a sanctimonious satrap of the Middle Brow Educational Establishment. He was the epitome . . ." A peal of laughter rang out from down in the bar. The young women had now formed a circle around the lolling oafs who were finding that they had less and less room to loll.

"Hideous," Bloxham muttered into his pint. Dryden glanced at him, wondering whether he was still referring to Cyril Bennett or whether that was meant as a comment on the behaviour down in the bar. In a strange way he was attracted to Bloxham who showed the most sincere hatred of Great Battley International School, yet he was still repelled by the man's shambling, arty-farty demeanour. It was easy to see why Bloxham would detest the school vehemently for what he considered were its threadbare middle-brow pretentions but then why had he gone there in the first place?

"Where were you before Great Battley, Nigel?" Dryden asked.

"Thetterington Grammar. The Royal they called it though I could never conceive of royalty ever setting foot in the place."

"I gather it was better than Great Battley, though?"

"Good God, yes. Some of the staff were even quite intelligent. Alcoholic, of course, but with flair. Of course, there was an oafish side I abhorred. Rugby and all that infernal nonsense but I could ignore that," he sighed wearily. "No money in it though. Needed cash. Always need cash. Drove me out in the end." Bloxham finished his pint, glanced at his watch and stood up abruptly, bumping the table.

"Got to get back, Pollock," he said. "Nice to chat though. Knew you had to be a fellow malcontent. Ought to found a movement or something. Anti-Bennett Society for the Prevention of Internationalism in schools. Invite that vulgar harridan Rosie Kennedy as guest speaker, eh?" He grinned, nodded a farewell and waddled out of the bar. With a sidelong glance at the women down in the bar, Dryden followed him a few minutes later.

CHAPTER SIX

"Where the fuck is the Rhine?"

"That's enough of that, Roger." Dryden glared at the pock-marked youth who was leaning over his neighbour's atlas.

"Where's the Rhine, Sir?" came another voice. "It's not on this map." Dryden sighed and peered over Gillian's shoulder at the map of southern Italy she was poring over in her quest for Europe's largest river.

"Page forty-five, Gillian. It doesn't flow through Italy." Gillian pulled irritably at the pages of her school atlas.

"You'll find it in the middle of a large green bit running from the top of the page to the bottom."

"Oh yeah. I found it."

"Good. Draw it on the map I've given you and then mark in the most important cities."

"Is Munich on the Rhine, Sir?"

"No."

Dryden watched them sullenly, playing with his pencil. What would Mr. Cyril Bennett, O.B.E., have said to this little lot, he wondered. He thought of Wendy who at that very moment was teaching Norway to another class. In his mind's eye he saw her bottom moving seductively beneath her tight-fitting skirt. That's what they'd all be looking at, the filthy little brutes. Oh, they'd pretend to be so interested in her talk of fjords and mountains, all the while feasting their piggy little eyes on her body. He glared at his class ferociously, daring any of them to reveal his or her sexual fantasies. Sarah, a rather sweet faced girl, glanced up at him and smiled. He reddened and felt ashamed of himself. He sighed deeply. Several others in the class looked up at him and grinned. He knew what they were grinning about. So what if this was the first lesson they hadn't been on the verge of mutiny? So what if he had spent an hour dreaming up the simplest possible task, an outline map on a banda sheet. Mark in this, that and the next thing. Write a paragraph on the river Rhine. He would then have to mark the damn things. Most of it would be complete rubbish, of course. They'd have Berlin marked on the Rhine, Warsaw and probably Brussels as well. Suddenly, every

33

damn river in Europe would have become the Rhine. One or two might have sorted it out reasonably well but the rest of them would put down the first thing that came into their heads. He didn't blame them. They were bored stiff with European Studies. They couldn't see the point of it and neither could he. It was a meaningless ritual they were all performing for the benefit of an ex-Chairman of the County Council who had got an O.B.E. and died of a heart attack. Three of his pupils looked up at him and frowned. He smiled. They seemed to be enjoying themselves with his feeble little map. Good God, he thought, a mere fifteen years before he had had to sit at a desk and write précis of Virgil. Perhaps he had stumbled unwittingly upon something of 'educational value'. If he had, he would do it all the time. It was worth missing an hour's evening drinking time to keep them this quiet. Maybe there was a bob or two to be made out of this sort of stuff. He picked up a copy of the banda sheet. He screwed up his eyes at it. It would have to look a bit more professional than that but it could serve as a basis. An outline map with a series of pertinent questions followed by a crossword puzzle, a few pics, call it a unit and he would be coining it. Unit One. The Rhine. The sheets could be made detachable banda masters for quick and easy duplication. Package the whole kit in a glossy cover together with an easy marking scheme and he'd have Pollock's European Studies Series. Quick, efficient and absorbing. A godsend to the harassed teacher. No, it was too easy. Too much of that sort of stuff around. Educational Aids was big business these days. And mercilessly cutthroat. Showing up in the market place with a few tatty banda masters was hardly a world beater.

The bell rang as he hastily collected up the worksheets, glancing nervously in the direction of the blotchy-faced Ian who looked as if he was about to appeal for help. Dryden had successfully avoided him so far that week, nipping out of the classroom door even before the kids and bounding away up the corridor. Like a herd of prehistoric creatures the class struggled tiredly to its feet and lurched towards the door. Dryden bundled the pile of worksheets into his briefcase and shouldered his way through the Saurian throng that was muttering and munching and grumbling its way towards fresh pastures of knowledge. He spotted Wendy emerging from a door at the other end of the corridor.

"Dryden." A voice called him from behind. "Have you got a minute?" Maurice Talbot touched him on the shoulder. Wendy vanished in the crowd.

"Just a word about the files. Have you got a minute?"

Dryden nodded wearily, cast a longing glance at the spot where, but a second or two before, Wendy had been and followed Talbot's tall, spare figure into the Resources Room. The Motts were sitting down to lunch, each of them with a neat stack of crispbread sandwiches wrapped in foil and a pot of some special health promoting yoghourt. Christine smiled at him as she bit into her Ryvita. Caught you, hasn't he? her eyes seemed to say. Maurice Talbot pulled open a drawer of the filing cabinet behind his desk.

"Dryden, I think you know this is where we keep our files on European Studies." Talbot's voice was silken, slightly menacing. "Now, it's absolutely crucial that these files are kept in tip-top order. Norway, Baroque, Rumania, see they're all colour-coded and properly labelled . . ." A numbness had settled over Dryden at the sight of the rows of manilla folders in the drawer. Talbot was fanatical about files. He spent hours clipping together bits of paper and inserting them into manilla folders.

"A few days ago," his voice was icier now, "I happened to be looking through our file on Rumania. And I found this." Between the tips of his long fingers he held up a banana skin. It was shrivelled and almost black. "I conducted extensive enquiries among the staff and as far as I can estimate no-one else was eating a banana for lunch on that particular day." Dryden felt a sudden vast hollow where a moment before his heart had been beating. He blushed crimson. Of course he remembered eating the banana and, in a sudden panic, when the bell rang and he was supposed to be in dismissing his class, he had not been able to find a litter bin, (the Motts saw noneed for litter bins in the Resources Room)—he had wrenched open the drawer of the filing cabinet and stuffed the skin into a file, fully intending to retrieve it later.

"It must have been me," Dryden stammered. He grinned sheepishly.

"It would seem so," Talbot frowned. "Now, you must realise how extremely unpleasant it is for other staff to find old banana skins in these files. Apart from the fact that it has left a nasty brown stain on the inside of the folder." He showed it to Dryden. Dryden felt hot and cold flushes all over his body. How could he do such a thing? It was tantamount to weeing in a Church. As if Talbot and the Motts didn't already have a catalogue of heinous crimes he had committed.

"There is another matter I feel I ought to bring to your attention, while we're about it, Dryden, if I may. Stephen found yesterday that the dust-cover had been left off the console in the language laboratory. A quick check of the timetable showed it could only have been you."

"You were in there with a class in the last period." Stephen Mott fixed Dryden with a baleful watery glare.

"Yes . . ." Dryden managed in a husky voice. "I'm sorry, I forgot . . ."

"Quite." Talbot pursed his lips. Oh, he was enjoying this, Dryden could tell, his rubbery face suffused with a faint pink glow of satisfaction. Dryden just stopped himself from kneeling on the floor at Talbot's feet and clutching his trouser leg in supplication. For a minute, as the sun broke through the clouds and shone through the window behind Talbot's head it seemed as if the Senior Co-ordinator of International Studies was surrounded by a halo.

"It's not good enough, Dryden," Talbot murmured at him out of a holy, shining mist. "Not good enough."

"The cover must be put back on the console as soon as you've finished

35

with it," Stephen Mott drawled from somewhere behind Dryden. He felt his legs going wobbly at the knees. Incompetence. The word flashed on and off in his brain. He, Dryden Pollock, was incompetent. And he was not just incompetent in the ordinary way. He was the epitome of incompetence. Swollen with pride, he had dared enter the realms of responsibility. Gently Talbot closed the filing cabinet drawer and moved round to sit down at his desk. Dryden backed away from the cabinet and left the room.

That afternoon he taught with a kind of desperation, as if he could make up for the months of carelessness and incompetence. As was only to be expected, his pupils reacted badly to this unexpected dose of committed teaching. They talked and laughed loudly, threw darts at one another, scraped their chairs noisily and paid not the slightest heed to his attempts at engaging their attention. He, in turn, struggled to resist the urge to give up altogether and let them play noughts and crosses while he sullenly dreamt of mass murder behind his desk. At last the bell put an end to this ordeal. Drained of all energy, he retreated to the staff common room, morosely smoked a cigarette and went home.

Later that evening after his usual meal of baked beans on toast, he sat down in front of the television to mark the maps his European Studies class had filled in. As he had expected, many of them had marked in countries as far from the Rhine as Portugal and India and put all sorts of strange cities along the river. On the television an earnest looking man in a smart safari suit was ranting on about the disappearance of unique Indian cultures in Colombia, while in the background the objects of his concern danced about gleefully in tracksuits and running shoes. These days it was only a matter of hours before the latest fads had taken root at the remotest corners of the globe.

Next day Dryden arrived at school in a state of profound depression. Plagued by phantoms that had closely resembled Maurice Talbot waving manilla folders at him, he had slept badly during the night. The sight of the fanatical Stephen Mott slipping yet another memo into his pigeon-hole filled him with foreboding. He waited until Mott had left the staff room before venturing to read it. It was a reminder to all staff to be punctilious about replacing the cover on the console in the language laboratory immediately after use. A few minutes later Maurice Talbot entered, a sheaf of memos in his hand. Without a word he handed one to Dryden. It concerned the care of files in the Resources Room—'Due to some recent irregularities in the filing system . . .' it began. Everyone would know to what and to whom Talbot was referring, of course.

Goldway arrived and greeted Dryden cheerfully. "Cheer up, mate. Think of the staff meeting this afternoon."

"What staff meeting?" Dryden's heart sank. Goldway tapped the side of his nose. "Thursday, the twelfth. Staff meeting. The agenda's on the board. And it's a beauty. I shan't be there, of course. Have fun, though, won't you?" And he slipped away into the crowd. Dryden loped round to the staff notice-board. There for all to see was one of

Basil's long, densely worded agendas. Dryden cursed. He had completely forgotten about it. Oh why, oh why . . .? He took out his pocket diary and flicked over the pages. It was completely blank, of course, save for an entry from the previous July when for some unaccountable reason he had religiously noted down a visit to the dentist. Things were going from bad to worse. After the banana skin incident the day before he was well and truly on the run and now he was faced with the bleak prospect of an hour and a half of Basil's incomprehensible speechifying. Then he spotted Wendy and smiled. She smiled back. Briefly, his spirits lifted. He would ask her down to the Spotted Dog that lunchtime. Suddenly, he was chagrined to see her walking off towards Devereaux. Dryden glowered at him.

"It's outrageous," a voice droned in Dryden's ear. It was Ken Tyler, the arch bore of the Science Department. Dryden peered at the agenda. He tried to read the first sentence but got lost. It was all to do with litter, he gathered. Next to promoting international understanding Basil's primary concern as Headmaster of Great Battley was his constant preoccupation with litter.

"Why the hell are we discussing that, for God's sake?" said another voice. "We never discuss anything important."

"Litter is important, mate," Rosie's voice boomed out from the other end of the staff common room. She was all ears was that woman. "You may think it isn't but I can tell you that if we don't do something about all the litter lying round the place this school'll go under. You haven't been out on the grounds and had a look round, mate. It's blimmin disgusting."

It is, too," came Devereaux's voice. Dryden scowled at the sound of it. Devereaux never lost an opportunity to publicly agree with the authorities.

"See, he knows the problem. He's got a finger on the pulse," Rosie declared. Devereaux smiled.

If only he had some excuse to get out of the meeting, Dryden thought. Pursuing his new policy of vacating the premises thirty seconds after the kids, he had been dreaming of a nice lie-down after school before the rigours of the evening's television.

"Isn't it riveting?" Goldway had re-appeared at Dryden's shoulder. "What a pity I shan't be there."

"What's your excuse?" Dryden muttered sourly.

"I'd already planned to attend a session for prospective fathers at our local pre-natal clinic, dear boy. The session starts at four."

Dryden stared at him in surprise. "Is Ruth expecting?"

Goldway put his fingers to his lips. "No, you duffer!" he whispered. "Well, if she is, I'm not responsible."

"Then how—"

"The midwife who runs the sessions is a mate of Ruth's. We scratch each other's backs occasionally. And dear old Basil fell for it hook, line and sinker. You know what a family minded old duffer he is."

"I'll tell, Goldway, I swear." Dryden swore.

"Tell all you like. ring the hospital if you like. My name's on the list." And with that Goldway darted off gleefully. He was so damnably well organised, Dryden reflected bitterly. Goldway meticulously copied down every meeting for the year (and there were hundreds), selected a suitable number to attend for appearance's sake and busily devised cast-iron excuses for the rest. And cast-iron excuses they had to be for Basil took an exceedingly dim view of staff trying to wriggle out of meetings.

Basil had meeting mania. He gave every sign of being terrified of people and encountering them anywhere other than in a meeting, he invariably behaved like a cornered animal but, with the peculiar logic of the bureaucrat, he immersed himself in a gruelling programme of meetings in order to pre-empt the accusation that his staff had not been consulted in the 'decision-making process'. He held meetings about everything. There were staff meetings, there were meetings of 'senior management', 'middle management' and 'junior management'. There were senior, middle and lower school pastoral meetings, Heads of Department meetings, year tutor meetings and senior and assistant co-ordinator meetings. If the staff were not to be found in a classroom or at home then they were almost certainly to be found in one of Basil's meetings.

Litter, Dryden grimaced, as he made his way as slowly as possible up towards his form room. It was now after nine and he was hoping the mysterious Head of Fifth Year would have arrived, stormed into Five Grigorescu and quelled the morning riot. Litter had never concerned him in the least. Yet it had pursued him relentlessly throughout his teaching career hitherto. Even at the grammar school they had talked endlessly about litter. There the Headmaster had even taken to patrolling the school grounds late in the evening, armed with a spike, hunting the little flocks of sweet papers that he firmly believed hid in the shrubbery during the day, only to come out in the evenings to dance like fairies on that holy of holies, the school cricket pitch.

He found Five Grigorescu sitting at their desks for once, looking sullen but subdued.

"She was in here," one of the girls muttered at him venomously as he sat down to take the register. "What a bitch she is."

"That's enough," Dryden screamed hysterically. Five Grigorescu grinned at one another. He recovered his composure and began calling their names, enjoying the temporary triumph of the forces of law and order over them. Temporary it was, for by the time morning registration ended, Five Grigorescu were lounging about the room in various stages of undress, making lewd comments to one another. Sex, all they ever thought about was sex, Dryden scowled at them, as the bell rang.

"Donnez-moi un bonbon," Stephen Mott was drawling when Dryden poked his head in through the door of the Resources Room.

"Voila," Christine shrilled. "Qu'est-ce que vous dites?"

"Merci, madame."

"Je vous en prie." Dryden realised they were rehearsing an audio-visual lesson. They had probably started it over breakfast back in their immaculate neo-Georgian semi.

"That was your tutor group, wasn't it, making that terrible row?" Christine had caught sight of him. "Poor old Pam had to come along and shut them up. You weren't here." Dryden smiled and shut the door. The Motts were now in full cry after yesterday's banana skin incident.

Contrary to his expectations the morning passed relatively peacefully, if somewhat tediously. When the lunch bell rang, Dryden nipped out of the door before the kids were even aware the lesson was over, hurried downstairs and lay in wait for Wendy. Ten minutes later she appeared, surrounded by a gaggle of teenage boys. Filthy swine, Dryden muttered to himself. He touched her on the arm and mouthed the words 'Spotted Dog'. She smiled. He had to wait a further five minutes before she managed to extricate herself from the group of fifteen year old sex maniacs.

"Do you have to put up with that all the time?" Dryden smiled at her cheerfully. Wendy frowned.

"They were having problems. They were wanting to know all about the Norwegian oilfields."

"I see. And what did you tell them?"

She smiled. "As much as I know. They're so eager to learn, aren't they? And so polite. They're always bringing me work they've done. Especially the boys. It makes me wonder if anyone's ever bothered with them before."

Dryden said nothing. How would she react when they started pawing her with their clammy little hands, he wondered. Would she see that, too, as a refreshing eagerness to learn? They walked into the staff common room. Rosie was bellowing in fury.

"He's done it again you know. Honestly, I don't know how he manages to do these things."

Arnold Scoresby, Dryden thought. Poor old Arnold. He must have ballsed something up again.

"I mean," Rosie shook her head, "he knew the geography staff were all away today. They told him, I told him, the Head told him. And still he forgot. He put them all down to cover one another's classes. It's hopeless."

"What was all that about?" Wendy asked him as they drove down to the Spotted Dog.

"Arnold Scoresby the deputy head. He's always making cock-ups."

Arnold had been known to entirely forget what day it was. Once, so the story went, he had not turned up at school in the morning and the Headmaster, ringing him up at home, had discovered Arnold was having a lie-in. He had thought it was Sunday. This sort of forgetfulness was a serious fault in a man, who, after all, was supposed to be responsible for the day to day running of the school.

Dryden's efforts that lunch time to steer Wendy's thoughts onto things other than school proved futile. She was still in a state of euphoria after her years at Charles Darwin.

"I'm really enjoying teaching for the first time, you know," she beamed. "I just love the kids. Even the working class ones."

"Working class ones? I didn't know we had any of those."

"Oh, there are a few," Wendy smiled. "I expect they slipped in somehow. After all, they don't have to be intelligent to go to this school, do they? That's what's so wonderful about it. It's really trying to do something useful. What vision that man must have had."

"Who? Cyril Bennett?"

"Yes. No wonder they gave him the O.B.E. If only he could see his school now."

"Wendy, what are you doing at half term?" Half term was some weeks off but Dryden thought of holidays long before they were due. He had already thought of the Christmas holidays and Easter. Mostly, he just drove aimlessly round the country getting drunk.

"Oh," Wendy grimaced. "I'm going to the West Country with my parents." She sighed. "I hate holidays. And I'll hate them even more now, I expect. I used to thank God for holidays when I was at Charles Darwin but here it's so different, isn't it? Time just rushes by. There's so much to do."

Dryden was considering whether his Viva might make it to the West Country. After a couple of days with Harry and Sue, he'd be needing a rest.

"Whereabouts in the West Country?"

"Oh, near Padstow. It's very lovely but there's nothing to do. Daddy sleeps most of the time and Mummy reads novels. I go for walks. Mind you, this time I intend to take my marking down with me." Her eyes positively gleamed at the prospect. Where the hell was Padstow? Dryden was thinking. He knew nothing at all about the West Country. He knew it was some sort of vague protuberance into the ocean but that was all.

"Ah, Padstow," he smiled, his eyes lighting up. "I know that place. It's lovely, isn't it? So peaceful."

"Dead would be a better word, I think," Wendy gave him a curious glance. "Mind you, Cornwall as a whole is nice. Not that I would want to live there." Ah, Cornwall, Dryden thought. That was the end bit of the peninsula. A few minutes later his lying had succeeded in eliciting from Wendy the location of her parents' house by the sea. He drove her back to school, very pleased with himself. That very afternoon he would rush out and buy a map of the West Country. It was then he remembered the staff meeting and cursed long and silently, as he parked the car and showed Wendy how to get into the school the back way, for the bell for afternoon school had already sounded.

CHAPTER SEVEN

At precisely four o'clock, Nathan Goldway was seen hurrying out of the school with a decidedly self-satisfied look on his face. Dryden roused himself out of his semi-comatose state in the staff common room and ambled along to the school library. Most of the staff were already there, having dashed in early to crouch in the back rows marking books or drawing pictures or reading catalogues of expensive educational aids or quietly dozing. In the front rows sat those people who viewed these occasions as an excellent opportunity to hold forth to a captive audience.

He decided to sit in one of the middle rows. He looked round and saw that Wendy was sitting next to Reg Devereaux. She gazed expectantly towards the large table where the Headmaster, Rosie Kennedy and Arnold Scoresby waited for the staff to assemble and settle themselves down. Dryden, of course, had forgotten his copy of the agenda. He had also forgotten his diary and anything else that might have helped him while away the next crashingly tedious hour and a half. He, therefore, took out his cheque-book and prepared to indulge in some truly infantile doodling.

Basil had clearly spent a great deal of time composing his agenda. Staff meetings in particular made him extremely nervous. He looked round furtively as if to check his distance from the nearest emergency exit. Without fully realising it, however, Basil had a very powerful weapon at his disposal. In the twinkling of an eye he was able to induce a state of stupefied boredom in large gatherings of people. The very sight of him up at the table nervously fingering his incomprehensible agenda induced a feeling of overpowering drowsiness. From all around Dryden came the sound of suppressed yawning.

A few minutes later the Headmaster began. Within seconds all save a few desperate souls, had completely lost track of what he was saying and were happily busy about their own affairs, some inspecting their nails, others ruminatively picking their noses, still others staring blankly at the library shelves around them. It all reminded Dryden of a Greek mass he had once attended by mistake. He had been looking for a lecture on Existentialism at the time and had suddenly found himself in a Church. A minute or two had elapsed before he realised that the celebrant's gorgeous robes and the smell of incense didn't really correspond to his vague notion of a lecture on Existentialism. Embarrassed at his own stupidity, he had nevertheless remained in the Church pretending he was a Greek Orthodox Englishman. Of the people around him, scarcely anyone had bothered themselves with the incomprehensible goings-on up at the altar. Indeed, the altar itself had been obscured from view by a screen. The congregation had happily busied itself with passing the time: chatting, pointing at other people, laughing, picking noses and even eating little snacks from time to time. It was then Dryden had fully understood what it meant to 'hear mass'. The mass itself meant no more than the pleasant twittering of birds in the bushes behind a family picnic. Now he was struck yet again by the resemblance of one of Basil's staff meetings to a Greek mass. The Headmaster was now well into his incomprehensible liturgy on item one of the agenda, his arms waving about in vague, airy gestures. He seemed to be addressing the Reference Section of the library.

Dryden glanced furtively at Wendy. The dear, delicious woman was frowning slightly as she concentrated on the Headmaster's peroration. Undoubtedly, she was the only person present who was actually trying to follow the drift of Basil's argument. Devereaux, sitting next to her, his arms folded, had a glazed look on his face. He had planted himself very visibly in a middle row, ready at any time to agree publicly with everything the Headmaster said.

"Well, I think I've said just about all I was intending to say on this particular item," Basil grinned sheepishly round the room. "Has anyone anything further to add?" There was a long silence. People had begun to stir, suddenly embarrassed that they had been caught napping or playing. An evil smile played round Rosie's lips. 'I don't know why the Head bothers, quite honestly,' Dryden imagined her saying to herself. 'All this blimmin' consultation nonsense. Look at 'em. They're all sitting there half asleep. He should just tell 'em what to do, mate. And make 'em do it. And if they don't like it, they can blimmin' well lump it. There's people queueing up to work here.' Alas, Rosie's frank despotism was decidedly out of fashion these days. Nowadays autocracy had been renamed the 'decision-making process'.

Basil frowned at his agenda. "Shall we go on to the next item then?" Several minutes of droning followed before he paused again. This time Ken Tyler, the arch bore of the Science Department got to his feet and held forth, rivalling Basil in all respects for sheer monotony. Tyler sat down. No-one else had anything to say. Basil moved on. Item number three: Middle Management stratagems re items number one and two. Someone else stood up and ranted vehemently, asserting that item three was really a question that ought properly to be discussed at a Middle Management Meeting. Item four: allocation of supervisory litter duties. Item five: litter in the neighbourhood of the school and the school's responsibility for it. Item six: more litter. Litter on weekends and public holidays, Dryden thought. Litter in London, New York, Paris and Rome. Litter and the Arms Race. Litter and the Middle East Question. The staff were prostrate. Rosie yawned long and loud.

Arnold Scoresby appeared to be sound asleep. From the back rows somewhere came the sound of gentle snoring. On and on Basil went. His eyes now had a fanatical look in them, as if he had completely forgotten where he was and was imagining himself addressing a rally at Nuremberg. Dryden glanced round at Wendy. She was looking at him. He reddened slightly and smiled back at her. She frowned. He shrugged his shoulders. There was a fleeting smile on her lips before she looked away and tried to concentrate on what the Headmaster was saying now. Finally, with a triumphant flourish, Basil came to a halt. He glanced at his watch, then stared at the staff with an expression of great satisfation.

"Any further business?"

Suddenly behind Dryden there was a slight commotion. He turned round. Bloxham, the Head of English Studies was on his feet, his hairy face red with anger.

"Headmaster: I have some further business." He looked round fanatically. There was an immediate stir as people suddenly woke up, exchanging furtive glances of horror or delight.

"We've sat here for over an hour listening to this unbelievable trivia about litter. At our last staff meeting we dealt with . . . uh . . ." Bloxham consulted a notebook, "the question of wet weather wear in corridor locker rooms. When are we ever going to get round to discussing worthwhile issues such as methods of assessment of pupils or the authority structure in the school or the desperate need to overhaul the curriculum?"

There was a long dangerous silence. Rosie's eyes had become two narrow slits. She hated Bloxham. He was a stirrer. In Rosie's ideal world he would have been strangled at birth. Basil had gone red in the face. He opened his mouth to speak but for a moment there was no sound. Everyone in the room was alert now. No more sleeping. Bloxham had fired off a very provocative broadside.

"I . . . uh . . ." Basil shifted uneasily in his chair, desperately searching for something to say. Suddenly a look of appeal came into his eyes. He turned to Rosie. Rosie nodded at the Headmaster almost imperceptibly.

"It's very late," she said. "I'm sure we've all got homes to go to, haven't we?" People shifted about restlessly and looked at their watches. Bloxham leapt to his feet.

"Oh no!" he shouted. "The meeting isn't finished yet. I have raised further business."

A few people had begun to murmur disconsolately. It was after half past five. Rosie looked at the Headmaster, who in turn looked at Arnold Scoresby, who went pale. The deputy head cleared his throat.

"I appreciate your point, Nigel," he began firmly, "but I think some of us would like to be clear on what it is you're asking for exactly?"

"I should have thought it was perfectly clear," Bloxham snorted. "I, for one, would like to know when we are going to have a staff meeting to discuss issues of some significance. Wet weather gear and litter are hardly issues of significance."

"Yes, but what is the point of your demand? What are you asking us to discuss now, Nigel? That's all we're trying to find out."

"All right," Bloxham said, "I am raising the question of staff meetings being reserved as a forum for important educational and pastoral issues, I'm sure I've made this point before but, of course, it has been studiously ignored like everything else in this school."

"I really don't see the point of this, Nigel . . . I must say," the Headmaster burst out angrily. "I mean . . . in the context of these staff meetings and as a result of the ongoing process of consultation, I would have thought it was perfectly clear that the sort of issue we turned our collective attentions upon, as it were, was not the sort of issue that could be excluded from the, shall we say, wider implicaions of the management structures that obtain, some might say, prevail within these four walls." He glared at Bloxham ferociously. "Furthermore, it is getting towards the end of the day and we're all very tired and I'm sure I speak for the majority of colleagues when I venture to make this statement, namely that such issues of what you and perhaps others may care to call issues of wider significance would be more appropriately, perhaps more effectively, raised within the context of a forum specially designated for this purpose, wouldn't you say?" Bloxham blinked owlishly at the Headmaster and shook his head. A few people were making for the door, nodding at Rosie who nodded back, an expression of grim determination on her face. Finally, Bloxham seemed to have made some sense of Basil's outburst.

"I consider a full staff meeting the ideal forum, Headmaster. It doesn't have to be specially designated as such by you or anyone else."

Basil sank back in his chair and shot a look of appeal at Rosie. She leaned forward threateningly across the table, her palms pressed together, her fingers intertwined.

"There's no time for this Blox . . . Nigel," she said. "People have got families to attend to. Meals to cook, kids to get to bed. It's blimmin' late as it is."

"Late because we've spent so much time on trivia," Bloxham roared back. He was white with fury. Cries of 'bloody nonsense' and 'sit down, you fat poof' were heard from the back rows. Dryden glanced at Wendy. She was looking pale and shocked. Devereaux was now on his feet.

"I agree, Head. I think we should call it a day. Some of us have got kids to feed and get to bed. This isn't the time to start bringing up things for discussion now, is it?"

"Crawler," someone shouted from the back. Devereaux looked round guiltily and sat down.

"Can't we take a vote on this, Headmaster?" droned a familiar voice. It was Stephen Mott. "That would be the proper procedure in the circumstances, I'm sure. I know that at my last school it was a regular procedure to vote on prolonging discussion of matters raised under Any Other Business."

The Headmaster, Rosie and Arnold went into a huddle up at the table. More people were getting up to leave. The library was rapidly emptying.

"May I put in a word here, Head?" Maurice Talbot stood up. The Headmaster nodded at him eagerly. "I think we're all aware what kind of forum a full staff meeting is and the context of the discussion. There's a pretty full description of it in 'Notes for Staff Guidance, Page Thirty-Nine, Section Ten, Subsection D . . ." Here he was interrupted by someone shouting rudely that 'Notes For Staff Guidance' was the biggest load of rubbish under the sun. Talbot gave a pained smile. "These, as we all know," he went on, "are issued to all staff upon their appointment" He waved a copy of the document. "I would refer you to it. It explains everything." "It explains bugger all," someone shouted from the back. "It's unreadable," said another voice. Talbot shrugged and sat down.

"I vote we take a vote on it," Bernard McGraw, the Head of Musical Studies said in his hee-haw voice. "Maybe then we can all go home."

"What do you say to that Nigel?" Arnold Scoresby said to Bloxham.

"Why do we need a vote on it? And on what?" Bloxham snapped. "It's ludicrous."

"We want to vote to see if we can all go home now. I vote we all go home," someone called from the back. "Vote! Vote!" other people started calling. "Let's have a vote." Basil stared at the remaining staff in unhappy, red-faced confusion. "Vote! Vote!" came the ragged call.

"Perhaps . . . that is . . . it would seem a sizeable majority of those present notwithstanding those colleagues who, for a variety of differing commitments, have already departed, might consider a vote the most appropriate course of action in the context of your suggestion, Nigel." Basil had recovered somewhat and smiled proudly at the success of this statement. Bloxham shrugged. He seemed to have given up.

A vote was taken among those remaining. Dryden raised his hand both times. No-one seemed to notice. Out of the confusion, however, it appeared that a majority had voted against Bloxham. The meeting came to an end. The Headmaster leaned back and wiped his brow. Rosie followed Bloxham's exit from the library with a venomous look in her eyes. The caretaker stood just inside the library door, scowling mutinously and glancing ostentatiously at his wrist-watch.

Dryden caught up with Wendy just as she walked into the staff common room.

"What did you make of that then?" he grinned. She gave him an anxious look.

"I don't know why people have to make such a fuss," she said. "I thought the Head handled it all very well." Dryden's grin widened. A few of the staff were standing around Bloxham, muttering in conspiratorial tones. Rosie clumped in and pretended to be busy about the notice-board, all the while swivelling her finely-tuned antennae in the direction of the malcontents around Bloxham.

"It's outrageous," Bloxham declared. "I've never seen anything like it. The man's mad. This absurdly autocratic behaviour has got to stop."

"He's running scared," said another. "And like all autocrats he reacts by going on the attack."

"The level of political consciousness in this staff room is minimal, of course." Bloxham pursed his lips. "Toryism is endemic. The 'they know best so keep your trap shut' brigade."

"Isn't there anything we can do to resist this mad despotism?" cried an eager young woman, a probationary teacher in the English Faculty. Rosie's eyes swivelled dangerously in her direction. For Christ's sake keep your trap shut, Dryden silently pleaded with the girl. Rosie'll have you supervising senior classes in motor mechanics.

"Somehow, we've got to make him realise that true consultation is more than just a ritual rubber stamping of his decisions," Bloxham said. "Which brings us back to the dialectic, of course."

The others nodded sagely at this. At this point no-one dared admit that they didn't have the faintest idea what a 'dialectic' was. But whatever it was, it sounded suitably ominous and revolutionary, a word that bestowed a nice scientific inexorability on any form of resistance to establishment oppression. Rosie clumped out of the staff room. She had heard enough.

CHAPTER EIGHT

'Bollocks loves Tits.' Dryden stared glumly at the words etched in letters an inch and a half high on one of the brand new desks in the language laboraory. Merciless little swine, he thought. It was an invitation to mass murder if ever there was one. Maurice Talbot inspected the letters distainfully.

"Done with a compass I should think. I made the usual enquiries, of course, and knew it had to be one of your group." In Talbot's phraseology everyone else had 'classes'. Dryden had 'groups'.

"I presumed that the first word was some kind of obscene pun on your surname," Talbot sniffed. "Who . . . the other person is, I have no idea. I think we ought to try and find the culprit. Have you any idea who might have been responsible, Dryden?"

It could have been one of a dozen kids, Dryden thought grimly. He had been indulging in one of his audio-visual lessons. The tape recorder had squawked and gabbled at high speed, the slide projector had blown a bulb and the black-out curtains had fallen down. It had been pandemonium. The class had milled wildly around the language laboratory, hooting and howling. Dryden had seriously considered using the broken projector as a weapon to restore order. Amidst all of this, there would have been plenty of time to etch graffiti at one's leisure.

"It's difficult," Dryden frowned.

"Your seating plan for the language laboratory will be in the file, won't it?" Talbot murmured, knowing perfectly well that it wasn't. Dryden shook his head.

"That's a pity," Talbot said. "That's why I ask colleagues to do them as soon as possible after the beginning of term, Dryden. It makes it so much easier to deal with this sort of vandalism, doesn't it?" Dryden nodded.

"Well, we'll just have to try and work from memory, won't we?" Talbot took out a slim pocket diary and a pen and glanced expectantly at Dryden who, in truth, had no idea which kid had sat at which desk, this due to the fact that none of them had spent more than a second sitting down during the whole lesson.

"Who was sitting in that row?"

Frantically, Dryden tried to conjure up the name of any pupil who had been present in his disastrous audio-visual lesson. But his mind had gone completely blank. Not only could he not remember the names of any of those particular pupils, he couldn't now remember the name of any single child he taught in any of his classes.

"Starting from that end," Talbot gestured with his pen. "Who sat there?"

"I . . . uh . . ." Dryden was on the verge of panic. "I . . . uh . . . Ryan O'Neal," he blurted, not daring to look Talbot in the eyes.

"Ryan O'Neal?" Talbot frowned. "Don't think I've come across him. What tutor group, do you know?"

"Four Dostoevsky, I think."

Talbot made a note of it. "And next to him?"

"Faye Dunaway," Dryden said confidently. "Blonde girl with grey, blue eyes."

"And next to Faye?"

"Hedda Gabler."

"Hedda Gabler? Isn't that the name of a poem or something?"

"She's . . . ah . . . part Norwegian, I believe," Dryden said hastily. "Nice girl, actually."

"Hedda Gabler," Talbot repeated, writing the name in his pocket diary. "O.K. Well that's something to go on, isn't it? I'll send a note round to form tutors to send those pupils up to me for a chat." God, what had he done? Dryden groaned. Talbot would be beside himself with fury.

"I think you'd better leave this to me, Dryden. It's a very serious matter."

Dryden's throat had gone dry. He picked up his briefcase and hurried out of the door. He had about two hours before Talbot would find out that Ryan O'Neal, Faye Dunawaye and Hedda Gabler were not pupils of Great Battley International School. He ran downstairs and made straight for the staff common room. Rosie was in there, with several others, including Reg Devereaux.

"I'd have blimmin' sacked him on the spot," Rosie snorted. "He's got a cheek. The Head's furious."

"I bet he is," Devereaux said. "Who does he think he is, saying what sort of things we ought to be discussing? The litter problem is one of the biggest issues facing education today."

"He's always been a stirrer," Rosie scowled. "I was against his appointment from the start. He was so blimmin' high and mighty. Talked on and on about world art and literature. The Head was taken in, of course. So was the Vicar. All that high falutin' stuff. I saw right away what an act the whole thing was. These grammar school types you know. You can't trust 'em. The Head's very upset."

"It was all so totally unnecessary, wasn't it?" Devereaux went on. "Still, I'm glad we had that vote. That put a stop to it."

"Vote?" Rosie stared at Devereaux aghast. "That was completely pointless. I dunno whose crack-brained idea that was. Fancy having a vote on whether we go on talking or not . . ."

"Yeah, that was really stupid, I suppose," Devereaux agreed hastily. "Pointless. I've never known anything like it . . ."

". . . my opinion the Head should have put his foot down there and then. He's far too gentle with the likes of Bloxham, y'know. All this consultation and what have you, it doesn't get us anywhere," Rosie said. "Tell 'em what to do, mate, that's the way. If they don't like it they can jolly well lump it. There are plenty of other schools they can go to. We've got people queueing up to work here, y'know . . ."

Dryden crept round to the notice-board. Pinned to the Headmaster's section of it was one of Basil's long letters to the staff, full of phrases like 'the functional parameters' and 'within the decisional infrastructure'. Dryden gathered it was Basil's answer to Bloxham's challenge. There were ominous references to 'school policy' and the famed 'Notes For Staff Guidance'. Poor old Basil. Under fire he became frantic, drafting endless counter-attacks and apologia. Below Basil's letter a copy of 'Notes For Staff Guidance' had been pinned to the wall for ready reference.

'Notes For Staff Guidance' was a lengthy, densely-worded document containing Basil's interpretation of Cyril Bennett's grand vision of Great Battley International School. Here everything from the ideals of Cyril Bennett's Internationalism to the correct procedures for disciplining pupils who had not done their homework were to be found. In theory, 'school policy', i.e. Basil's decisions ceased to be a bewildering succession of seemingly irrelevant and contradictory edicts and regulations if understood in the context of 'Notes for Guidance'. 'I would draw colleagues' attention to page such and such, paragraph so and so . . .' was one of the Headmaster's constant exhortations. The trouble was, very few of the staff had ever bothered to read the thing.

In the first flush of enthusiasm for his new job, Dryden had thought of reading it but he had been so utterly bewildered by the first sentence that, as usual, he had given up and watched a soap opera on television. His mental sloth where official looking documents were concerned bordered on the criminal. However, unlike Bloxham, who contemptuously consigned anything 'official' to the nearest waste-paper basket, Dryden guiltily stored up large sheaves of official documents, some in various corners of his house, some beneath the back seat of his car or in the boot, others beneath his raincoat in his staff common room locker. He kept them against the day when someone would approach him with the ringing challenge: 'It was in the document I sent round last May.'

It appeared to be Basil's firm conviction that Cyril Bennett's vision of internationalism could best be realised in a truly majestic tide of paper. Several secretaries were employed full time to keep pace with the

Headmaster's mammoth production of notes on this or that, reports on this or that, minutes of this or that meeting or indeed the thousands of memoranda he circulated every week. At times a veritable tidal wave of memos from Basil engulfed the staff. They ended up drifting about the school like autumn leaves, turning up in odd places like the car park or the hockey pitch. They piled up in corners or stuck to one's shoes, yellowing and curly-edged. Dryden sometimes had a nightmare vision of driving home to Winkworth and being suddenly blinded in a blizzard of Basil's memos, descending out of an otherwise placid evening sky.

"So, I missed the fun." Goldway appeared beside him. "Sounded an absolute hoot."

"We had a vote to see if we could all go home," Dryden whispered. "You've heard the Inquisition round the corner. Rosie's baying for Bloxham's blood."

"I try to pick my meetings carefully but I missed out this time," Goldway murmured. "I think I'll come to the next one. Pity. I had a terrific excuse."

"Oh? What was that? Grandmother died in Tel Aviv?" Dryden snapped tartly.

"Nothing so obvious, Pollock old chap. Nothing so obvious," Goldway grinned.

"You're unprincipled, Goldway. Is nothing sacred?"

"Getting out of one of Basil's terrible meetings is, old boy," he chuckled.

Throughout the lunch-hour the staff common room buzzed with conversation. Dryden had never seen people looking so animated. Bloxham made a brief appearance, glanced disdainfully round the room and left. Though his superior and condescending mannerisms had never endeared him to his colleagues, there were those who thought his direct attack on the Headmaster had been the best thing that had ever happened. For too long they had worked in the cloud of incense that Basil had continually wafted round the altar of 'school policy'. The rituals of the 'decision making process' had been publicly denounced as meaningless and irrelevant.

Rosie's eyes darted in all directions at once, spying out the groups of the disaffected, making mental notes of facial expressions, gestures, etc. for future reference. Since the Headmaster invariably went into hiding when anything went wrong, Rosie considered it her special duty to make an accurate appraisal of staff reaction. One slip of the tongue and one could be condemned to hours of substituting with difficult classes, to bus duties in the pouring rain or to double doses of after school detention supervision. Keenly aware of this possibility, Dryden kept well out of the range of Rosie's roving eye.

As the lunch-hour drew to a close, Dryden became more and more nervous. Maurice Talbot would undoubtedly have spent the whole lunch-hour on one of his dogged investigations into crime and indeed must now know that Ryan O'Neal, Faye Dunaway and Hedda Gabler could not be held responsible for the graffiti on the new desk in the language laboratory. In the staff common room Dryden felt relatively safe. Outside he was in mortal danger. He decided to concentrate on evasive action for the remainder of the afternoon.

"Dryden, a word please, if I may." For a split second, Dryden was on the verge of fainting at the sound of the voice. But it was David Hepworth, the Co-ordinator of Religious Studies.

"I've just caught one of your boys smoking in the High Street. Michael Kelly it was. I challenged him, of course, and he was—well—terribly rude back to me. He ran into the Spotted Dog, is it? He's under age, of course." Hepworth glared down at Dryden, his smooth face creased in a frown. Hepworth was a young, very tall and rather effete individual. Behind his back he was usually referred to by the nickname 'Auntie Marge' on account of his fussy, old-maidish ways. His effeminacy, however, belied the fact that he was an extremely dangerous human being. Dressed in a blue cardigan and immaculately pressed slacks, he conducted an unceasing campaign against all forms of deviance from prescribed rules and regulations. He was the sort of person who reported total strangers to the police if he saw them weeing in a park or picking flowers on public property. He was an ardent admirer of traditional authority, positively drooled over the Royal Family and quite openly admitted he would like to see all Socialists, Libertarians, Atheists, Ne'er-do-wells, Working Class People, Blacks, Pakistanis, Drunks, Smokers and most Children put to death. Dryden hastily stubbed out his cigarette.

"Really?" He feigned outrage. "He's a proper little hoodlum, that kid." Hepworth's eyes were examining Dryden carefully, noting every sign of irresponsibility and dissipation about the person of the Assistant Co-ordinator of European Studies.

"What are you going to do about it?" Hepworth asked. "I've written a report on it for the authorities. Shall I pass it on to you?"

"Yes. Do." Dryden nodded eagerly. Written a report? Hepworth was a compulsive informer. IRA supergrasses were nothing by comparison. He had apparently once reported a bus driver for braking too heavily and skidding on a wet road. His written report to the relevant authorities had almost got the driver sacked.

"You'll do something about it, I hope. He shouldn't be allowed to get away with it. He was terribly rude to me."

"Sure, David. I'll deal with him straight away."

Seemingly satisfied with this, Hepworth glided away towards the common room door. The bell rang. Dryden fetched his register and made his way slowly up to Five Grigorescu. They grimaced as he entered. Michael Kelly was there, a long, gangly youth with green streaked teeth, sweaty hands and wearing a short leather jacket with a cluster of swastikas on the back. Dryden called the register. There were grunts in reply.

52

"Michael Kelly. Can you see me at the end of registration please," Dryden said calmly and tonelessly. The youth darted a venomous look at him and promptly went into a huddle with his two sidekicks. With the bell, Five Grigorescu stretched, yawned, mumbled and stared sourly at Dryden as they sauntered out of the room. He suppressed the usual urge to go utterly berserk, throttle half of them with his bare hands and hurl the other half of them out of the windows. He smiled at them instead, through clenched teeth, and closed the door. Michael Kelly sat on a desk at the back of the room.

"Would you come here please, Michael." Very slowly, the youth got up and as insolently as he could strolled up to the desk. Dryden controlled a desire to kick the loathsome little swine in the testicles without further ado and instead put on his 'seriously concerned' face. "Mr. Hepworth was talking to me just now. You were smoking in the village, weren't you?" The youth looked out of the window. For an instant, Dryden reflected how much easier and saner it would be if he and the youth got together and carefully planned David Hepworth's murder instead. But the world wasn't made that way. Dryden and David Hepworth were on one side of the front line while Michael Kelly was on the other.

"There's no use denying it. He's written a report. I'll have to see the Head of Fifth Year about it, I'm afraid. You know the rules."

"Do what you like. I don't care."

"Okay, fine. That's settled then. You'll no doubt be hearing in due course." He gathered up the register. The youth stared at him mutinously.

"You smoke, don't you?"

Dryden hesitated. "Yes, I do. I don't see what that's got to do with it."

"You must feel pretty stupid getting me into trouble for something you do yourself, don't you?"

The youth's gaze was steady, unflinching. Somewhere in that ghastly conglomeration of acne, limbs and unwashed pubescence a brain was at work, Dryden thought.

"You know the rule, Michael. Mr. Hepworth's quite right. He's asked me to deal with it."

"Hepworth's a faggot, a poofter and an arsehole."

"That's enough!" Dryden narrowed his eyes, trying not to let the youth see that he agreed with him wholeheartedly.

"Okay, Sir. I ain't got long in this dump anyway. But I'll tell you what—Sir—if ever I get the opportunity to blow this stupid place sky high, I'll do it." With that Michael Kelly, yet another fifteen year old terrorist (one of thousands) heaved his ungainly teenage body upright and stalked out of the room.

Peace and love, Dryden raised his hand at the youth's back. Then he

53

tiptoed along the corridor and peered in through the window in the Resources Room door. The room was empty. His heart pounding, he darted in through the door, quickly collected up what he needed and was just on the point of going out when the telephone rang. For a second or two he hesitated. Then he went to Talbot's desk and lifted the receiver.

"Hello? Hello?" Dryden recognised the voice as belonging to Arnold Scoresby, Great Battley's diminutive deputy head. "Hello? Is that you Basil? Look, I've finally decided I'm going to step down after all. I think it's probably the best thing to do in the circumstances as you and Rosie were suggesting. I know Maurice Talbot will probably be in line for the job and I'll certainly be submitting an application for Bloxham's position. I'll have to pop in sometime this afternoon and have a chat with you about it. When can you see me, do you think?"

Dryden was sweating. He stared aghast at the receiver. The deputy head had dialled the wrong number.

"I . . . uh . . ." He made his voice sound like Basil's. "Shall we say three forty-five?"

"Hello? Hello? I'm sorry Head, I didn't hear the time you said."

"Three forty-five," Dryden said gruffly into the receiver.

"Fine. That suits me fine. Thanks. I'll see you then." And Arnold hung up. Trembling, Dryden replaced the receiver and fled from the Resources Room. As he tottered down the stairs, his mind in a whirl, he remembered a long document that the Headmaster had circulated to all staff soon after Dryden's arrival at Great Battley. This document had been entitled 'Towards Efficient Communications'. By the time he arrived at the door of the classroom where he was due to teach, the tears of mirth were rolling down his cheeks.

CHAPTER NINE

It was the first day of the Autumn Half Term and an east wind was blowing. There was a vague malevolence in people's eyes at the prospect of yet another raw, grey winter. Dryden descended the steps into one of the many underpasses that permitted access from one half of Winkworth to the other. A strong smell of vomit and urine assailed his nostrils. As he approached the other end he pondered momentarily on the significance of the graffiti scrawled across the concrete wall. 'Millo is a wanker' someone had written in large black letters. Various attempts had been made to erase this but without success. Who was Millo, Dryden wondered. Whoever he was, his reputation was now indelibly inscribed in the minds of thousands of stolid Winkworthians trundling through the underpass with their kids and their shopping trolleys. Near the top of the concrete wall was another graffito: 'The Gay Vicars'. This one conjured up visions of tipsy clergymen scrawling a memorial to themselves as they passed by after a particularly uninhibited sherry party.

Schlack's Bessarabian Riesling clanked cheerfully against the tins of baked beans in Dryden's shopping bag. He gloated at the sound. Ninety-nine pence a bottle. It was perfect.

He had been invited to stay in London at his brother and sister-in-law's place for a couple of days during the half term week. Dryden's elder brother, Harry, was a hugely successful accountant in the city. In fact, Harry had never been anything other than hugely successful. For as long as he could remember drawing breath Dryden had lived in awe of his older brother. Harry's career at grammar school had been brilliant. He had won prize after prize. He had barely been in the place for more than a month before there was talk of Open Scholarships and the comparative merits of Oxford and Cambridge. At fourteen years of age Harry had talked airily of Magdalen, Sidney Sussex and Jesus College as if they were grocery stores in the High Street. Pollock mater and pater had looked upon their eldest son, in fact, as the culmination of centuries of careful, selective breeding (beginning with a cross-eyed Fenland farmer, Dryden had suspected bitterly). Dryden, however, was not. Dryden was the culmination of something else, the underside of ambitious breeding, like a third leg or an extra thumb. He was the concentration of all those useless Pollock genes that had been dispensed with in the making of Harry. As was only to be expected, Dryden's career at grammar school had been undistinguished. His marks had been average and, try as he might, he could never get them to move any higher. His school reports had contained comments like 'tries hard and achieves creditable results' or 'has estabished a solid basis for good average marks at 'O' level'. Harry's reports on the other hand had been a testimony to his unfailing brilliance. 'A rara avis indeed', the grammar school headmaster had written. Dryden had never forgotten it. Harry was a rare bird. Dryden was an ordinary, common or garden sparrow.

Harry had won a scholarship and gone to Oxford. Graduating with an excellent degree in Ancient Languages (notably Hebrew and Sanskrit), he had decided against the academic life and joined a large firm of city accountants. Within minutes, or so it seemed to Dryden, his older brother was virtually running the show. He was dining with the rich and famous, he was invited for weekend house parties in Yorkshire or in France, he was on first name terms with people who were in the news. Then he got married. At first his marriage to Sue had been regarded as something of an error, since Sue's genetic inheritance was undoubtedly inferior. She had not been to either Oxford of Cambridge, in fact, she hadn't been to University at all. She had worked as a kindergarten teacher (though in a fashionable establishment) and had apparently stopped Harry in his tracks as he was careering through a succession of glittering parties in West London. Harry had been carted off very smartly to the nearest Church and had been hitched up to Sue at a truly astonishing speed. Though this had given mater and pater Pollock some cause for concern, their new daughter-in-law had successfully ingratiated herself with her parents-in-law, reassuring them in every small way that their social ambitions were very much in keeping with her own. Thus they had consoled themselves with the thought that brilliant Pollock genes might well benefit, in fact, from an infusion of sturdier, though duller, Brandon genes to create in the next generation, who knew, another Gladstone or another Churchill. Thus, what had been seen as a slightly downward kink in Harry's career had gradually been turned into another brilliant achievement and Sue had joined the Pollock family's quest for distinction.

At first Dryden had desperately tried to ingratiate himself with the new member of the Pollock family, in the pathetic hope that she might appreciate and understand his difficult position with regard to his ferociously ambitious parents and his paragon of a brother. Alas, it was not to be. Sue had happily adopted the family attitude towards her useless brother-in-law but then she had gone one step further. She had declared war on him. Thus, for years it seemed to Dryden that his sister-in-law regarded him in much the same way as a powerful empress might regard one of her royal children who was an idiot. Only Sue was in no position to have Dryden permanently incarcerated in the East Wing. Instead, she devoted her energies to devising nifty little ways of making him feel extremely small.

Now, as he made his way home from the supermarket, he envisaged the scene: his sister-in-law serving up a dinner of tinned spaghetti bolognese to celebrate her brother-in-law's arrival, while out in her vast kitchen there were freezers crammed full with pheasant, quail and whole salmon. No wine would be served with the meal, while in the larder there were shelves of expensive French, Spanish and Italian wines gathering dust. Dryden would suddenly remember that he'd bought a bottle of wine to go with the meal. Out to his Viva he would go, fetch the bottle of Schlack's Bessarabian vinegar in its brown-paper bag and place it triumphantly on the table. Oh, revenge would be sweet. How many times in the past had he bought bottles of expensive wine for one of Sue's dinners. How long had he nurtured the vain hope that she would realise he, too, was a person of taste and culture. But the last time he had been there she had served up a dinner of cold left-overs, snatched his bottle of St. Emilion Vendange Superbe and Exquis, put it away in the larder and planted a bottle of indescribably cheap and poisonous vinegar on the table instead. Well this time, he thought, he was going to be well prepared for that sort of calculated insult.

He reached home and placed the wine reverently on the back seat of his car. He went inside, finished his packing and decided to set off for London there and then. It was early afternoon. He'd get in a few drinks at a pub before turning up at his brother's place. He needed something to steady his nerves. His sister-in-law's smile of welcome was enough to freeze a blast furnace.

An hour later he reached the outskirts of London. The traffic was hideous. He sat back in his seat, lit a cigarette and thought of Wendy. She was no doubt on her way to Cornwall, reflecting on her first few weeks at Great Battley. For a minute or two he experienced grave doubts about his plan. Was it really him, doing that sort of thing? It was a very great risk. Wendy and her parents might slam the door in his face. The traffic moved and he drove across the river into sister-in-law territory. A few minutes later he parked the Viva and strolled nonchalantly into a pub.

Two hours later he emerged into the chill of the early evening, slipped effortlessly out of his parking space and drove boldy around to his brother's house. It was a large, imposing detached house with Greek pillars on either side of the front door as befitted the residence of a successful accountant. Dryden walked up the path and rang the bell. A few seconds later the door opened.

"Oh, it's you. Hello. I'm busy bathing the kids. Go through will you? Harry's just getting changed." His sister-in-law hurried back upstairs. Dryden wandered into the house.

"Harry, your brother's here," he heard his sister-in-law call from upstairs. It was the way she said the words 'your brother' that sent a slight shiver of apprehension down Dryden's spine. Sue never used his name if she could help it. He found himself in the vast living-room, wondering whether he should sit down or remain standing. He remained standing. He looked around. There was no doubting his sister-in-law's good taste, if you liked that sort of thing. Sombre, sober furnishings with little etchings of country houses on the walls. Sue was always visiting country houses, picnicking in their parks, inspecting their collection of furniture. He had tried that angle too. He had trotted out to a few places and boned-up on the country house scene, yawning his way through the musty interiors, tramping round gardens just so he'd have something to say on the subject. It hadn't worked. Sue had glanced at him balefully and started talking about something else.

"Hullo Dry." Harry walked into the living-room. He was sleek and rosy cheeked. "How was the drive?"

"Fine. Traffic was heavy though," Dryden smiled. In his brother's presence he found himself lapsing into a mock Oxford undergrad. accent, a sort of laid-back, 'isn't life boring, let's go and get pissed' way of talking. At Dryden's University the speech patterns had been Northern and determined, the talk of future railway engineers and technologists. Harry frowned and stared at his younger brother.

"Drink?" he said eventually. Harry crossed to a large cabinet and threw open the doors. A vast array of bottles: gin, Scotch, brandy, vermouth, vodka. Dryden's eyes lit up. He decided on a gin and tonic. That would do nicely on top of the moderately large intake in the pub earlier; Harry poured out two large gins.

"Well, how's school then?" Harry raised his glass. Dryden felt his carefully imbibed courage slipping away. Why did everything his brother had to say make him feel so small and ordinary? Simply because Dryden as yet had not outgrown his vast inferiority complex towards Harry. "School's fine" he said. From upstairs came the sound of children's voices. Harry and Sue had two children. Dryden rarely saw them. He firmly believed that his sister-in-law was determined to keep them away from him. Uncle Dry was a misfit and a no-hoper. Besides, he smoked. In this house there were no ashtrays. Visitors in Sue's house either smoked out in the garden and took their butts away with them in their pockets or they didn't visit. Dryden studied his brother. Every time he saw him he looked fitter and wealthier. He had taken up jogging and squash.

Sue poked her head round the door. "Can you get me a drink, Harry? I'll be in the television room."

Harry nodded, fixed a drink and left the room with it. Dryden stared unhappily at the deep pile carpet. He felt like a rather low class playmate of a pampered rich kid. He was being kept in quarantine for the duration. Harry re-appeared, smiled and closed the door carefully behind him. Maybe he could make an excuse and slip away now, Dryden thought miserably. Off out into the cold, windy evening. Suddenly, the thought of Schlack's Bessarabian Riesling gave him no comfort at all. It seemed ludicrous and outrageous. He couldn't win in this household. He began to wish he had bought something decent.

"I'll show you your room," Harry said. Dryden followed his brother upstairs. At the end of a long landing Harry opened a door and they stepped into a large room with a camp bed in one corner. There was no light, unfortunately, Harry said. Sue was in the process of re-decorating it. Dryden smiled at the ladders, pots of paint and other paraphernalia scattered about.

"I've got a torch you can use," Harry said, reassuringly. "Sorry it's in such a state but Sue's determined to get it all done. I tried to persuade her to get a professional decorator in but you know what she's like." Dryden smiled and nodded. He looked round. The room was bare and cold. He was a waif, he thought, self-pityingly, a vagabond whom his brother and sister-in-law were magnanimously offering shelter to for the night. He thought of his warm, cosy bedroom in Winkworth from where he had an excellent view of the huge police building in the town. It blazed light from dusk to dawn, reassuring the people of Winkworth that the local constabulary was keeping watch over them throughout the hours of darkness.

"This is fine, Harry," Dryden said mournfully. He dumped his bag next to the camp bed. He was a soldier on an exercise in the Brecon Beacons, toughening up for a tour of duty in the Falklands. Soldiers died sometimes in the Brecon Beacons. A gust of wind rattled the window panes and the air lifted the sheets of newspaper off the floor.

"Hope you'll be warm enough," Harry smiled. Dryden repeated it would be fine. In any case, he didn't like being too warm.

They went back downstairs.

"I'll get the kids to bed and we'll have supper," Sue said from the television room.

"Is that Uncle Dry?" a child's voice called.

"Yes dear, that's Uncle Dry. You'll see him tomorrow."

Back in the living-room Harry poured out another drink and seemed to be musing about something. He was frowning. He glanced up at Dryden and sighed. Dryden shifted uneasily in his chair. There was something wrong, he knew. His arrival seemed to have brought about a state of deep depression in his brother's household. His visit already seemed to have acquired the character of an unwelcome intrusion. Harry sighed again. He was looking miserable. Dryden squirmed at his brother's expression. Then it suddenly occurred to him. Had he got it all wrong? He thought of the room upstairs that Sue was in the midst of re-decorating. Oh God. Of course, that was it. He had made a mistake. He cast his mind back to the telephone call he had made all those weeks ago. Maybe Sue had said the twenty-fifth and not the fifteenth. Half term breaks varied from county to county. And, typically, Dryden hadn't written it down. What a blunder. Sue would never forgive him for this. The sweat broke out on the back of his neck. They were embarrassed. It was all falling into place. Sue in the midst of re-decorating that room, they hadn't been expecting anyone. And now he had gone and committed the worst crime in his sister-in-law's catalogue of social gaffes. He stood up.

"Look, Harry . . . it's just occurred to me . . . I'm sorry . . . oh God, what can I say?"

"Don't worry about it Dry," Harry said quietly. "It's okay."

"No but I forget these things. My damn memory is like a sieve. Oh Hell, I'd better go and talk to Sue, hadn't I?"

"No, no, don't be stupid. She doesn't mind. Honestly. When you can."

"No, look, Harry, I'd prefer to make a clean breast of it. I would. We can't just pretend it's all okay. You see I . . ."

"Harry," came Sue's voice from the kitchen. "Could you come and give me a hand, please?"

Harry shrugged at Dryden, leapt to his feet and hastened out of the room. Dryden sank down into his armchair, crushed by the weight of his own dreadful stupidity. She had said the twenty-fifth and here he was turning up on the doorstep as bold as brass on the fifteenth. But why hadn't she said anything to him at the door? Maybe he hadn't made a mistake. If not, what else could it be? He sat there in cold anxiety, feeling like a suspect awaiting police interrogation.

He reached for his gin. The glass toppled off the table and rolled over the deep pile carpet. The ice cube skittered away under Harry's armchair. In a panic, Dryden got down on his knees and began feeling round under the chair. The living-room door opened.

"Would you come through to the dining-room now please." His sister-in-law stared at him in alarm.

"I spilt my drink." Dryden gave a sheepish grin. "I'm sorry . . . the ice cube's melting away under the chair."

Sue raised her eyes Heavenward. "Congratulations. You've just won the prize for being the first person to spill something on that carpet," she turned and shouted through the door.

"Harry, get a cloth will you? Your brother's spilt his drink. Leave it to Harry," she said to Dryden. "He'll clean it up. Come through to the dining-room. We're ready to eat." Shame-faced Dryden followed her through to the dining-room.

"There's ice under the armchair. You'll see it. It's melted," Sue said to his brother who passed them in the passage-way clutching a dish-cloth. Dryden's face now felt as if it was permanently contorted into the rictus of a sheepish grin. Suddenly, he made a loud sucking noise. Sue glanced back at him, startled. God, what she must be thinking. And how right she was. If indeed, as he suspected, he had come on the wrong day, then he had doubtlessly put her in the extremely embarrassing predicament of having to put him up in the unfinished guest room, provide some sort of dinner at a moment's notice, and then had to stand by as he fished about on her expensive carpet for the remains of his drink and had now been startled by a strange sucking noise he had made for no reason at all. What an oaf she must think he was! Not only an oaf but also something of an archetypal slob. Almost unconscious with shame he sat down at the table at his designated place. He was momentarily aware that the meal was rather scant: one piece of fried chicken each,

60

one jacket potato and a bowl of lettuce salad. Next to each plate was a roll that was still half frozen from its over-wintering in one of Sue's gigantic freezers. He shook his head. Poor woman. In the circumstances she had probably done what she could. He stared at the elegant silver cutlery and the gracefully curved wineglasses. What she had been unable to provide in the way of a meal at short notice she had made up for with the table setting. It was like one of those pictures out of a Habitat catalogue. Simple, tasteful elegance. Quality, nothing showy. He remembered the bottle of Schlack's Bessarabian Riesling on the back seat of his car. How low could you get, he muttered contemptuously to himself under his breath. If he didn't have such a distorted view of the world, he might conceivably have had the grace and good sense to buy a bottle of excellent wine. That, at least, might have gone a little way towards easing the embarrassment of his own stupidity and forgetfulness. He cursed himself. He picked up his knife and stared at it. If this had been Japan he would already have sequestered himself in some back room and would be deep in meditation preparatory to committing seppuku. At least that was the impression Yukio Mishima gave. The Japanese had an extraordinary sense of honour and a highly sensitive code of conduct. Social gaffes of the sort Dryden constantly committed were dealt with in the severest possible manner.

"There's a programme I want to watch at nine," Sue said, breaking into her brother-in-law's Japanese reveries. "You two can do the dishes."

Harry nodded solemnly as he sat down.

"Help yourselves," Sue said with a sour look at Dryden who was slumped in his chair. "There's one piece of chicken each and a potato. And, oh, I've forgotten the Slimline. Harry, get the Slimline, please." Sue detested butter. It was fantastically unhealthy. Similarly, sugar, sweets, chocolate, ice-cream, were banned from this house. Once she had held forth very sternly on the subject of unhealthy food to Dryden who had dared to be flippant about all this fanatical concern for what went into one's body. The lettuce salad would be eaten raw. French dressing was highly calorific and Mayonnaise was a word that never failed to evoke a flash of fury in Sue's eyes. On a number of occasions over the years Dryden had sneered at this sort of thing, of course. He loved to relate his chance discovery of one of Sue's children's 'Early Learning' books, which, however cleverly designed to promote infant prodigies' reading ability, had committed the horrendous error of displaying pictures of cakes and cream buns on several of its pages. Sue had glued these pages together. Dryden had gleefully pulled them apart and replaced the book in the bookcase. Of course, it was a typically childish act on his part, yet another example of his silly campaign against good, wholesome, responsible living.

"And the wine please," Sue said sharply as Harry, having deposited the Slimline on the table was in the throes of sitting down to the meal. It was strange, of course, that Sue never condemned alcohol for its calorific content or its damaging effect on the body. Maybe that was

Harry though. Dryden could imagine Harry meekly surrendering on everything else but booze. Harry loved booze. He had once confided to Dryden that he would consider it the purest pleasure to drown in a vat of gin.

"What shall I get?" Harry frowned slightly.

"You know," Sue said impatiently. "Left hand cupboard, front row. It's always in the same place, isn't it?"

Harry nodded. He got up and left the dining-room. Dryden kept his eyes on his plate. He knew it would have occurred to Sue that he had probably brought a bottle of wine. But he couldn't. Not after the fiasco of arriving and spilling his drink on the wrong day. Schlack's Bessarabian Riesling indeed. Really!

Harry came in with a bottle and an opener.

"Okay?" He held out the bottle to Sue. She nodded. Dryden instantly recognised the label. It was Schlack's Bessarabian Riesling. Harry grimaced as he plunged the corkscrew into the cork.

"These ones are always hard to get out." He screwed up his eyes. "It's probably the one they bottle in Weston-super-Mare. The ones they bottle in Swindon are usually much easier."

"Yes, all right, dear," Sue said irritably. "We don't need a lecture on the bottling factories, do we?" Harry extracted the cork. The wine fizzed ominously. He poured some into each glass and placed the bottle on the table. The astonishingly lurid label ill suited the fine linen tablecloth and the elegant cutlery.

As they began to eat, Dryden considered how he might best broach the business of some sort of humble and contrite apology to his sister-in-law. This was extremely difficult for Sue did not take kindly to apologies. She rarely apologised. Yet Dryden knew that if he didn't apologise for something (for turning up on the wrong day, as he suspected) an ominous atmosphere would prevail all evening. His very presence would be an affront to all standards of good taste and decent behaviour. Harry would sit and sigh, at a loss as to how to cope with an angry and resentful wife and a hopelessly gauche and guilt-stricken brother.

"Sue," Dryden began on a sudden impulse. "I feel I must apologise." There, he had said it. He had broken the spell. His sister-in-law looked up at him puzzled.

"Apologise? What for?" She shot a glance at Harry. Harry looked anxious and clasped his hands.

"For . . . turning up like this. I feel terrible," Dryden continued hastily. "My memory for dates is just . . . well, I'd convinced myself it was the fifteenth you see."

"It is the fifteenth, isn't it?" Sue replied, a tone of exasperation in her voice. "What are you talking about?"

"I remember you must have said the twenty-fifth and I got the fives mixed up. Half term, we're on half term you see." He gazed at Sue helplessly.

"Well, of course, it's half term. The fifteenth. That's what we'd arranged, wasn't it?"

Dryden glanced at his brother who was looking nonplussed.

"I thought . . . well . . . I thought . . ." he mumbled. "I thought I'd made a mistake and come on the wrong day, you see."

"Well, you haven't. We'd arranged the fifteenth and here you are. The twenty-fifth would have been impossible. That's when I'm going up to Nottingham with my Feminine Consciousness Group."

Dryden was dumbfounded.

"I think," Harry smiled, "that there's a mix-up here somewhere. Dryden was upset before and well, I thought, he was thinking about . . . well . . . you know . . . Christmas."

""Christmas?" Sue stared at her husband. "Oh, that," she smiled and nodded. "Yes, well, I had forgotten about it actually . . ."

Dryden felt a pang of anxiety. Christmas? What about Christmas? He had determinedly put the memory of that right out of his mind. It had been gruesome. His sister-in-law had been in a vile mood for three whole days and nights. Harry had slunk about the house like a dog that had been repeatedly thrashed for worrying the chickens. The children had whined and shivered in the cold, since Sue insisted it was not cold enough to waste money on the central heating, the turkey had been undercooked and she had thrown things around the kitchen in silent fury. The Christmas tree had dropped its needles in a transport of sheer terror and Dryden had been ordered to spend hours vacuuming the carpet. He had slept on the floor of the study and shivered miserably all night, unable to sleep. Christmas had been sheer purgatory.

"Sorry," he said, "I didn't realise there was . . . well, Christmas. I'd forgotten about it actually."

"Trust you to bring it up at the dinner table," Sue snapped at Harry. "You've got no sense of timing have you?"

"I . . ." Harry then gave up. He set about dissecting a wilted lettuce leaf.

"What is it, Sue? Please tell me. I hate to think I might have forgotten something." Sue shrugged and smiled at her brother-in-law.

"Your brother thinks I'm annoyed because you left without paying your share of the turkey. Honestly, I'd forgotten all about it. It's so trivial," she laughed.

"But I thought I'd paid my share," Dryden said. "I wrote a cheque for twenty-eight pounds, didn't I?"

"Yes, you did," Sue said slowly. "It bounced too, I think, Harry? Wasn't that the one that bounced?" Harry nodded.

"Anyway," Sue went on, "We got the money eventually. No, that twenty-eight pounds was for the booze and the decorations and other extras. The turkey was separate. It's all Harry's fault. As usual, he didn't explain it properly. I put it down to all this 'money's no object' sort of attitude he has. Honestly, for an Accountant he's so damn casual about money. God knows how he manages to keep track of all those millions he transfers out to tax havens all over the place."

"That's different," Harry protested. "That's a challenge, it's my job."

"Frankly, Harry, I don't see what's different about it." Sue was suddenly flaring. "It's all money, even if its millions in one case and two pounds twenty-seven in the other. The only difference is the amount, surely?"

"Was that . . ." Dryden began.

"There's a vast difference, Sue," Harry said haughtily. "You can't forget about tens of millions of clients' money for a start. They'd be down on you like a ton of bricks."

"Who said I'd forgotten about his two pounds twenty-eight? Twenty-nine actually, wasn't it? Just because it's my housekeeping money, that's considered totally unimportant."

"Two pounds twenty-nine?" Dryden asked. He began feeling in his pockets. Damn it. He'd had a fiver but most of that he'd spent in the pub that afternoon. He had sixty pence left. His cheque book was in the car.

"You said you'd forgotten about it," Harry fumed across the table. "Just now."

"Well, if I had, it still doesn't change the fact of your attitude to my housekeeping money, does it?"

"Of course your housekeeping money is important. I never said it wasn't."

"No but you did imply it isn't to be considered as important as all the millions you're busy salting away for your clients. If it was their two pounds thirty we were talking about, you certainly wouldn't overlook it then, would you? Oh no, that's your job. That's a challenge. The big man out in the big wide world screwing the Government and the tax-payers. Little wifey at home, though, that's different. She's only operating a household budget. What's two pounds thirty or forty between friends? Or family? Honestly, Harry you are incredible at times." Dryden sat looking shame-faced. How much was it for God's sake? The amount seemed to be increasing by the second.

"Well for all the high-minded principles of your Feminine Consciousness, Sue, you benefit from my job, don't you? I mean, it's what we happen to be living on."

"Oh, ah, of course. The enormously successful Accountant. I'm sorry. I've insulted the master and breadwinner. So, the housekeeping comes out of your income but how far does it go? Think of that for a minute. You've never thought of it before, have you? I'm supposed to run this house, buy food, keep the kids in clothes and toys and then on

64

top of that provide big, slap-up meals for house guests. You've never thought of that, have you?"

"So, the housekeeping isn't enough. You need more?"

"No, Harry, I didn't say I needed more now, did I? You've not listened to a word I've been saying. It's not a question of the amount, Harry. It's the attitude behind it. The sort of easy-come easy-go attitude you hold towards my housekeeping money, whereas you wouldn't dream of that in your job, would you? In my opinion Mrs. Thatcher speaks for all women at home when she talks about running the country on the principles of the family budget. She knows all about it. It is a family budget. On a bigger scale, of course, but the same principles apply. She would know exactly what I'm talking about. Your brother's owing us two pounds forty for the turkey last Christmas is no different from someone owing the country millions or this country owing someone else millions. It's the same principle at work, isn't it. Two pounds forty or two billion forty thousand. It's all the same."

"If you like," Harry shrugged and morosely sipped his wine. "Maybe you're right."

"Of course I'm right," Sue snapped. "Anyway, there's a pot of yoghurt in the 'fridge if anyone feels like dessert."

"What flavour?" Harry asked.

"It's plain, Harry. You know I don't get flavoured yoghurt."

"You want yoghurt, Dry?"

"Ah, no thanks," Dryden smiled. "Look, I'm sorry about the turkey business. I honestly didn't realise. I've only got sixty pence on me at the moment. If you like I could write you a cheque."

"Oh, don't worry about it," Sue waved her hand. ""Harry's not worried about it, so it seems. And if he can't be bothered about it, then neither can I. Look, if it's going to upset you, then send us a postal order or something. I'd prefer that to one of your cheques. Besides, a cheque for two pounds fifty is ridiculous."

"Two pounds fifty, is it?" Dryden asked.

"Yes. That'll do. That'll cover most of it, I think. Anyway, let's forget about money for Heaven's sake. People are obsessed with it. One of the joys of being married to a successful Accountant, I suppose." She glanced at her watch. "Oh look, it's almost nine. I want to watch a programme on television. You two are doing the dishes, aren't you?" Harry nodded and poured out the last of the wine.

CHAPTER TEN

Large, wet snowflakes were falling on the windscreen as Dryden drove up the slip-road onto the M4 bound for the West Country. He lit his third cigarette within half an hour, drawing on it deeply, revelling in the damage he was no doubt doing to himself. The car heater had begun to warm him now after an almost sleepless night on the camp bed at Harry and Sue's. The wind had rattled at the windowpanes, gusts of cold, damp air had billowed into the room. At one stage he had just drifted off to sleep when a particularly violent gust had lifted several sheets of newspaper off the floor and deposited them on the bed. He had been too tired to move them, had drifted off toe sleep again, imagining himself cosily wrapped in cartons and old newspapers underneath the Arches by Charing Cross Station, with a belly full of hot Salvation Army soup and bread inside him and a couple of bottles of wine.

Sue had pretended to be puzzled and hurt when he had announced his departure, as he clasped a mug of lukewarm coffee in his hands to stop himself shivering at the breakfast table.

"You don't have to go you know," she said crisply. "We were expecting you to stay a couple of days at least."

"I know, Sue, but they're expecting me in Cornwall today, as early as possible," Dryden lied. "They're very hospitable, you see, and worry all the time if people don't turn up on invitation. Besides, I've never been to Cornwall."

"It's cold and miserable and bleak at this time of the year, you know. I wish you'd said something sooner."

"I know. I should have. It went clean out of my mind," Dryden said lamely, hoping his sister-in-law might swallow that outrageously feeble excuse. She gave him a quizzical look.

"I'll send you that money by postal order as soon as I get back to Winkworth," Dryden said, quickly changing the subject.

"Oh, don't worry. I feel awful now. I wish Harry hadn't brought the whole thing up. It's only two pounds sixty after all."

"Well, I think I'd better be heading off," he had smiled, wondering if the circulation would ever return to his legs.

Sue and the kids waved at him from the portalled doorway as he had driven off. Never again, he had solemnly declared to himself as he had put the car into third gear. Never again. But he knew that wasn't true. Somehow he would end up going back there, enduring more sleepless nights, gnawing hunger and damp chills. As he had lain on the camp bed he had wanted to rage and howl, to construct scenarios of humiliation and torture but he had been too tired and too cold. Besides, there was a peculiar satisfaction in his own total annihilation. You had to hand it to Harry and Sue. They never did anything by halves.

At mid-day he stopped at a motorway cafe for a roll and a cup of coffee. In the toilet a man addressed him in a broad West Country accent. He was almost there, Dryden thought, as he left the building. He had very little idea of where the West Country began. Apparently, it had begun already. Except that he hadn't seen any signs. Still, it was like that all over the show now, wasn't it? Borders being done away with, everyone wearing tracksuits and carrying Adidas bags. Great Battley's internationalism was well on the way to being realised. The thought of Great Battley suddenly dampened his spirits. Maurice Talbot had been seething over the graffiti business in the language laboratory.

"I still have no idea who's responsible for this," he stared coldly at Dryden and tapped the end of a pencil on the top of his desk. "It's a serious matter I'm afraid, Dryden, and your flippancy has done nothing to further the investigation. As it happens, I have found almost all of the people in that group of yours and they all swore they hadn't seen anything. They also told me the lesson had been something of a riot."

"Everything broke down," Dryden murmured contritely. He thought of clutching Talbot's grey trouser leg beneath the desk but decided against it. "It was chaos, I must admit. I just wasn't prepared for it."

"I see." Talbot narrowed his eyes. "Still, that's part of our job, isn't it? Being prepared for anything. We can't let the children take over, you know. I must say, Dryden, I've become more and more concerned these past few weeks. I get the impression your attitude to our work here has altered somewhat. Correct me if I'm wrong."

"No, of course not, I mean my attitude hasn't changed at all, Maurice," Dryden protested earnestly.

"I'm sure I don't have to remind you that as Assistant Co-ordinator of European Studies you have something of a primary sector responsibility as regards the aims of this school. That responsibility must be taken seriously."

"I do take it seriously, Maurice. You mustn't think I don't."

"All right then. Just remember we're looking for that drive and enthusiasm you so impressed us with at your interview. Hedda Gabler, by the way, is a play by the Norwegian dramatist, Ibsen. Ryan O'Neal and Faye Dunaway are film actors. You may think all this is very funny, Dryden, but I'm afraid the humour is lost on me in this particular instance. Serious vandalism is no joke."

Dryden's abject submission had restored things a little. Talbot had even said 'Good morning' to him the following day. The Motts, however, continued to regard him with undisguised hatred.

As he drove further into what he now realised was the West Country, the weather grew steadily worse. A curtain of heavy rain blotted out the road ahead. He almost missed the turning beyond Bristol. But the distance between him and Wendy was lessening by the minute. He longed to see her. He turned on the car radio and began to sing.

It was dark when he reached Cornwall. It turned out to be a rather larger place than he had expected. He was irritated by this. It was his education, of course, learning all about Latin and French verbs when he should have been discovering the size of Cornwall.

At eight-thirty he pulled up in front of a guesthouse in Padstow. A rather severe looking woman with a bun looked him up and down at the reception desk and promptly charged him twelve quid for bed and breakfast. He was staggered. He looked round. The place seemed deserted. Clearly, he was the only visible source of income at that particular moment. The woman showed him to his room. A few minutes later he was lying on the bed wondering at the absurdity of his own actions. The air was damp and cold. The wind rattled at the windowpanes. Outside, the rain poured down. Yet, in a strange way, it was all very beautiful. Padstow was beautiful, though he had seen almost nothing of it. Cornwall was beautiful, he sighed, because at this particular moment it contained the person of Wendy within its bounds, somewhere not far away she was there, with her sleeping father and her avid reader of a mother. What was she doing now, he wondered. Sitting by a window perhaps, gazing wistfully out to sea?

Exhausted, he undressed and climbed into bed. Marvelling at the warmth of a heavy pile of blankets on top of him and a large pillow that threatened to smother him with softness, he fell asleep within minutes.

* * * * *

The next morning the worst of the bad weather was over. The town was bathed in a watery sunshine. Dryden tucked into the large breakfast the severe woman served him in the deserted dining-room. Behind her severity was a kindly soul, he thought. Ah, Cornwall, he sighed. It sounded so romantic.

"Excuse me, but I'm hoping to see some friends of mine today at a place called Polzeath? Can you tell me if it's far from here?"

"Polzeath?" The woman frowned. "Well, it's not far as the crow flies but it takes a while by road. There's a ferry, of course. That's quicker."

A ferry? Good Lord! He was sure it had all been joined up. A vague suspicion that he might not be in Padstow at all crept into the back of his mind. No, that wasn't possible. He had seen the road signs. Perhaps, though, there were two Padstows. If there were, then Dryden Pollock was sure to have come to the wrong one.

"'Cross the estuary. Polzeath's the other side," the woman went on.

"Lovely place that. Who do you know over there?"

"The Bashfords," Dryden said confidently, imagining everyone probably knew everyone else in Cornwall. .

"Bashford? No, mind you, the place is swarming with foreigners nowadays."

"Oh, they're not foreigners. They're English. Bashford."

The woman suddenly laughed. "Foreigners is English, my love. We Cornish folk call English people foreigners, you see."

"Oh, I see," Dryden laughed, not really understanding what on earth the woman was talking about.

"First time in these parts is it, my love?" The woman had dropped three more sausages into the pan. Dryden listened to the sizzling with growing alarm. How much was each sausage, for Heaven's sake? He imagined a meter somewhere busily clocking up the extras.

"Yet it is. It's beautiful. I never realised."

"Oh, you haven't seen it at its best. Spring is the best time of year actually. I wouldn't live anywhere else and that's for sure. Very romantic it is. Full of legends. King Arthur and all that. You want to go to Tintagel while you're here, my love. It's beautiful. Buy yourslf a nice souvenir. Like this one here, see?" She emerged from the kitchen with a tea-towel. "Lovely, in't it?"

Dryden nodded. The woman came and got his plate and reloaded it with eggs, bacon, mushrooms and sausages.

"You looks as if you need a good breakfast, my love, if you don't mind my saying so. You people from the East always looks a bit peaky. All that filth, I expect." She walked away with a shudder.

An hour later Dryden boarded the ferry to Polzeath. The morning was brightening rapidly. On ferryman, he murmured to himself. On to my fair Guinevere at Polzeath. A short while later he stepped off the ferry and walked up to an elderly gentleman who was quizzically examining some weeds in the sand.

"Excuse me, Sir. Can you tell me if this is Polzeath?"

"Polzeath?" The elderly gentleman frowned. "That's up the coast a ways. Quite a long way if you're on foot. You've just come off the ferry have you?"

"Yes." Dryden's heart sank. He wasn't in Polzeath.

"This is Rock, you see," the old gentleman explained. "Without a car, oh, I'd say it'd take you a couple of hours maybe to get up there."

A couple of hours? How big was Cornwall, for God's sake?

"It's a lovely walk though. Some of the finest seascape in the country up that way. You want to make sure you get out Pentireglaze way. Oh, it's beautiful. Fulmar colony there."

Damn and hell, Dryden swore as he walked away from the elderly gentleman. There wasn't a ferry back to Padstow for another hour.

Here he was stuck in some place called Rock which happened to be miles from Polzeath. Maybe he would just walk it anyway. The old boy probably meant two hours at his arthritic pace. For someone younger it was probably only half an hour or so. He set off rapidly.

An hour later, near exhaustion, he collapsed at the bottom of a little round hill. He had no idea where he was except that he didn't seem to be in Polzeath. He raged at his own incompetence. Then he lit a cigarette and gazed bleakly out over the muddy estuary. Romantic indeed, the place was a desert.

Another hour and he rounded a headland. Was this Polzeath? He asked a child who was playing with a dog.

"That's Polzeath, Mister. There." The child pointed at what seemed to be a densely populated suburb above the sea. Dryden showed him the name of the road. The child shrugged and ran off. This was hopeless, he thought miserably. He had had no idea it would all turn into such an ordeal. He was about to make his way up towards a rather splendid neo-Georgian home to ask directions when he suddenly espied a figure in the distance. The figure of a woman. Not daring to believe it could be, yet at the same time certain it was, he limped off along the track after her, his heart beating faster with every step.

"Wendy!" he called. "Wendy!" The woman stopped and looked round in astonishment.

"Hullo. It's Dryden, isn't it? Heavens, what are you doing here?"

"I was just out for a walk and happened to see you." Dryden struggled to control his excitement. Wendy looked stunning in a sweater, slacks and black Wellington boots.

"I didn't know you were coming down here?" She stared at him in amazement.

"Well . . . I . . . uh decided at the last minute. I'm staying over in Padstow."

"Oh, yes. You said you'd often stayed there. That's our place up there by the way, the one with the green verandah. That's Daddy there, see, that little blob. He's asleep. Mummy's still in bed reading."

"Where are you off to?"

"I was going up to Pentireglaze to see the fulmars." What on earth were fulmars, Dryden wondered.

"Mind if I join you?" he grinned. Wendy smiled. At that moment and in blissful ignorance of just how far it was to Pentireglaze, Dryden swore that the hundreds of miles he had driven, the twelve pounds he was paying for bed and breakfast and the last two hours of footslogging round the North Cornish coastal path were a small price to pay for the company of the woman with whom he was head over heels in love.

* * * * *

It was mid-afternoon when they finally came in sight of the house with the green verandah again. Dryden was sure he was going to die. He

70

hobbled along bravely in Wendy's wake, wondering in fact if he would ever be able to walk properly again. Pentireglaze had been spectacular and strenuous. They had watched the fulmars wheeling and diving round the cliffs, for Wendy, it had emerged, was an enthusiastic bird watcher.

"Daddy." Wendy shook her father's arm as they stepped up onto the verandah. "Wake up. We've got a visitor." Wendy's father opened his eyes and stared vacantly at Dryden.

"Daddy. Meet Dryden Pollock. He teaches at the school in Great Battley."

"Where?" Wendy's father frowned in puzzlement.

"Great Battley, Daddy. You know, the school I'm at." She glanced at Dryden. "He's a bit deaf," she murmured.

"School? What d'you mean, girl?"

"The school I teach at, Daddy. Dryden teaches there too. This is Dryden." Dryden held out his hand. The old man shook it, bewildered.

"What's the time?" he frowned.

"It's a quarter to three, Mr. Bashford," Dryden said.

"Good Lord. I haven't had any lunch. Where's that mother of yours?" He struggled to get out of his chair. Wendy helped him up.

"You shouldn't sleep so much, Daddy. You're not supposed to need so much sleep at your age." The old man walked across the verandah and opened the glass doors. "Sarah! Sarah"!" he shouted. From inside the house somewhere a toilet flushed. Then a tall, thin, elderly woman appeared reading a book.

"Mummy." Wendy pushed Dryden into the large sun lounge. "Mummy, I want you to meet Dryden."

"Hello, Dryden." The woman held out her hand. "Lovely to meet you. What's that old fool bellowing about?"

"He hasn't had his lunch. He must have been asleep all day."

"Thank God for that!" Mrs. Bashford murmured, sitting down. She turned a page of her book.

"Sarah!" The old man stared ferociously at his wife from where he stood by the windows. "Do you realise it's three o'clock and we haven't had any lunch? I don't know. We've always had these problems, you know." He turned to Dryden. "She's read close on six thousand books, you know. Six thousand."

"Shall I make us all a cup of tea?" Wendy suggested.

"You do as you think fit, dear," Mrs. Bashford murmured from behind her book.

"Ah me!" Wendy's father shook his head at the view from the windows. "Missing out on lunch. It's not worth it."

"Shut up," Wendy's mother suddenly said loudly. She turned another page.

"Watch your language, woman," Mr. Bashford scowled. "She's only a girl you know."

"Go roast your head," Wendy's mother murmured. "Bloody fool."

Dryden felt himself reddening.

"Swears like a trooper, that woman," Wendy's father murmured at the window-pane. There were several minutes silence, broken only by the sound of Mrs. Bashford turning the pages of her book. Dryden decided he had to sit down before he fell over. He sat down.

"That's it. Sit down. Take the weight off your feet," Wendy's father muttered to himself.

"God, how I hate missing lunch. It's a waste of time."

"It's a lovely view you've got from here, isn't it?" Dryden said.

"Six thousand books. Half of them at least in this house." The old man turned away from the windows. "She skips whole chapters sometimes. I've seen her. She doesn't think I have but I have. Always reads the end though, takes her time over that."

"Tea's up." Wendy came in from the kitchen carrying a tray with the tea things. She placed it on a low table in the middle of the room.

"Tea, Daddy?"

"I ought to, I suppose." Wendy poured out a cup and handed it to her father who stared at it, fascinated.

"Tea, Mummy?"

"Just a little, dear, Why doesn't he go back to sleep? He's a bloody nuisance." Wendy handed her mother a full cup of tea. She then poured out two cups of tea for herself and Dryden.

"Dryden and I went up to Pentireglaze," she said. "There were lots of fulmars."

"I expect there were, dear. Did you count them?" Wendy's mother turned another page.

"It was quite windy but the sun was warm, wasn't it Dryden?"

"Yes, it was. Quite warm."

"I'm not going back to sleep," Wendy's father said. "Not for anyone. She can say what she likes. It's far too early," he sighed. "She can be very sweet when she wants to be."

"Help yourself to biscuits, Dryden." Wendy smiled and gestured towards a large plate of biscuits. "You must be hungry."

"A bit," Dryden grinned. "I had a large breakfast actually."

"Did you now?" Mr. Bashford stared at him with great interest. "Where was that?"

"In Padstow. That's where I'm staying."

"Good Lord! How many eggs did you have then?"

"Ah . . . three eggs, I think. At least. It was very large."

"Very large," Wendy's father repeated. "Not too large though."

"No." Dryden smiled.

"Why doesn't someone lock him outside. It's not too cold, is it? I can't stand it," Wendy's mother said vehemently. "Silly bastard!"

"Mummy . . ." Wendy went pink.

"Well, he is, isn't he? I'm sorry, my dear, but it's the too, too painful truth. Everyone knows that. He's well overdue."

"More tea, anyone?" Wendy smiled at them.

Wendy's father grimaced. "I think I'll go for a walk. Get the cobwebs out of my brain."

"That's a good idea, Daddy. Be careful though, won't you? It's quite windy."

Wendy's father went to the doors, opened them wide and stood out on the verandah. He stretched out his arms, then shook himself and promptly sat down in his chair. Wendy got up and closed the doors.

"I thought he was going for a walk?" Dryden grinned.

"Oh, he will. He always does. He'll probably go after tea though," Wendy said. "How's the book, Mummy?"

"It's very exciting, dear. Don't disturb me now or I'll miss something. It's beautifully written." Dryden stood up. "I think I'd better be heading back actually. It's quite a long way."

"Oh, do you want Daddy to drive you?"

"Ah, no thanks. No, I think he's gone to sleep anyway."

"Oh, that doesn't matter. I'll wake him up."

"No, no, don't bother. Really, I'll enjoy the walk."

"Are you sure? You were hobbling before."

"I think I've recovered. Thanks for the tea, Wendy."

"I'll come with you some of the way." She went out of the room to fetch a jacket.

"Nice to meet you Mrs. Bashford," Dryden said.

"Yes, very nice," the old woman said. "Did you like the tea?"

"Yes, thanks."

* * * * *

They walked off down the track towards the cliffs. Wendy's father had been dozing in his chair as they had crossed the verandah. The sun was now quite low in the sky and a nasty, chill wind was blowing in off the sea.

"I can't get over what a coincidence it was meeting you here," Wendy said. "It's never happened to me before. Nobody at Charles Darwin ever came to these parts for their holidays. Most of them seemed to use the time to have operations. The local hospitals were booked up years in advance."

"Your parents are nice," Dryden ventured.

"Yes, they're very sweet. Only it is a bit boring sometimes being with them. They don't do much, you see. We haven't been anywhere yet, this time."

"How about us going for a few drives? Up to Tintagel, maybe?"

Wendy looked at him in surprise, then smiled. "That would be nice. It's quite far though."

"How about tomorrow then?"

"Yes, I'd like that. We'll set off quite early. Say around nine o'clock?"

Dryden nodded.

"I think this is as far as I'll come with you, if you don't mind, Dryden," Wendy said.

"Wendy . . ." He stopped and stared at her. Was this the moment?

"Yes . . .?" She looked at him in surprise, bordering, it suddenly seemed to him, on alarm.

"I . . . uh . . . I'll be down here for a few days. Maybe we could take a few drives together. What do you think?"

"Why not?" she smiled. "There's a lot to see around these parts."

She turned and waved at him as he plodded on around the path towards Padstow . . .

That night he slept fitfully, plagued by flickering dreams of Wendy, her parents, the Motts and his sister-in-law. Several times he woke up and thought he heard the rain beating against the window-panes and the wind howling anew but the morning dawned bright and clear and he had the impression the bad weather in the night had been no more than his imagination.

"I'm going up to Tintagel, today," he said to the severe woman who seemed intent on rendering him incapable of moving after her huge breakfast.

"Oh, that's nice. Don't forget to get yourself a souvenir now, will you, my love?"

"No, I won't."

"I showed you my tea-towel, din' I?"

"Yes. It was beautiful."

"You be careful up Tintagel way now, won't you dear? It can be very dangerous." She deposited a huge lump of liver onto his plate. He groaned inwardly.

"And see you don't get mixed up with them hooligans up there."

"Hooligans?"

"Oh yes. Were in the paper yesterday evening. Big camp or something up at Tintagel. I don't know what for but the police's very

74

nervous. There'll be hundreds of 'em. All on motorbikes and what have you?"

"Good Heavens. What's all that about?"

"As I say, I dunno, my love, but there's likely to be trouble. They're comin' from all over the West Country, Devon, Somerset, Dorset, even some from Wales I think. Some sort of protest. Ah me, time was our little Cornwall were far away from all that sort of thing. We always had our visitors, of course, our foreigners but they were nice, respectable folk like yourself and your friends. Kept themselves to themselves. Not any more, we get the worst types down here now and our own worst types joinin' up with 'em. Sort of misrule, I reckon. The Kingdom of Misrule. And up at Tintagel, too. It's deliberate, I reckon. Sort of, I dunno, an attack on things as they are. Tintagel means a lot to folk in a funny sort of way. Old Cornwall, if you know what I mean."

Dryden nodded sympathetically. He had no idea what the woman meant. He managed to get through half the liver before he had to give up.

It took far longer than he had thought to drive round to Polzeath. In Wadebridge he got stuck in a long line of cars piled up behind a gigantic lorry that seemed to have got into trouble trying to get round a corner. There was a great deal of confusion when the lorry driver decided he was going to reverse out of his predicament. The long line of cars that had quietly been waiting for something to happen erupted into a demonic, melée of hooting horns, red-faced drivers, everyone yelling violently at everyone else. The lorry reversed inexorably back over the narrow bridge, squashing the traffic up onto the footpaths and into the side-streets of the little town. Three quarters of an hour passed before the lorry finally lumbered off the way it had come looking for fresh traffic jams to cause. Boiling with fury, Dryden drove at breakneck speed along the narrow roads to Polzeath. It was almost ten o'clock when he finally arrived at the Bashfords.

"Mummy wants to come with us," Wendy said in a slightly sorrowful voice. "She hasn't been to Tintagel for years, so she says. "You don't mind, do you?"

"No, of course not," Dryden said, just managing to smile reassuringly.

"Daddy's gone fishing with a friend of his from the village, you see, and Mummy doesn't like being in the house all day on her own with no-one to talk to. By the way, I've made us a picnic lunch. You do like sweet pickle, don't you?"

"I love it," Dryden said. He helped Wendy pack a large wicker basket into the boot of the car. Wendy's mother appeared, dressed in a long, bright yellow raincoat. She carried a large Sainsbury's bag full of books.

"Good morning," she smiled. "I've completely forgotten your name, I'm afraid."

"Dryden. Dryden Pollock."

"Nice to meet you, Dryden. I'm Sarah Bashford, Wendy's mother. You were here yesterday afternoon, weren't you?"

"That's right."

"I thought so. I must apologise for my husband's behaviour. He's very unused to young people. He's gone fishing today, thank God. With luck, the silly swine might drown now, mightn't he?"

"Mummy, please . . ." Wendy said. Dryden opened the rear door and Wendy's mother settled herself in the back seat.

"Off we go then," she suddenly shouted.

"Just wait, Mummy. We're not quite ready yet," Wendy scolded. A few minutes later Dryden backed out of the driveway, turned and drove off towards the main road. He glanced in the rear vision mirror. Mrs. Bashford was reading. Wendy had spread a road map across her knees. Dryden was immeasurably thankful for her forethought. As usual he didn't have the faintest idea of where they were going. He was on the point of turning right at the main road, then suddenly sensing Wendy's puzzlement, he turned left. A car behind him honked abuse. "Sorry" Dryden muttered at the rear vision mirror. Wendy glanced at him. Had she guessed his guilty secret, he wondered, reddening. He had never been to Tintagel before in his life. The traffic on the main road was light and they made good time. After some slight confusion over the turning beyond Camelford they eventually found themselves on the right road. As they neared the coast they began to see more and more police cars. Dryden thought of what the severe woman at the guesthouse had told him that morning. Suddenly, within sight of the sea, they arrived at a roadblock. A policeman approached the car. Dryden wound down the window.

"May I see your driver's licence, Sir?" The policeman peered into the car. Dryden fished frantically in the glovebox and found it to his immense relief. The policeman examined it curiously then returned it.

"Thank you, Sir. Are you or have you been at any time a member of the Communist Party?" Dryden stared at the man in astonishment.

"No, I haven't."

"What about the ladies?" The policeman glanced suspiciously at Wendy's mother in the back seat. Wendy looked embarrassed.

"Nineteen thirty-two," Wendy's mother murmured from behind her book. "I was a Red agitator in the fight against Fascism, Constable."

"Officer . . . we're on our way to Tintagel for a picnic," Wendy said. "My mother was a Communist years ago. She isn't now. We're staying at our house in Polzeath. This is a friend of ours who is staying in Padstow."

"I'm sorry, lady, but I'm going to have to ask your mother to get out of the car for a few minutes." The policeman opened the back door. "Madam, if you don't mind." Wendy's mother was escorted to the side of the road and was soon deep in conversation with a Police Inspector.

76

"What's all this about?" Wendy glanced round nervously.

"I think it must have something to do with a big protest meeting here today. The woman at the guesthouse where I'm staying read about it in the paper last night."

"I don't see what all this has got to do with us," Wendy frowned. "Or has it suddenly become a crime to picnic at a National Monument?"

"They're probably checking everyone. Visitors included."

A few minutes later Mrs. Bashford returned to the car, accompanied by the Police Inspector. "Much obliged, Madam." He touched his cap as he opened the door. "Have a lovely day, won't you." He peered in at Dryden. "Sorry for the hold-up but we're under strict orders. Security, you understand."

Dryden started the car and nodded at the Inspector who touched his cap again by way of a salute. A short while later they drove into Tintagel. The village swarmed with people, mainly elderly folk on day trips judging by the row of large coaches parked along the street. Dryden almost knocked down an old man who tottered across the roadway in front of them, oblivious to the traffic. They parked the car in a large car-park at the end of the street.

"What shall we do first?" Wendy asked. "Go out to the castle or have a cup of tea?"

They decided to go out to the castle. Dryden helped Mrs. Bashford out of the back seat.

"Isn't it romantic?" the old woman murmured. "My, the seas rough, isn't it?"

"I hope Daddy knows what he's doing," Wendy murmured as they set off down the path leading to Tintagel Castle, Mrs. Bashford's raincoat creaking loudly as she walked. They found themselves in a long line of people heading for the castle. Twenty minutes later they arrived in Merlin's Cove. The sands swarmed with people, photographing the sea or picking up pebbles and slipping them furtively into their pockets.

The castle was no more than a few vague ruins on top of a rugged promontory. Here the wind was violent. It was hardly the sort of place for a picnic. Wendy had brought along her binoculars in order to inspect any bird colonies that might have survived the onslaught of the tourists. Mrs. Bashford stood on the highest point of the promontory, staring out to sea, her yellow mackintosh flapping noisily in the wind.

It was Dryden who first noticed the fires burning on the clifftops a mile or so away from the village.

"Wendy, can I borrow your binoculars a minute?" She handed them over. He re-focussed them and trained them on the clifftops. Hundreds of tiny figures were milling about in a paddock. They seemed to be dancing. On the wind Dryden fancied he heard the faint sound of heavy metal rock music, a strange, intermittent and sinister thumping.

He handed the glasses back to Wendy. "That must be the protest," he shouted in her ear. Wendy trained the glasses on the clifftops. Then she turned and trained them on the base of the cliffs.

"There's a fulmar, Dryden," she shouted. "Look, you can tell by the way it flies. They look very like gulls you know. Have a look." Dryden took the binoculars and looked for the fulmar. But he could see nothing but black cliffs and the grey, raging sea. The fulmar had vanished.

"I'm dying for a cup of tea," Wendy shouted. "Mummy, we're going to get a cup of tea."

"Isn't it?" Wendy's mother beamed down at them. She stood facing into the buffeting wind, her eyes closed. Wendy climbed up to her.

"Tea, Mummy. It's cold."

Mrs. Bashford clambered down off her rock and the three of them made their way down off the rugged promontory. They skirted Merlin's Cove and climbed up the narrow defile to the village. Mrs. Bashford picked some flowers and put them in the buttonhole of her yellow raincoat.

They entered the premises of King Arthur's Teashop in the village and squeezed round a table in one corner. A large, dark-faced woman, heavily made up appeared to take their order.

"There's something odd here," Mrs. Bashford suddenly whispered. "I don't like it. Let's go home."

"Mummy, we've just arrived," Wendy said crossly.

"That woman is a gipsy," Mrs. Bashford exclaimed loudly. "Or Jewish. Look at the size of her nose!"

The woman turned round. Wendy reddened. The woman sniffed at them disdainfully and marched away towards the rear of the teashop. The place was full of elderly folk. Huge platefuls of chocolate éclairs, cream buns and sponge cake vanished down their throats in a twinkling. They chattered amongst themselves excitedly, pouring one another cups of tea and casting suspicious looks at Wendy's mother in her bright yellow raincoat with the wilting flowers in the buttonhole. The large, dark-faced woman re-appeared with a tray and served them noisily, dumping the tea things on the table so that the fragile china cups jumped about on their saucers and a bun hopped off the cakeplate. The woman fixed Wendy's mother with a venomous glare. Mrs. Bashford seemed to be hugely enjoying it all, a slight smile playing on her lips. Wendy's mother was a troublemaker, Dryden decided.

Just as Wendy was pouring them each a cup of tea, they became aware of a vague rumbling sound in the distance. A thunderstorm? The conversation round them died down. One or two people went to the window to look, then shrugged and returned to the serious business of scoffing cakes and buns. Gradually, however, the rumbling grew louder. Suddenly, everyone in the teashop knew at once what it was. Motorbikes. The large, dark-faced woman hurried to the door and closed it.

"Can I have your attention a minute please, ladies and gentlemen," she said loudly. There was an immediate hush. "There is no cause for alarm. The police assure us that they have the situation in hand. We have been expecting something like this. Please remain seated."

The rumbling had become a throaty roar. A few seconds later dozens of motorcycles roared into the village, figures in black leather and helmets, flashing past the teashop windows. Dryden thought he glimpsed several skulls and crossbones, several clusters of swastikas. The street was soon full of motorcyclists wildly revving their machines, circling about, roaring back up the road only to turn at the top and roar back down again. The teashop windows rattled with the noise. On the tables the crockery tinkled merrily with the vibrations. The large, dark-faced woman stood by the windows peering through a narrow gap in the lace curtains.

For several long minutes the din continued unabated. Then suddenly, above the roar of the motorcycles came the sound of police sirens. The woman turned and nodded re-assuringly at the elderly folk in the teashop. The sirens wailed louder and louder and then stopped. The motorcyclists revved their engines violently and seemed now to be tearing back up the street at breakneck speed. There was shouting and uniformed figures dashed past the teashop windows. People got up and crowded together round the woman by the windows.

"They've got 'em," a voice shouted gleefully. "That's it. Beat the living daylights out of 'em."

"Hooligans."

All at once the elderly folk at the windows seemed to be in a transport of demonic glee. They jumped up and down, banging the window-panes and shouting encouragement to the forces of law and order outside. Dryden got up and went to one end of the windows. An extraordinary sight greeted him in the street outside. Swarms of policemen dashed about the roadway, wielding their truncheons, as motorcyclists wove their way back up the street, trying to dodge the blows. Some of the police, uniformed, helmeted, bulky with padding, stood in the middle of the roadway, seizing riders and pillion passengers, dragging them off moving motorcycles and clubbing them to the ground. There were screams and shouts, figures darting in all directions, others being dragged towards the waiting police vans.

"Filthy larrikins," the large, dark-faced woman howled. "That's it. Round 'em up." Dryden returned to the table. Wendy glanced at him anxiously. Mrs. Bashford was staring at the people by the windows, her face expressionless.

"It's incredible." Dryden shook his head. "There's a full scale riot going on out there." He poured himself another cup of tea. He had never seen a riot before in his life. Gradually, the terrible din in the street outside was subsiding. There came the sounds of heavy doors slamming as the police rounded up the last of the motorcyclists. The large, dark-faced woman went to the teashop door and opened it. A helmeted policeman with a gigantic truncheon entered. He look round, smiling.

"Cup of tea, officer?" several voices said at once. The policeman shook his head. "Later, thanks. Sorry for this disturbance, ladies and gentlemen, but we seem to have things under control now. I suggest you keep within the town for the next hour or two, just to be on the safe side. There's still a few of them roaming round the countryside."

"Grand work, officer," said an elderly gentleman with a bristly moustache. The policeman smiled, nodded and strode out of the door.

The teashop emptied. Dryden, Wendy and Mrs. Bashford made their way back towards the car-park. Groups of elderly folk stood round in the street chatting to the police. The last few motorcyclists were being handcuffed and pushed into police vans.

"Power to the people," one of these individuals suddenly shouted. A truncheon descended. There were cheers and applause from the old folk. The van started up and drove away up the street.

At the entrance to the car-park stood a wizened old man in a uniform.

"Have you got your ticket, Sir?" He smiled and touched his cap. Dryden stopped, embarrassed.

"No . . . I'm sorry . . . I didn't realise . . ."

"It's not a free car-park you know, Sir." He pointed to a sign fixed to a wall high up. Camelot Carpark, Dryden read. Fifty pence. He fished in his pocket and gave the little man fifty pence.

"Here's your ticket, Sir." He handed Dryden a ticket. Dryden pocketed it and took a step towards the entrance.

"I'm sorry, Sir, but can I have the ticket back? It has to be ripped in two." Dryden returned the ticket. The little man ripped it deftly in two and handed Dryden one half.

"Orders, Sir, you understand. Security. You saw what happened. Much obliged." He waved them into the car-park. Three policemen in helmets and nursing truncheons stood round checking car-park tickets.

"Much obliged, Sir." The policeman took Dryden's half ticket, glanced at it and touched his helmet with his truncheon. Beneath the thick plastic visor Dryden recognised the constable from the roadblock.

"Have you had your picnic, Sir?"

"No, not yet," Dryden said. "We just managed to get out to see the castle before . . ."

"Quite. We're sorry about that. They found an old track we didn't know about. Neither did the Ramblers' Association apparently. Still, we got here eventually, didn't we? Ah, Madam, Inspector Rayburn sends his regards."

"Is the road out clear now?" Dryden asked.

"It will be soon, Sir. They've moved in on the camp, the last I heard. The army's lending a hand. Should be all over in let's say twenty minutes or so." He glanced at his watch. "Give it half an hour and you should be all right. Have a pleasant day now, Sir, won't you? The weather's supposed to improve later this afternoon.

Dryden found a leaflet stuck under the windscreen wiper. It was a cyclostyled sheet, calling upon the British people to rise up and throw off the yoke of oppression.

"Give me that." Wendy's mother fished about in her Sainsbury's carrier bag for her glasses.

"Ha, this brings back memories."

"Mummy . . ." Wendy murmured. "The police."

"Oh stuff the police." The old woman tapped the sheet with her finger. "So much for three decades of mass education. The grammar's terrible." She screwed up the leaflet and flung it away.

"Let's go," Mrs. Bashford said, opening the car door and plumping herself down on the back seat. As they drove out of the car-park, Dryden saw in his rear vision mirror, one of the helmeted policemen stroll over, pick up the leaflet and deposit it in a nearby litter bin.

CHAPTER ELEVEN

" 'From summit identify stone wall on far side of moor below, leading off left from patch of trees. Scramble down over rocks and make for any point along wall.' Can you see the wall, Dryden?"

Wendy stood up and gazed down into the valley below them. "There it is," she pointed triumphantly. "Come on." She shouldered her knapsack and started away down the hill. Dryden quickly stubbed out his cigarette on an ancient rock and struggled to his feet. She seemed to be already halfway down the hillside. He watched the way her body moved as she skipped from stone to stone.

"Come on," she turned and yelled up to him. "It's easy."

As he walked or rather stumbled down over the dozens of rocks that seemed to have been put there for no other purpose than for people like him to stub his toes on, he silently rehearsed the little speech he was going to give when he was certain the right moment had come. First of all, it involved a humble admission that he had never been to Cornwall in his life, a fact he was sure Wendy must have tumbled to already. Heading for the moor that very morning he had again turned right instead of left. She had stiffened in the seat beside him as he swerved recklessly about the junction, narrowly avoiding the oncoming traffic.

Having got that over with, he would then ask her if she had any idea as to why he might have chosen to come to Cornwall at this particular time. If she did have any idea, then she would smile that mysterious smile women smiled when they knew a man was trying to tell them he was in love. If she had no idea, then he would have to tell her, simply, directly, without shame or deceit. It was at this point that the scene, as he imagined it, could take any one of a number of turnings. Would they drift into each other's arms, drawn by the magnetism of their physical instincts for one another? . . . Wendy had stopped, he saw. She was peering among the ancient rocks, in her hand the Observer's Book of Wildflowers.

"What is it?" He had caught up with her. His legs were feeling like rubber.

"I think it's Crowberry," Wendy frowned. "Look"—she pointed to a drawing in the book.

"Except that, according to this, it's not supposed to be here, is it?" she said slowly.

"Isn't it?" He was Wendy's pupil where the World of nature was concerned.

"Well no, Dryden." She glanced at him as if he were a particularly dense child. "If you read the entry, you'll see it's supposed to be in Devon or Dorset, Not Cornwall."

"That's strange," Dryden nodded solemnly.

"It's probably the right sort of environment I suppose," Wendy mused. "I do wonder about the soil though." She dug her fingers into the ground around the weed. "Do you know anything about soils, Dryden?" He shook his head. She glanced round furtively. "I'm going to take some of this with me," she said in a low voice. "I'll get Margaret to do a test on it. I just don't understand it." She lifted out the weed and laid it together with some of the soil in her handkerchief. Dryden watched her, fascinated. She might have been stealing the Crown Jewels. She tied the corners of the handkerchief together and deposited the whole bundle in her knapsack.

"I hope they don't mind too much," she whispered. "I know it's an area of outstanding natural beauty but I'm so curious to know if this really is crowberry. Daddy might know, of course. Then we could drop it back up here tomorrow, couldn't we?" Dryden smiled and shrugged. "Sure."

"I feel like a criminal," Wendy giggled nervously. "It's awful isn't it? I wonder how many people do this sort of thing. Hundreds, maybe thousands? No wonder they go on about it."

"They? Who are they?"

"The Authorities. The people that run these places."

"These places are run?" Dryden gazed round bewildered at the vast tracts of bleak moorland.

"Why, of course they are, Dryden. They have to be. For the benefit of the nation as a whole. The ecological balance has to be kept. Otherwise, there'd be chaos."

It looked pretty chaotic as it was, Dryden thought. All those stones lying around. He said nothing, however, as he plodded off after Wendy. They reached the stone wall.

"Follow wall left . . ." Wendy read aloud. They followed the wall left, down to gate and bridge over stream.

"See. That's Brown Willy," Wendy pointed upwards. Dryden stared aghast. The track they were following snaked away up the rough, steep mountainside. "And there's the trig station," Wendy said. "You can just see it. Come on. This is lovely."

It was a brighter, clearer day than the day before and the contours of the moor stood out in sharp relief. Bodmin Moor had been Wendy's idea, generated partly by a strong desire to get away from it all. Tintagel had been a disaster. As Wendy had said, one did not go picknicking at National Monuments expecting to be caught up in a full scale riot. Not that they had come to any harm, of course, safe as they had been in the sanctuary of King Arthur's Teashop. But it had been an unpleasant experience, especially as they were on holiday and, therefore, quite removed from the country's political and social problems.

That evening Dryden had watched the news on television back at the guesthouse in Padstow. A formidable array of politicians, policemen and social commentators of various hues had generally agreed that the Tintagel Riot was a frightening challenge to the Rule of Law. There were forces at work which seemed determined to undermine the very fabric of society. Peace-loving, law-abiding citizens of all political persuasions could only throw up their hands in horror at the mindless violence of these motorcycle borne hordes who demonstrated a horrifying contempt for the ordinary democratic processes. In essence, a retired general declared, they were following the path of terrorism, holding society to ransom, etc., etc. Who they were, no-one was quite sure. That they were no credit to the overwhelming majority of peace-loving, law-abiding young people was however an established fact. Such a challenge as they were offering to law and order had to be countered by the severest possible measures. The Government, therefore, was proposing to speed up the construction of juvenile prisons and detention centres. This last declaration had provoked an extremely violent debate between the Blue Team and the Red Team, the latter asserting that the Government was now trying to lock up the unemployed. To blot out this disturbing spectacle the next day's weather report had been hastily moved onto the screen.

Half an hour later Wendy and Dryden reached the summit of Brown Willy. Dryden collapsed onto a stone and lit a cigarette. He inhaled deeply, filling his lungs with the fresh, invigorating smoke.

"You shouldn't smoke so much, Dryden." Wendy sat down beside him. She had already been all over the summit, checking this or that detail in her walker's handbook.

"I know," Dryden murmured. He didn't mention that on expeditions like this it was the only thing that kept him alive.

"This is real, fresh air," Wendy beamed. "Oh, I'm so glad we ran into each other on the Greenaway, Dryden. I'd have never got out so much otherwise. I haven't been up here for ages. And it's so beautiful."

"Wendy . . ." Dryden turned to her. The wind tore the smoke from his lips. Was this the moment? Up here on Brown Willy, with the moor stretching away bleakly in every direction? He made a poor Heathcliff, of course, with his pasty face and his addiction to toasted tobacco, but whatever else the moor meant, for the romantically inclined it was utterly private. No Wendy's mother, no police, just the wilderness busily maintaining its ecological balance.

"We should eat our sandwiches here, you know," Wendy smiled. "We're about half way."

"His passion subsided. He nodded glumly. Briskly, Wendy unpacked the sandwiches and a thermos of tea.

"One for you, one for me," she said, handing him a sandwich. The sweet pickle had made the wholemeal bread soggy.

They sat eating their sandwiches, gazing in silence at the wild sweep of the moor in all its sombre shades.

"Oh, look," Wendy suddenly pointed. "There are people down there." Dryden gazed in the direction of her outstretched arm. Barely visible against the background of moor vegetation, unless one looked very hard, a long line of figures was moving slowly towards what seemed to be a large bog. They looked like beaters flushing out the grouse for a shooting party. He glanced then at the other side of the bog. He stood up and stared in astonishment. There were tanks driving through the heather.

"It's the Army," he said. At that instant there was a loud report and a puff of smoke from the turret of one of the tanks. Then, from just below them on the hillside came the rattle of machine-gun fire.

Wendy, too, was on her feet now, her half-eaten sandwich in her hand. "It can't be."

"It is," Dryden said. "And they're close, too."

"But this is an area of outstanding natural beauty."

"Not today, it seems."

They watched, fascinated, as the cluster of tanks drove round the bog, their guns firing. The line of figures on the other side had flattened themselves in the heather. There was more machine-gun fire from just below them where they watched on the summit of Brown Willy.

"This is outrageous," Wendy shouted. "I didn't see any signs, did you?"

Dryden shrugged. "No, Wendy, I think we'd better leave. If I'm thinking what they're thinking, then they're about to attack this hill."

"I don't believe it," Wendy breathed. "Who do they think they are?"

"There's nothing we can do about it. Come on, we'd better pack up." He threw away his sandwich and gathered up the remainder of their picnic and the thermos. Wendy stowed them away in her knapsack. Suddenly, they heard a new sound. Dryden looked up fearfully. Bearing down on the summit of Brown Willy out of the northern skies were three helicopters. He felt the panic rising. Helicopters terrified him, even on television. It was something to do with the relentless whirring of their rotor blades.

"Come on," he shouted. They scrambled off along the summit of Brown Willy, ducking back and forth among the lichen covered rocks. Dryden had a glimpse of another line of figures on the hill's southern flank, climbing up towards them. He gritted his teeth. The noise of the helicopters was louder now. He was on the verge of hysteria. He'd never do in a war, he thought miserably. The sound of the first helicopter and he would instantly surrender. Please God, he prayed, don't let them be using live ammunition. He grabbed Wendy's arm and pulled her down behind a large rock. The helicopters were now overhead, hovering. They crouched, shivering, as the huge machines drifted back and forth above them. Suddenly they heard the crackle and rasp of a loudspeaker: "You there," came a harsh voice. "Come out and show yourselves." Dryden stared at Wendy. She was staring back at him, her eyes filled with tears. Oh God. It was a nightmare.

"Show yourselves," the loudspeaker boomed. Shakily, Dryden got to his feet. They moved out into a grassy clearing among the rocks.

"Right out into the clear," the loudspeaker bellowed. "Hands on your heads. Don't move."

A helicopter drifted towards them above the rocky summit. A door in the side of it suddenly slid back and a rope dropped down. Within seconds four men in combat fatigues and with blackened faces were sliding down the rope, landing on the grass with catlike grace. They were armed. The rope was pulled back up into the helicopter, the door slid shut and the machine drifted away.

"Stay where you are." The soldiers surrounded them, rifles at the ready, faces set in an expression of grim determination beneath the black camouflage.

"What the hell are you doing here?" One of the soldiers stepped forward. An officer, Dryden thought, judging by the plummy Public School accent.

"We . . . we were out walking," Dryden stammered. His voice was high and nervous. Thank God it was the British Army. For a second or two he had had the wild idea the Russians might have invaded.

"Didn't you see the signs?" the officer snarled back. "The moor's closed to the public for three days." Dryden shook his head.

"This is public property, isn't it?" Wendy said beside him. The officer stepped closer.

"We're borrowing it, lady. Everyone's been informed. Except for you two it seems. Keep those hands on your heads, will you?" he suddenly screamed. "Have you got any identification? Driver's licence, birth certificate, I.D. card?"

"No," Dryden shook his head. "We were just out walking. Honestly, officer, we didn't see any signs."

"I find that very hard to believe, my friend," the officer said quietly. "Certain people would be very interested in information on this exercise."

Oh God, Dryden thought, suddenly panic-stricken. He thought they were spying. Russian spies pretending to be out enjoying a harmless ramble on Bodmin Moor. It was a nightmare. Then he suddenly remembered.

"I've got my Access card, officer."

"Access card?"

"Yes," Dryden murmured. Then he remembered that he still hadn't paid off his monthly bill. Would this have any bearing on his present situation, he wondered desperately.

"Find it," the officer commanded. Dryden gingerly lowered an arm, fished in the pocket of his jacket. The officer snatched it out of his grasp.

"D. K. Pollock?" Dryden nodded.

"What about you?" the officer rasped at Wendy.

"I think I might have my Youth Hostels Association membership card on me." The officer nodded at her. Wendy felt her pockets, then shook her head.

"You're not Communists are you? Socialist Workers' Party, anything like that?"

"No, no, of course not," Wendy said. "We're both teachers at Great Battley International School. Near Winkworth."

"Never heard of it, lady. Anarchists? Tribunites?"

"I'm a Social Democrat," Wendy ventured nervously.

"All right. Who is the member for Taunton East.?"

"I don't know," Wendy murmured helplessly. "I only joined the party recently."

"Okay. Hands on your heads. Don't move. We're going to search you," the officer barked. A soldier stepped forward and ran his hands over Dryden. Then he did the same to Wendy. Finally, he undid the flaps of Wendy's knapsack. He took out the binoculars and held them up.

"For bird-watching," Wendy said. The soldier extracted the packet of sandwiches, held them up and threw them on the ground, then the thermos, a map and finally he found the bundle in Wendy's handkerchief.

"What's that, lady?" The officer stared suspiciously at the knotted handkerchief. Wendy reddened.

"It's a specimen. I think it's Crowberry but I'm not sure." The soldier conducting the search had undone the knots and shaken out the weed together with its clump of soil. "Just a weed, Sir," he reported. "She's clean. Just sandwiches and stuff."

"Okay." The officer seemed to have made up his mind. "Right, you two, you realise you've just brought a vital military exercise to a complete halt. All civilians have been barred from this area for three days. Now, I could charge you with Regulation two two four. Interfering with Her Majesty's Armed Forces. That's pretty serious, I hope you realise. Apart from that, you clowns could have easily got yourselves shot. You happen to be in Argentinian held territory. Now, as it happens I'm not going to put you two in detention for the duration of the exercise. No. You two are going to piss off down this hill—thataway—just as fast as your little teachers' legs will carry you. See that stone circle down there? You've got half an hour to get that far. At that point you will follow the stream that runs round the flank of Roughtor and takes you back up towards the car-park and the road. Deviate from that course and I'll have you arrested. Is that understood? Don't try any tricks. Just as soon as we've taken this hill, we're moving on to Roughtor." He glanced at his watch. "That gives you about an hour, all told. Now, get the hell out of here."

Dryden picked up the sandwiches, the map and the thermos, stuffed them hastily into Wendy's knapsack, tied the flaps and the two of them set off at a trot. Behind them they could hear the sounds of explosions and the relentless, hostile whirr of the helicopters. Half an hour later they collapsed, exhausted, at the stone circle. Wendy was in tears.

"There was no need for it," she sobbed. "No need for that whatsoever."

Dryden glanced back at Brown Willy. The Argentinians had apparently relinquished their hold on the hill and were doubtless in the throes of regrouping on Roughtor. He took Wendy by the arm. "Come on. We'd better keep moving or we'll be surrounded."

"It's unbelievable," Wendy wailed. "They've got no right. This moor's a public area. It always has been. They don't give a damn for the ecology of places like this. They just blast their way through no matter what the cost in wildlife. It's obscene."

They plodded on hastily, spurred by the distant rattle of machine-gun fire from the foot of Roughtor. Following the stream the Army officer had designated, they soon found themselves in a bog, up to their knees in mud.

"Oh my God," Wendy howled. "This is impossible."

"We've got to keep moving, Wendy," Dryden shouted. "They're on Roughtor already. God knows where they'll stop."

They dragged themselves through the mud, their legs making loud sucking noises in the ooze. Around Roughtor the battle raged on. A helicopter appeared and flew low over them. No doubt checking that they weren't deviating, Dryden reflected grimly. He stopped and waited until Wendy had floundered her way through the bog to him. Then, supporting each other as best they could, they stumbled on, their trousers soaked, their feet huge clumps of mud. At last they reached firmer ground, freed themselves as best they could from the bog's tenacious slime and hurried up to the car-park. Dryden was immensely relieved to see that his decrepit Viva hadn't yet been mistaken for an enemy tank. On Roughtor there were soldiers everywhere, darting in and out of the rocks, scrambling up through the heather, while on the lower slopes tanks careered back and forth, their guns blazing.

"Look." Wendy suddenly pointed to something in the grass. Dryden went across to her. In the scrub at the edge of the car-park lay a large notice on its side. It was a notification to the public that the moor was closed for three days. Someone had deliberately torn it out of the ground and thrown it away. Across the notice in big red angry letters were scrawled the words 'Militant Ramblers.'

CHAPTER TWELVE

The next day the Bashfords left their house in Polzeath and drove back to London. Dryden discovered he had suddenly lost interest in Cornwall, aside from the fact that it seemed to have become a ferocious battleground, and decided to leave the guest house in Padstow and return to Winkworth. The bill for his little jaunt to Cornwall was astronomical, he knew. The severe woman, he suspected, had charged him a little extra for the maternal concern she had shown him throughout his stay.

"Pity about them hooligans," she said yet again, as she made out his receipt. "First time in these parts an' you have to run into that." She sighed and shook her head. "Still, my love, you can't say as you weren't warned were you now? Cornwall's a very different place from what her used to be in the old days."

If only she knew, Dryden thought bitterly, thinking of the fiasco of their ramble on Bodmin Moor. He hadn't mentioned anything about that to her. Though she was in her way a kindly soul, she was not above ringing the police 'just to put matters in the clear'. Thankful, he climbed into his car and drove out of Padstow. He was feeling weak and bleary. The worst of it all was that he hadn't found the right time to tell Wendy of his feelings for her. The Army had seen to that. Wendy's father had been sound asleep on the verandah while her mother had been out, apparently at an afternoon tea organised by the Cornish Society. Dryden had not been surprised to learn that Wendy's mother had taught herself Cornish some years before and was now involved in various subversive activities to do with re-establishing Cornwall as an independent state. That woman was an agitator from way back.

It was late in the evening when he arrived at Winkworth. The police building was a blaze of light. He smiled at it.

Somehow it was a welcome sight after the horrors of Cornwall. He negotiated the one-way system of the town with consummate ease, reassured that in his days away from it he hadn't forgotten how. For Winkworthians, forgetting the one-way system of their town was something of a worry during prolonged absence. It could take hours of blundering up cul-de-sacs and driving round and round in circles before one finally got home.

He carried his suitcase inside, dumped it in the bedroom and then ran downstairs. On a sudden impulse he opened the bottle of Schlack's Bessarabian Riesling. Throughout his Cornish holiday it had remained on the back seat of the Viva, enduring a variety of climatic changes from the warmth of Mrs. Bashford's behind on the trip to Tintagel to the chill of the night air outside the guest house in Padstow.

"To Cornwall," he grinned, raising his glass westwards. "Her ain't what her used to be." Schlack's Bessarabian Riesling he decided had improved with age. He glanced at the label. It had been bottled in Swindon. Obviously superior to the Weston-super-Mare variety. He drank the whole bottle, then suddenly raging with thirst, he started on the half bottle of Vodka he had left in the cupboard. That went in no time. Fairly drunk, he finally staggered upstairs and went to bed, heaving an enormous sigh of relief.

The following Monday he arrived at Great Battley early, hoping to nab Wendy for a little chat before school. He glanced at the substitution list and his heart sank. Wendy was absent and would be so for several days. A scrappy note in Rosie Kennedy's hand informed colleagues that W.J.B. (Wendy) had contracted a severe chill. Bodmin, Dryden thought bitterly. Maybe her mother would sue the Army for medical expenses incurred. His eye strayed over the notice-board and suddenly stopped. There, on the Headmaster's section of the board, was a neatly typed letter. It was Bloxham's answer to Basil's answer to Bloxham's 'uncalled for' provocation at the staff meeting.

"You're early." Rosie's deep voice chuckled from behind him. "Makes a change."

"I'm never late, Rosie. Well, seldom."

"That's not what Five Grigorescu tells me, mate. They're always complaining. Have a good holiday?"

"Yes. Hectic but a nice change."

"Where'd you go?"

"Cornwall."

"Cornwall, eh? That's where what's 'er name was, Wendy Bashford. You weren't down there with her, were you, mate?"

Dryden went red. Rosie regarded him suspiciously.

"Yes, well, we did meet once or twice."

"She's away for the next two days. Got a chill or something. I hope you didn't make her ill, mate. We don't approve of that sort of thing here, you know. Here, look, you seen that?" Rosie pointed to Bloxham's letter.

"Yes. I was just looking at it."

"The Head's just seen it. He's furious. Bloxham's resigned you know."

"Yes. I'd heard."

"Darned good job too, I reckon. He's a stirrer if ever there was one.

Look, you read that blimmin' letter." She shook her head. "I dunno. The things people think of." She clumped off. Dryden heard Bernard 'McGraw's hee-haw voice from round the corner. He screwed up his eyes and concentrated hard on Bloxham's English. It was sprinkled with fancy phrases, 'Spero meliora' and 'simplex munditus', the significance of which was completely lost on Dryden whose six years of Latin now, alas, permitted him only to conjugate the verb 'moneo' in all its tenses. Bloxham's letter, however, for all its pretentious allusions was a persuasive attack on poor Basil's notions of running a staff meeting. Bloxham concluded that it was fatal to pretend that vast problems did not exist within Great Battley International School and indeed in the world at large. There were forces at work that could not be ignored, under-currents that had to be openly and honestly acknowledged. One ignored that at one's peril.

'Forces at work' Dryden thought remembering the array of politicians, policemen and retired Army generals discussing the riot at Tintagel. There had been 'forces at work' in Tintagel.

"That man's off his head," Reg Devereaux exclaimed, seeing Bloxham's letter. "He should be put away."

Soon the crowd round the notice-board had swelled to several dozen, everyone straining to read Bloxham's elegant, if rather overblown prose.

"Basil's hiding, I suppose," Goldway grinned. "Aprés-moi le dèluge syndrome. Poor old man. Bloxham's right, of course, though I can't stomach the man. Things aren't as they should be. I wonder what Basil will do about it?"

"There isn't much he can do. bloxham's resigned, hasn't he?"

"The trouble is, though," Goldway sighed, "he's mnanaged to stir up quite a hornets' nest. All the malcontents are behind him, including, so I hear through the grapevine, a lot of the Sixth Form."

"What the hell has the Sixth Form got to do with it?"

"Bloxie's told them everything. He's been agitating for years. Apparntly," here Goldway lowered his voice, "there has been talk of a petition, signed by staff and Sixth Formers, calling upon the Headmaster to agree to a number of demands."

As the bell rang, the staff seemed to be in a fever of excitement and it was some time before the little groups discussing the letter could tear themselves away to go up and supervise morning registration.

Five Grigorescue glowered at him as Dryden walked into the form room. A whole harvest of new hairdoes and other, less visible signs of disobedience greeted home. One or two seemed to have dyd their hair a bright yellow, reminding him of Mrs. Bashford's conspicuous macintosh. Chains clanked ominously as some of the boys heaved their bodies into a sitting position. Dryden was surprised by this, then realised that of course the Head of Fifth Year was out and about. Indeed, a brief glimpse of her was enough to give the toughest little thug in Five

Grigorescue food for thought. He called their names and completed the register. The class had just begun to spread themselves out in their usual, insolent way, when the Head of Fifth Year appeared in the doorway and beckoned to Dryden. She was a deceptively mild-looking creature was Pam but behind her quietly-spoken manner was the ferocity of a drill sergeant.

"Dryden," she almost whispered. "There's a uniform inspection in five minutes. The Head's at the other end of the corridor now. Get that lot into some sort of shape, will you?" And she hurried away. Dryden went dold. Some sort of shape? He couldn't even get them to sit down. He walked with measured tread back to the front of the form room.

"Uniform inspection," he shouted. "In five minutes."

No-one heard him. He took a deep breath.

"Uniform inspection," he screamed. "Five minutes." There was a brief lull in the general conversation. "You know what that means, I trust?" He suddenly had an urge to laugh at his own pompousness but he daren't. Five Grigorescue would trample him underfoot for it.

"That's it. You tell us, Sir," Michael Kelly grinned. Dryden kept his voice calm. "It means, Michael, that chains, swastikas and other anarchist paraphernalia are to be invisible. Understood?"

"Do we get a prize for the best dressed boy or girl, Sir?" piped a sweet-as-sugar voice from the front row. My God, Dryden thought, even little Caroline was becoming a revolutionary. Until half term she had been the only one in the class who had ever listened to what he said.

"No, you don't Caroline," he said bitterly. Sweet, gentle, timid Caroline looked at him with undisguised scorn.

"Tell you what, Sir. We'll do it for you," came another voice. It belonged to a gigantic youth who had stepped straight out of a late night horror film. He looked as if he was a composite being of some kind, the product of a mad genetic scientist's laboratory.

"I don't care," Dryden snapped. "Just do it, for God's sake."

Five Grigorescu began divesting themselves of their ornaments. One of the boys had emptied a satchel and strolled round the room receiving the badges, buckles, chains and even one or two small knives. There was a middle-class orderliness about the proceedings that Dryden found vaguely reassuring. In the thug society of the future there would still be class distinction. Five Grigorescu sat down and waited, looking as uniform as they ever would. Dryden permitted himself a slight smile of appreciation for their efforts, a smile that vanished instantly when he noticed the gigantic youth's leer. Presently. Basil appeared at the door, accompanied by the Head of Fifth Year. He hesitated before coming into the room, directing a guilty smile at Dryden.

"Stand!" the Head of Fifth Year roared. All stood.

"At ease, everyone," Basil murmured, looking round nervously. There was an immediate slouch.

"Up straight!" the Head of Fifth Year screamed. Five Grigorescu snapped to attention. She was truly terrifying. Basil clasped his hands behind his back and walked up and down the rows. Some of Five Grigorescu were grinning.

"Wipe those smiles off your faces!" the Head of Fifth Year barked. The smiles vanished. Basil, confident of her devastating effect on any collection of teenage hooligans, now began to strut like a South American General inspecting his palace guard. He lifted the corners of blazers, deftly raised a few sleeves, pinching the cloth between thumb and forefinger. "Hmmmm," he said to himself, pausing for reflection. "Hmmm."

"Hmmm," went most of Five Grigorescu.

"Enough!" screamed the Head of Fifth Year. She looked round venomously. Basil returned to the front of the room.

"Well, apart from one or two discrepancies, or perhaps I should say one or two deviations from the prescribed attire, there seems to be no particular lack in garments conforming to the accepted mode and colour that I would want to, as it were, initiate a dialogue with your parents upon. You may resume your prior positions." Baffled, Five Grigorescu slumped in their chairs.

"I didn't invite you to resume a fully seated posture or am I perhaps mistaken in . . . in . . ."

"On your feet!" screamed the Head of Fifth Year. Five Grigorescu leapt to their feet.

". . . in your cognisance of the verbal import within . . . within . . . the context of my reference?" Basil winced as he finished. He looked round sternly at Five Grigorescu, as if the severity of his facial expression could compel them to understand what he had said. Five Grigorescu looked contrite. The Headmaster sighed, nodded at Dryden and walked out of the room.

"Quick, give me my chains," yelled a voice. "Come on, you pratt, that's my swastika!" "It's not! It's mine!" "'Mine's got a little nick on it, see?" "Where's my other chain?" wailed yet another voice. "Scunge took it, I think." "Hey, Scunge, give me back my chain, you thief." The bell rang and in a last frantic scramble Five Grigorescu re-attached their beloved emblems and lumbered out of the door. Dryden saw that the fanatical Stephen Mott was lying in wait for him, a crisp sheet of paper in his hand.

"Dryden. Maurice has asked me to check that everyone's filled in a seating plan for their classes in the language laboratory." There was a slightly sardonic smile on the man's lips as he said this. "I think you're the only one left who hasn't."

"Sure," Dryden said cheerfully. "I'll get it done as soon as I can." He reached for the sheet of paper. Stephen Mott drew back.

"Maurice wants these all in now. Because of that incident before half term I suppose."

"Well I can't do it now," Dryden smiled. "He can wait, can't he?"

"Mott shook his head. "I'm sorry Dryden but he was quite insistent. Can't you do it off your register?" No, of course he couldn't. In the first place he didn't know where it was and secondly he wouldn't have the faintest idea of who sat where until he saw them.

"Actually, I haven't got my register with me at the moment," Dryden smiled.

"Where is it? I could do it for you. I'm free this period." A cunning Mott ploy to expose Dryden for the lazy incompetent that he was. Aha, Dryden narrowed his eyes at the man and mentally wagged his finger. Don't think I don't know your game, Mott. You're trying to get me to admit I haven't kept my register and I haven't a clue what kid sits where.

"Wendy Bashford's got it," Dryden felt instantly hot at this appalling fib. "She borrowed it to enter marks for the Norway test." Triumph! Mott's face fell. He was up against one of the most consummate liars in the business.

"She's away isn't she?" Mott said, crestfallen.

"I believe so," Dryden sniffed. "She got a chill in Cornwall. Tell Maurice I'm sorry, won't you? Couldn't be helped." He walked away with the sheet of paper.

"He won't be pleased you know, Dryden," Mott said lamely. "This should have been done ages ago."

"I know." Dryden feigned sorrow. "I just overlooked it I guess. Still, I'll get it done as soon as I can."

So, hostilities had been resumed with a vengeance, Dryden thought as he descended the stairs. Well, he had won himself a bit of time. He would make out the seating plan later in the day and have it in Talbot's 'IN' Tray by the end of School.

By lunchtime Basil had prepared his answer to Bloxham's challenging letter and had had it posted on the board in the staff common room. In a welter of verbiage it eventually made clear that Basil's only defence now was to pull rank. As Headmaster, he was the custodian of 'school policy' and as such bore the total responsibility for the realisation of the school's mission as envisaged by the late Cyril Bennett, O.B.E. Basil was St. Peter to Bennett's Jesus. He was, therefore, in a manner of speaking to be regarded as infallible. Rosie had taken up her post by the staff notice-board and was smiling evilly at the staff who came to read the head's answer. Her little eyes darted everywhere.

"That's ridiculous!" someone cried before he noticed Rosie.

"That's how it is I'm afraid, mate," Rosie snapped. She glared intently at any others who might dare to show signs of outrage. "The Head's the Head. He's in charge. That's where all this silly business stops, I'm afraid."

"Oh no, it doesn't," said a voice. It was Bloxham. He was red in the face but his tone was confidently superior. "As it happens, Miss Kennedy, I have just handed a petition to the Headmaster, signed by a sizeable proportion of the staff and most of the Sixth Form. It's a call for genuine democracy, Miss Kennedy, if you happen to know what the word means." Rosie was caught off balance. A lurid gleam came into her eyes. For a moment it seemed she might spring at Bloxham and claw his fat face. Dryden watched her, fascinated, as she fought to regain control of herself.

"A petition?" she snorted contemptuously. "That doesn't make the slightest difference, mate. As for democracy, it doesn't work. Not here."

"It certainly doesn't seem to, does it?" Bloxham smiled. "We aspire to internationalism but abhor democracy. Threadbare, utterly threadbare. This place seems to be determined to remain a symbol of ideological bankruptcy. In that, of course, it is entirely in step with the country as a whole." There were smiles among the other staff. Bloxham mightn't be the most likeable person in the world but there was no denying his boldness and eloquence. Rosie, seething turned on her heel and clumped off. There was a round of quiet applause. A few seconds later the staffroom door slammed shut, followed by the sound of Rosie's office door slamming shut. Bloxham had her on the run.

"I don't think we need regard this pharisaical nonsense," he gestured airily towards the Headmaster's notice, "as the last word in this matter."

"Down with autocracy," someone shouted.

"Down with the decision making process," came another voice. "It's just crap."

"Schools should be run by the people," said another. "Basil's an incompetent idiot. He's got to go."

"To be replaced by another incompetent?" Bloxham raised an eyebrow. "No, that's not the answer. The answer is to re-distribute power, to make an effort to set up proper consultation, to ensure that important decisions are genuinely collective decisions."

"Hear! Hear!" Dryden swung round in surprise. It was Reg Devereaux's voice. And he was applauding Bloxham. He had changed sides. It was extraordinary.

"I've always voted Labour," Devereaux went on, seemingly quite carried away by the mood of popular revolt. "This is our chance to bring in a few Socialist principles right here, isn't it? Grass roots Socialism they call it: build upwards and outwards."

"You won't get anywhere," came a melancholy voice. It was the Head of Art, a decidedly gloomy individual who loved pouring cold water on grandiose schemes. "Basil's got a few cards up his sleeve yet, don't you worry. This sort of thing happens quite often round the country and it never succeeds. Basil can bring in County, the Unions, the whole kit and caboodle. At best you can get some sort of compromise. That's the English way. It never fails to work.

Bloxham reddened slightly. He stared pensively at the Head of Art.

96

"It's that sort of attitude that is guaranteed to ensure that things will never change. Resignation won't get us anywhere."

"But you've resigned, haven't you?"

"I don't mean that," Bloxham suddenly looked flustered. "I don't mean resignation in that sense. I mean a resigned attitude. Even though I have resigned, my attitude isn't resigned."

"What happens if this goes on into next term? You won't be here, Bloxham."

"I shall be here in spirit. And you can be sure I shall be working hard on yet another front."

"Oh, and where's that?" It was the Head of Art. There was a morbid gleam in his eyes.

"I . . . um . . . I'm . . . uh . . . doing research actually," Bloxham stammered.

"Research? On your own?"

"Of course. How else does one do research?"

"Into what?"

"I shall be researching the . . . uh . . . influence of French mediaeval poetry on . . . uh . . . English poets."

"Oh, very inflammatory. That should bring down the Government."

"Don't be ridiculous," Bloxham retorted. He coughed nervously. "My research has nothing whatsoever to do with this . . . business. Besides, I didn't notice any of you standing up to take the bull by the horns. I thought it was time someone did. This place is ludicrous. A ramshackle anachronism. Who wants Cyril Bennett's brand of internationalism anyway? It's nothing more than a pretext for the man's insatiable ambition to be immortalised. Huh, some monument!"

"He's right, you know, none of us stood up to say what he did. And he's shaken them too. You should have seen Rosie. She was about to have a pink fit. She'll be in reading the Telegraph soothing her wounds with the Leader."

"She reads the Guardian actually. Swears by it."

"That's even worse. How can a Guardian reader behave like her?"

You don't have to be a Socialist to read the Guardian, you know. Lots of Tories read the Guardian.

Throughout the lunch-break the staff continued discussing the growing confrontation between Bloxham and the Headmaster. Those who had mis-spent their days at University joining in protest marches, nostalgically re-lived their memories. Those had been the days. Vietnam, South Africa, Chile. There had been hope then. Hope that the ramshackle old clump of scrap iron, old tyres, sellotape and bits of cardboard that was S.S. Britain was on its way into drydock for a re-fit. There had been the glimmer of a new dawn on the horizon, the promise of a new era of justice and freedom. Alas, there had been no dawn. Everything had quietly fallen to bits. There had been no new Golden Age. It was now the Age of the Receiver.

"I don't know what they're worrying about," Goldway mused. "We're all a lot of has-beens, you know. The Sixties is Ancient History. Did you read about that business in Cornwall over half term? Tintagel or somewhere, I think it was."

"Yes," Dryden murmured. Goldway glanced at him, curious.

"That's what the Eighties are all about. One half of the nation beating hell out of the other half. All this pussy-footing about with petitions and letters is futile."

"You're a supporter of widespread hooliganism then?" Dryden raised his eyebrows.

"I'm not a supporter of anything, mate," Goldway grinned. "Except myself. I intend to survive whatever happens. By the way, did you have a good holiday?" Dryden nodded.

"I see young Wendy is ill. How are you progressing in that direction?"

"Sometimes, Goldway, I wish you'd mind your own business." The mention of Wendy's name was enough to provoke a twinge of yearning. Goldway shrugged. The bell rang and the staff room emptied. Dryden was just about to go and collect his register when the door opened and the Headmaster peered in furtively.

"Hello, Dryden, I . . . uh . . ." Basil grinned sheepishly. Dryden suddenly felt sorry for him. The Headmaster looked ill. "You haven't seen Nigel Bloxham, have you?"

"No, Headmaster. I think he's teaching."

"Oh goo . . . I mean, that's a pity." Basil stammered. He gazed round anxiously at the empty staff room. Then carefully he made his way round to the notice-board, in his hand a sheet of paper, closely typed. Dryden loitered round the pigeon-holes, pretending to be looking for something. He would be late for registration but he was burning with curiosity with regard to Basil's reaction to Bloxham's latest broadside, the petition. For several minutes Basil shuffled about beneath the notice-board, no doubt checking to see if any more calls to revolution had appeared during the lunch-break. Then he rapidly retreated to his office. Dryden could have sworn he heard the Headmaster lock his office door behind him. He hastened round to the notice-board and drew in his breath sharply at the sheet of paper Basil had just pinned up. In his haste, the dear man hadn't realised it was lop-sided.

'Litter' Dryden read. Beneath this heading, which had been drastically underlined in red ballpoint, there followed a devastating attack on the litter problem in Great Battley. On and on Basil ranted about the grave crisis the school was now facing as a tide of litter threatened to engulf it. Not only were there piles of sweet papers accumulating in every conceivable corner of the school buildings but there were cans and bottles and throw-away containers of every kind lying about. In vain, the school caretaker struggled to contain this deluge. It had now got to the stage where the harshest measures would have to be employed to counter this appalling threat to the school's well being. Those among the staff who mistakenly believed that litter was somehow irrelevant to their curricular and pastoral concerns were exhorted to reconsider their position very seriously. If the pupils of Great Battley were not immediately and ruthlessly reminded of their civic responsibilities regarding the proper disposal of litter, then there was little hope for the school's survival as an institution devoted to the nurture of decent, considerate citizens for the world of tomorrow. To this end, a staff working party was to be formed to investigate the problem, teams of staff and pupils were to be dragooned into a routine of litter clearance at morning breaks and lunchtimes and anyone taking it upon his or herself to neglect this duty would face stern disciplinary measures. In a further almost hysterical paragraph, the Headmaster went on to express his horror at the general slackness and nonchalance in matters of uniform, personal hygiene and courtesy. Threatened as every school was by the shock waves of youthful hooliganism, as instanced at Tintagel, Great Battley must strive to the utmost to protect the enduring values of civilised behaviour. Henceforth, there would be daily uniform inspections. Discourtesy of any kind was to be ruthlessly stamped out. Chains, swastikas, badges, expressing subversive opinions or obscene suggestions were to be confiscated without further ado and their youthful bearers dealt with as harshly as possible.

Dryden let out a long low whistle. This was Basil's answer to Bloxham and his petition. This was a ruthless re-assertion of power. Basil had slipped off the woolly mittens of his 'decision-making process' to reveal the mailed fist of dictatorship.

CHAPTER THIRTEEN

"The Head's right, of course," Reg Devereaux exclaimed loudly. "You can't beat the old, decent values, can you?"

"Too right, you can't, mate," Rosie squinted in the watery sunlight shining in through the Staff Common Room windows. She chuckled. "I bet that's given old Bloxham and his ragged band something to chew on. I told the Head to throw that stupid, blimmin' petition in the bin where it darn well belongs but I suppose he's gone and filed it as usual. Still, at least he's decided to call the Sixth Form together for a special meeting. He'll tell 'em what's what then I should think. I know what I'd do. I'd suspend the blinkin' lot of 'em. By their heels in the gym." She chuckled. "Honestly, I don't know what the world's coming to. Did you read about that riot in Cornwall over the half term.

"Yes." Bernard McGraw clucked his tongue. "I thought it was absolutely terrible. My Granny took me there once as a kid I remember. Lovely place, Tintagel. Lots of old people, teashops and things. Matter of fact, we've got a tea-towel at home showing King Arthur and all his knights sitting down to a meal at the Round Table. That's what I can't fathom, you know. Why Tintagel? It's harmless. What are these hooligans protesting about?"

"They say it was some sort of rock-and-roll jamboree to start off with and they just went wild," Rosie said. "If you ask me I think what we need is another war."

"Another war?" Bernard McGraw carefully peeled the end of a cucumber. "But we just had one last year."

"Yeah, but that was only a little one, wasn't it?" Rosie shook her head. "What we need is a good long one to bring people to their senses. Not a nuclear one, of course, but a good long fight with somebody. Something that'll pull the whole country together and stop all this silly nonsense about riots and protests. There was precious little of that when we were fighting Hitler I can tell you. People got on with the job, they didn't moan all the time like they do now. I mean, I'm all for internationalism of course, otherwise I wouldn't be here but you've got to admit all this blimmin' adoration of foreigners hasn't got us very far. People need someone to hate you know. It's healthy. Far better if they can hate a bunch of foreigners in my opinion. Otherwise they just take it out on their own."

"Cyril Bennett'd have a fit if he heard you saying that, Rosie."

"He would too," Rosie laughed. "Mind you, he'd have probably changed his mind by now if he was here to see what a mess all this internationalism has got us into. He'd be the first out there waving the flag when the Task Force came home, I'll warrant. All this E.E.C. nonsense and what have you. It's a terrible waste of time really," she sighed. "As for all this nonsense here. She waved her hand in the general direction of the Common Room Notice-Board. "There'd be none of that in a good long war. Bloxham and his crew'd be out manning a shore battery. They wouldn't have time to stir up trouble with their crackpot ideas. Any of those tendencies and they'd be whisked away very smartly."

However drastic Rosie's solution for the likes of Bloxham and his fellow agitators might be, it was still a very remote possibility. Far more immediate was the veiled threat to them that lay behind the Headmaster's announcement of a vigorous campaign against litter. Indeed, litter had become a symbol in Basil's mind, a symbol of all that indifference to civilised values, that lack of respect for public property, lack of respect for authority, that he now perceived among a certain proportion of the school staff and in the great majority of pupils. In Basil's mind those who littered were little short of anarchists and those who chose to regard litter as trivial and irrelevant held his own judgment, therefore his own authority, in contempt. And he was not going to stand by idly while the likes of Bloxham set about undermining that authority. The implied threat behind the announcement had not gone unnoticed. Those of the staff who might have been tempted to climb aboard Bloxham's bandwagon, just for the hell of it, had quickly fallen into line, awed by the Headmaster's verbose fury. Indeed, there had been something of a dash to sign up for the new Working Party on the Litter Problem. The time was nigh when people were having to stand up and be counted.

Dryden had been disgusted to catch Nathan Goldway in the very act of signing up for the Working Party.

"It'll be a hoot," Goldway had beamed. "Go on, put your name down." Dryden shook his head.

"It's ridiculous," he murmured. "A working party on litter? Whoever heard of such nonsense?" Goldway performed a gleeful little dance in front of the notice-board. The Head of History considered himself a connoisseur of what he called 'hooty scenarios.' The 'hootiest' scenarios in Goldway's eyes were those forms of human inter-action, committees, working parties, conferences, etc., that actually endeavoured to achieve something. Goldway signed up for anything that promised to reduce him to helpless mirth.

"You'll regret it, old chap," Goldway grinned. "Bitterly. Sign up, for God's sake!"

"No," Dryden grimaced. "It's appalling rubbish. I'm keeping my distance from this whole ridiculous business."

"As you like, mate," Goldway frowned. "But I think you're making a mistake." And the Head of History galloped away, looking very pleased with himself. Dryden stared at the list. Goldway had an unerring instinct for the most advantageous move, it was true. No, he would not be party to any of these absurdities. Best to keep right out of it. Remain invisible.

"Dryden, may I have a word, please?" He turned round and met the smooth, round anxious face of David Hepworth. Hepworth drew him away to a remote corner of the staff common room, for the Head of Religious Studies was obsessively discreet. He took a crumpled piece of paper from between the pages of a book and presented it to Dryden.

"I found this beneath the door of my flat," Hepworth pursed his lips in distaste. Dryden read the note. 'You are an arsehole of the first order. We are out to get you. The Lone Rangers.' The message had been put together out of words from the newspaper.

"You think it's—?"

"Michael Kelly." Hepworth wrinkled his nose in disgust. "He's the only one it could be."

"The Lone Rangers," Dryden murmured.

"I'm sure he's one of that little gang, Dryden. The Great Battley Lone Rangers."

"I'll have a word with him," Dryden said.

"If you would. I've written a report," Hepworth whispered, "if you need it."

Kelly, Dryden remembered, had accepted his last dose of punishment without flinching. Typically, retribution had been ruthless. The youth had had to perform all sorts of absurd duties, write pages of lines, report to the Head of Fifth Year thrice a day; in short his life had resembled that of a captive monkey forced to perform a series of tricks in order to earn alms. Much as Dryden lived in fear of spotty, fiendish youths like Kelly, he couldn't help feeling that the boy had demonstrated an admirable strength of character in the onslaught Drill Sergeant Pam had unleashed upon him. Since that episode, Kelly had maintained a stoical silence. Now he was to be hauled before yet another tribunal. That afternoon after registration Dryden summoned him.

"What is it this time?" Kelly rolled his eyes Heavenward as if he had decided he was to be Martyr of the Decade.

"I was just wondering, Michael," Dryden began, "about your gang." He pushed the note across the table. "Mr. Hepworth gave it to me. He found it under the door of his flat."

The youth stared at the crumpled piece of paper. There was a flash of amusement in his eyes as he read it but he kept control of his facial muscles.

"He thinks I wrote it, does he?"

"Yes."

"Well, I didn't. Who are the Lone Rangers?"

"You tell me!"

"I've never heard of 'em."

"The Great Battley Lone Rangers? A local gang, so Mr. Hepworth told me. He thinks you're a member."

"Who, me?" the youth laughed bitterly. "I'd never be seen dead with a bunch of wallies that called themselves 'The Lone Rangers'."

"You deny you had anything to do with this then?"

"Of course I do. Why does he think it's me?"

"You tell me, Michael." Dryden sat back and smiled. Maybe he'd missed his real vocation, he thought to himself. Inspector Pollock of the Yard.

"He hates me. He always has. He'll do anything to get me into trouble."

"I see." Dryden was enjoying this. Youths like Kelly were always the innocent victims of some persecution campaign or other.

"Hepworth—"

"Mr. Hepworth to you, Michael."

"Mr. Hepworth, Sir, hates kids like me." Dryden studied the hideous apparition in front of him. Out of an acne-ravaged face, topped by a mop of greasy hair, a pair of sharp blue eyes stared back at him. Kelly had an earring in each ear, he noticed, a sure sign of criminality.

"See, Sir," the youth began slowly. "I can't cope with him. With what he is."

"Oh? And what is he?" Dryden had said it before he realised what the ghastly youth was driving at. He suddenly sat bolt upright.

"One of those."

Dryden coloured deeply. He looked very sternly at Michael Kelly.

"I got nothing against 'em in principle, Sir," the youth mumbled, "but—well—I can't play along with it. Like some kids can. I never want anything to do with that sort. As far as I'm concerned they got to keep to their side of the line. And—well—Mr. Hepworth sort of feels I can't stand the sight of him."

Dryden felt as if an abyss was opening up under his chair.

"Maybe he wrote the note himself, Sir."

Dryden cleared his throat. "Wrote it himself? I hardly think that's possible, Michael. People do not write threatening letters to themselves."

"People kill themselves, Sir. If they can do that they can threaten themselves . . ."

"Michael, I really don't see where all this is supposed to be leading us
. . ."

"I'm just trying to explain why he's told you he thinks it's me, Sir."

"Yes, well you've denied it, haven't you?"

"But you'll still send me to her, won't you?"

"Well—I—at the moment it's your word against Mr. Hepworth's I'm
afraid."

"And you think that's fair? He's a teacher and I'm a kid. People'll
always believe him before they believe me. Have you ever read any
Freud, Sir?"

"Freud? Well—some years ago, but what's that got to do with all
this?"

"Mr. Hepworth has an anal obsession, Sir."

"Michael, I find all this quite irrelevant to the problem facing us here,
I'm afraid . . ."

"But, Sir, that is the problem."

Dryden stared at the top of his desk. Hells bells, this lout had an
answer for everything. Anal obsession? Sixteen year olds weren't supposed to know about such things. Dryden himself knew very little about
anal obsession. It was a Freudian theory that had been carefully omitted
from the 'Student's Guide to Freud' he had leafed through one lunchtime many, many years ago.

"Now look, . . ." he coughed and gazed severely at the spotty youth
on the other side of the table. 'Let's just leave it at that, shall we? I'm
sure Mrs. Vernon will be very interested in your theories about Mr.
Hepworth."

"Oh, very interested, Sir," Kelly retorted sarcastically, "But I
thought you might be. You see, Sir, people with an anal obsession
worry a lot about what other people think of them. In the case of an
individual like Hepworth—Mr. Hepworth—It's all sublimated in his
work. He wants kids to love him, especially boys, to see him as a sort of
kind old uncle or auntie. That's the image he's put together for himself.
If he sees that someone sees through all that, he gets really vindictive,
see. Lashes out in whatever way he can. Self protection. 'Cause he
thinks I'm out to persecute him."

Dryden closed his eyes. God in Heaven!

"So he thinks you're persecuting him and in turn he persecutes you.
Is that it?"

"Something like that, Sir."

"Could it be, Michael, that you just think he's persecuting you?"

"Oh, you mean . . ." The youth was animated now. He leaned across
the table. "Have I got an anal obsession? No, Sir, I haven't. I've
thought about that a lot. I've got some of Freud's obsessions, sometimes I think I've got an oral one, but I haven't got an anal one."

"That's encouraging, I must say," Dryden murmured helplessly.

"It's a relief, Sir, to tell you the truth," the youth smiled. "Freud had me sweating there for a bit."

"Michael, do you think it might be an idea if you stopped reading Freud and started doing a bit for your 'O' levels? Your last report wasn't too good as I remember." This was a shot in the dark, of course, since Dryden couldn't remember any reports but it would probably hit home.

"What about Marx, Sir? Have you read any Karl Marx?"

"Michael, did you hear what I just said?"

"Yes, Sir. You should read him. One of the world's great thinkers."

"Quite," Dryden parried. He had borrowed Das Kapital from the University library once. It had gone back with a large coffee stain on the fly leaf. The librarian, incensed, had fined him a pound.

"It puts everything in perspective, Sir. Systems of power, I mean."

"Michael, I don't think Marx figures prominently on the 'O' level syllabus, does he?"

"Knowledge and control, Sir . . . you see, the 'O' level syllabus is the first part of a whole system of knowledge that's designed to keep people in line . . ."

"Look. That may all be very interesting, my young friend, but I don't see that any of this is getting us anywhere. Mr. Hepworth is not interested in your theories. In his eyes you are the Lone Rangers. What I'm trying to get through to you is that you stand accused of writing this note or having some part in writing it, quite apart from whether you did it or not."

"I know that," the youth shrugged. He sat back and scowled. "So, I'll get done. I don't mind. Only goes to show how right some people's theories are, doesn't it?"

"Are you saying you're happy to be punished for something you maybe didn't do?"

"If it'll help."

"Help who?"

"You, Sir. See, it's really your problem not mine. Mr. Hepworth's the problem and you're trying to find some way of solving it. Like you did the last time. Wash your hands of it."

Maybe he was just dreaming, Dryden thought grimly. Maybe he would wake up in a minute and meet the real Michael Kelly, the spotty, vicious, inarticulate youth who should be crushed. He bit his finger. The dream continued.

"Do you really think I had anything to do with this?" Kelly pointed to the note.

"No," Dryden sighed. "Probably not."

"I wouldn't stoop that low, Sir," the youth grinned. "I don't give a damn about him really. Just as long as he keeps away from me, see.

Leaves me alone."

"Well, I think we've established you had nothing to do with it."

"Course not. It's the work of some mindless teenage yobbo."

"Michael, in some people's eyes you are a mindless teenage yobbo."

"I know," he shrugged. "I know I look like a thug and a punk, Sir. I like looking like that. I've also analysed that. See, Freud wrote that . . ."

"That's enough Freud, I think, Michael. And Marx. And all the rest of your little theories. I suppose I could try to persuade Mr. Hepworth that you had nothing to do with any of this. But I can't promise anything."

"I know that. See, Sir, he's obsessed. He's getting you to do his dirty work for him while he hides behind the system and uses it against people, kids, like me, who don't—can't think that he's anything more than a pervert. You should read Freud and Marx, Sir. You read stuff like that and you begin to see what's really going on . . ."

"And where is it getting you, my young friend? Precisely nowhere!"

"I don't care. They can expel me if they like. It'll give me more time to educate myself."

"Educate yourself?"

"Yeah. We don't learn anything interesting in school, Sir. The stuff's boring, the teachers are boring and where does it all lead? Qualifications? For what? I don't mind being on the dole as long as I can borrow books from the library, books I want to read, that is. See, Sir, I'm bright. I know that. Bright as hell. Brighter than most of those morons that go to selective schools. Maybe one day I'll be a writer or something. Anyway, I'm not going to just sit around learning a lot of boring, useless stuff that other people think I should learn. I don't care what they think of me. So as far as I'm concerned Mr. Hepworth can have his revenge. It won't change my opinion of him. And that's where I've got him, see. I can just sit there, watching him, analysing him as a good example of somebody with an anal obsession and he's terrified."

Dryden felt an almost overpowering urge to put his head down on the table top, close his eyes and imagine he was on holiday somewhere, far, far away from Michael Kelly, David Hepworth, Karl Marx and Sigmund Freud. Damn, damn, damn them all, he murmured to himself. Educating himself? There was nothing more dangerous than that.

"Michael, you can go—" he waved his hand feebly towards the door. "I'll have a talk with Mr. Hepworth."

""Okay," the youth shrugged, picked up his bag and headed for the door. He turned round.

"Sir, I knew you weren't a complete fool," he smiled sympathetically, "we're all part of a system, aren't we?"

"Go. Just go," Dryden groaned.

"See ya, Sir." The youth pulled open the door and disappeared.

Dryden stared at the space that but a few moments before had been occupied by a sixteen year old youth with a brain far too big for his own good. Suddenly, he realised how appallingly late he was for his first class of the afternoon. Wearily, he gathered up his briefcase and his form register and hastened out of the room.

CHAPTER FOURTEEN

That night he slept badly. David Hepworth and Michael Kelly had now taken up residence in his mind along with all the other horrors that frequently plagued him. Next day, however, Wendy was returning to work. Oh, how he longed to see her. Despite the fiasco of his holiday in Cornwall he had now persuaded himself that between them a bond of some kind had been established. Hadn't they witnessed the Tintagel riot together? Hadn't they endured the dreadful experience of Bodmin Moor, supporting each other as they dragged themselves through the marsh?

And next morning there she was. His heart leapt at the sight of her. For an instant he had the odd impression she was shorter and fatter than he remembered her but it took no more than a few seconds for his memory to adjust itself to the real Wendy.

"I've missed you," he said with what he hoped was a casual smile. Wendy glanced at him in irritation.

"I've got so much to catch up on," she said bitterly. "Mummy and Daddy couldn't believe it, you know. I've still not recovered from the whole ghastly business," she sneezed. "It was outrageous." She shook her head. ""You seem to be all right?"

"What's that?" His eye suddenly alighted on a badge in the lapel of Wendy's jacket. She looked round furtively and mouthed something at him. Rosie Kennedy lurked in the vicinity.

"Uh?" He bent his face towards Wendy's. For a moment he thought he was going to kiss her on the lips. A sudden panic seized him.

"Militant Ramblers' Association," Wendy whispered. She coughed. "I joined up as soon as we got back to London." Dryden studied the badge. It was a clenched fist rampant in a wreath of wildflowers. He drew back.

"They were the ones who pulled down the sign, weren't they?"

"Yes," Wendy murmured. "Some of them are in prison awaiting trial. We're taking a collection for their legal expenses. They're very brave."

"They were arrested?"

She nodded. "Some of them were up on Roughtor apparently.

Hiding under a big rock. If only I'd known, I would have gone back and joined them."

"You'd have been shot, Wendy," he grinned, "or run over by a tank."

"So? It might have put a stop to the Army destroying wildlife just when they feel like it. If only the public knew what's been going on. Still, there'll be other occasions, I'm sure."

"Sure to be. Did your mother suggest this?"

She gave him a hurt look. "Of course not. Mummy's not a rambler. She hates the countryside. She couldn't care less if the Army turned it all into a desert. But, of course, she supports me in principle. Daddy doesn't know though. He'd be very worried if he thought I was getting mixed up in politics."

"Spotted Dog at lunch?" His heart missed a beat. "I'd like to know all about this association." Wendy's eyes gleamed.

"Really?"

"Yes." He frowned. "I think it's a cause I could wholeheartedly support."

"I didn't think you were a 'cause' sort of person."

"After what we went through Wendy, I think I've changed too," he said solemnly.

"I'll see." She frowned. "I've probably got a lot of work to catch up on."

"Meet you at one in here then?"

She nodded. Dryden slipped away. Rosie was eyeing them both with intense curiosity. As he went out of the door, he suddenly saw Reg Devereaux making his way over to Wendy. Dammit, he was still pursuing her. Still, Dryden smiled to himself, what would an idiot like Devereaux make of Wendy's new political consciousness?

Later that morning Dryden saw the Sixth Form returning from a special assembly. The expression of amusement on their faces told him everything. Basil had read the riot act. Still later, just before one o'clock, he passed a line of Sixth Formers returning from Basil's office. They were laughing and joking with one another.

In the Spotted Dog he told Wendy all about it. How Bloxham had written a powerful letter attacking the Headmaster's sacrosanct authority, enshrined in 'Notes for Staff Guidance', how Basil had replied with his Declaration or War on Litter, which was really to be interpreted as a flexing of headmasterly muscles and an unmistakable warning to the disaffected. He told her about the petition and about the special assembly for the Sixth Form that very morning. Wendy listened to it all intently. There was a strange light in her eyes. He had the impression he was in the presence of a woman transformed.

"It's only a temporary setback," she said solemnly. "Reg told me all about it. He's one of Bloxham's strongest supporters you know. But he has to work very discreetly you see. As a Head of Department he's in a key post. I think it's all rather exciting actually. Suddenly, it seems as if a fire has been started."

Dryden was aghast. "He told you that?"

"Yes. He was very interested in Militant Ramblers. I told him all about Bodmin and Tintagel. He was shocked."

"Good grief."

"He's been hammering away at the Establishment for years in his own quiet way, Dryden."

"Has he?"

"Of course. You wouldn't think it, would you? He doesn't look the type. But then they never do, do they?"

"Who?"

"The real revolutionaries. The people who are working for radical change from inside the system, like Reg."

"Wendy. Reg Devereaux is not a secret agent for the revolution," Dryden stared at her in desperation. "He simply says whatever he thinks will give him the maximum advantage at any given moment. I've heard him. You've heard him, for God's sake. He's an opportunist."

"Look, Dryden, Reg has been a terrific help to me since the beginning of term. He's dedicated."

"To himself, he is."

"You're wrong, Dryden. To education, to genuine curricular reform, everything—he's one of Bloxham's staunchest allies."

"Wendy, he's spinning you a line."

"What's that supposed to mean?"

Dryden reddened. "He wants to get you into bed Wendy. He'll tell you anything just to manoeuvre you between the sheets."

She stared at him then stood up.

"Oh, Wendy please. Sit down. Look, I wanted you to tell me all about this association you've joined. Please, I'm interested."

"Oh and I suppose you'll tell me you're the real secret revolutionary now, will you?"

"No—no, I'm sorry, I said that about Reg Devereaux. Honestly. Just ignore it. Sit down, please. I'll get us another drink."

She sat down reluctantly while Dryden leapt up, pushed his way through to the bar, shouted at the barman who took this as a cue to walk back and forth from the beer pump as slowly as possible, and finally pushed his way back to the table with the drinks.

"Now," he smiled, "tell me all about it."

Wendy proceeded to tell him all about Militant Ramblers. It had been formed several months before, breaking away from the main

110

association which over the years had compromised itself ideologically. Militant Ramblers was Marxist and loosely linked with the extreme left wing of the Labour Party. The association was formally committed to resistance on all fronts. Bodmin Moor had been a baptism of fire, Wendy explained, a testing ground for the movement's strategies. There were those in Militant Ramblers who even advocated systematic sabotage of Army exercises all over the country and who talked of buying arms and missiles from the Libyans in order to defend Britain's network of footpaths. The majority, however, was against this sort of action. If he was really interested, she said, she could lend him the movement's manifesto. There was also a magazine entitled 'The Revolutionary Rambler' which the Army was apparently trying to have suppressed.

Dryden was fascinated. This was not the same woman he had fallen in love with before the half term break. The woman now sitting a mere two feet away from him was a political agitator, a Rosa Luxembourg of the rambling world.

"Are you interested?" Wendy narrowed her eyes at him.

"Of course." Dryden hastily roused himself. "It sounds very committed."

"What's that supposed to mean?"

"Committed to high ideals," he smiled.

"You've got to be, Dryden, to get anywhere in this world of ours," sighed Ludmilla who looked as if she had just returned in triumph from defending the Kolkhoz against a horde of White Russian Dragoons. A vague doubt crept into Dryden's mind. Could he love a revolutionary? Yes, he could he decided, particularly with Reg Devereaux trying to get his mitts on her.

"Well if you really are interested, Dryden, there's a meeting next Monday." Wendy glanced round furtively as if an Army spy might be lurking in a corner. "Coffee costs seven pence a cup," she added. "There'll be a collection for our brothers and sisters in Bodmin gaol, so bring more than seven pence, won't you?" He nodded.

"Oh Dryden," she said, a strange passion in her voice. "I can't tell you how important this has become for me now. Maybe it'll become as important for you, too, since you were there, after all. The countryside needs us Dryden. People just don't know what's going on. Hedgerows being ripped up everywhere, paths being ploughed under, rare species of wild flowers disappearing for ever. It's a tragedy of human folly, Dryden. And it's got to stop. Within ten years there may be nothing left for the people to enjoy." She glanced at her watch. "Heavens, is that the time already?" She rose and walked purposefully out of the bar and into the car park. Dryden followed her meekly, feeling ashamed that all he could do, even now, was feast his eyes on that bottom moving seductively beneath her tight-fitting skirt.

CHAPTER FIFTEEN

That very evening Dryden settled down to read the copy of the Militant Rambler's Manifesto Wendy had lent him. It began with a lengthy extract from Marx about 'alienation'. The masses, alienated from their natural selves by the demands of Capitalism, were also alienated from 'true leisure'. One important aspect of 'true leisure' the manifesto rapidly deduced was a natural enjoyment of the natural world that existed around the masses. In a thousand different ways the Capitalist system restricted the individual's access to the world of Nature, not just by imprisoning workers in huge cities full of tower blocks and motorway interchanges, but also by having incorporated the countryside into the system of private ownership. National Parks, areas of outstanding Natural Beauty, Wildlife and Safari Parks, etc. were no more than a sop to a largely anaesthetised working class. The masses were led to believe that large parts of the countryside were a national asset, open to the enjoyment of all. Television wildlife programmes reinforced this illusion. In reality, Nature was totally in the control of the Bourgeois Capitalist state and its lackeys (too numerous to mention). Wild, free, untamed, uninterfered with Nature was a myth. She was, in fact, in chains, her head bowed, watching aghast as Capitalist Corporations felled her forests, ploughed up her earth, dammed her rivers, dug huge holes in her for minerals, bulldozed her mountains and drove tanks all over her heaths. The Capitalist bourgeois state and its institutions were per se the enemies of Mother Nature. The organisations they set up that were supposedly concerned with the preservation and protection of wildlife, virgin forests and those few wildernesses still extant in the modern world were nothing more than a façade, i.e. the World Wildlife Fund, the Royal Society for the Protection of Birds, the National Ramblers Association, etc. Militant Ramblers saw revolution as the only valid solution. Capitalist organisations had to be resisted and finally overthrown. Only then could Nature be liberated from exploitation and decline. Only then could the true nexus between the working masses and the countryside be restored.

Dryden felt his eyelids growing heavier. Determined to fight off sleep, he pulled himself together and read on doggedly, the print blurring before his eyes as his mind grappled with the relentless onward march of Marxist argument. An hour later he laid the manifesto aside and fell asleep, only to wake up guiltily a short while later and address himself to the Association's monthly magazine, 'The Revolutionary Rambler'. He glanced at the leading article which seemed to be a violent attack on bourgeois suppression of something called 'Badgerdom'. The second article dealt with something called 'Foxdom' and appeared to be a lengthy discussion of foxes as symbols of anarchy in the bourgeois mythology. They were also red, the article concluded, which had not helped their image in Capitalist society. Dryden couldn't make head nor tail, metaphorically speaking, of any of it. He leafed through the magazine to the back and was reassured to find the usual pages of advertisements (for health food shops) and general notices. Militant Ramblers, it appeared, were not above holding the odd jumble sale to raise funds. What sort of jumble? Dryden wondered. He sincerely hoped they firmly refused offers of old fox furs and crocodile skin handbags. On the very last page he spotted a small notice under Meetings: 'Militant Ramblers, Bonnington Branch. Thirty-five Wickham Avenue, Bonnington, Monday, October 20th. 8.00 p.m. Members only. Coffee (7p).'

He mustn't forget, he thought to himself. He must get himself properly organised and not suddenly discover that the petrol tank was empty as he was about to set off in the Viva or absent-mindedly wander off to a pub in Winkworth High Street.

Next morning he returned the manifesto and magazine to Wendy with a flourish.

"Compelling stuff," he grinned.

"Did you read the article on foxes?"

"Yes. Very penetrating I thought."

"Jason's into foxes, of course. In a very big way."

"Who's Jason?"

"Our local branch leader. He sees foxes as a symbol of resistance to manipulation. Foxes have moved into the suburbs, you know. They've taken up residence. And they're increasing in numbers all the time."

"Are they?"

"Oh yes. It won't be long before there's a massive reaction. They'll round them all up and exterminate them. Rabies or some such pretext."

"Has . . . uh . . . Reg Devereaux read these Wendy?"

"Oh yes. He's keen on foxes too. Unfortunately, he can't make the meeting on Monday evening. His wife's got a rehearsal. What about you?"

"Oh, sure. I'll be there. I'm looking forward to it actually."

"Good."

Dryden had been watching her face for any signs of private, personal pleasure at his willingness to go to the meeting. There were none. The light in Wendy's eye was evangelical, the joy on her face that of a missionary winning a new soul for the faith. His heart sank. His hopes were ebbing away. Was passion leading him yet again along the same old path, the one signposted 'Disappointment'?

The response to the Headmaster's Campaign on Litter that everyone had been expecting from Bloxham did not materialise. Each morning the staff had gathered round the Common Room notice-board eagerly awaiting the posting up of yet another eloquently devastating letter. None appeared. Bloxham's revolt, it seemed, had fizzled out.

The Campaign on Litter had begun in some confusion. Arnold Scoresby, the deputy head, had got himself in a muddle over what he was pleased to call 'task forces' and no-one had been able to make head nor tail of his 'flow chart' detailing how squads of teachers and pupils would work their way over the premises on a rota system, picking up litter. It turned out, too, that staff who had long since resigned, died or moved on elsewhere had been assigned commissions in the Headmaster's Campaign. Finally, Rosie, in a fit of exasperation, tore down poor Arnold's lists and 'flow chart' and consigned them contemptuously to the bin.

"I dunno," she shook her head. "I just don't know how on earth he does it. He can never get anything straight, that bloke." Arnold tried again. This time it all made more sense. The campaign could begin. Just to be on the safe side, politically, Basil had cancelled the next staff meeting.

"He's got a driving lesson," Rosie announced to the staff in a booming voice. "He can't miss that. He's doing his test in a few weeks time."

Reading Arnold's lists, Dryden found himself at the head of a small brigade of Fifth formers, a subdivision of the veritable army commanded by Pam, the redoubtable Head of Fifth Year.

"This is your logbook," Pam smiled, handing Dryden a booklet of cyclostyled forms. "One for each day of the week. You'll see your duty rota marked there with a cross. It's all been worked out on the computer now, you see, thank God. I'd hate to think what would have happened if Arnold had tried to do it all himself."

"What do I do with this?" Dryden stared glumly at his 'litter log'.

"Fill out one of these forms for each day, details of kids' attendance, performance, area covered, a rough estimate of litter disposed of, that sort of thing," Pam smiled. "Don't worry, Dryden, if you do happen to forget, just make it all up."

It was ludicrous, he fumed, as he deposited the log in his satchel. Not only was Basil's litter campaign an outrageous imposition on both staff and pupils but also, as usual, bureaucracy had run amok.

"Tsk, tsk," Goldway grinned. "You should have got your name down for the Working Party, mate, We're exempted from all this."

"I suppose this was your idea?" Dryden fumed.

"As it happens, yes. Actually, the Working Party has been working overtime. This is just the beginning, mate. Talk about Five Year Plans and Final Solutions. Our first report is due off the presses tomorrow. All twenty pages of it."

"Bloxham's right, isn't he? Basil's not interested in education. That's the last thing he's interested in," Dryden flared. ""How you can even pretend to take all this seriously is beyond me, Goldway."

"I love it." Goldway executed a few dance steps round the floor of the staff common room. "Look at you, Pollock, trailing round the grounds with a bunch of rioting kids picking up sweet papers and tin cans. That's what happens when you don't get yourself in on the business end of the 'decision making process'. There we are, the Working Party, drinking tea and scoffing biscuits in the plush surroundings of Basil's den, devising new and ever more elaborate campaign strategies for you lot to carry out."

"Is there anything you wouldn't do, Goldway, I mean as a matter of principle?"

"Very little, old chap. One or two things, I suppose. Oh look, let's go down to the 'Spotted Dog' at lunchtime to cheer you up. My shout."

Naturally Dryden refused. The prospect of sitting in the saloon bar listening to Goldway's gleeful gossip about the inner workings of the Working Party was depressing. Besides, Goldway would be unable to stop himself gloating over Dryden's unfortunate errors of judgment.

* * * * *

"David, I've had a chat with Michael Kelly about that letter. He denies having anything to do with it."

"Naturally." Hepworth's smooth face stared up at him, its eyebrows raised as if to say 'What did you expect?'. Dryden frowned. Anal obsession, eh? he thought to himself. He wondered what it felt like to have an anal obsession. Hepworth shifted uneasily on his chair.

"The point is, David, I find it difficult to accuse him of something he maybe didn't do."

"How do you know he didn't?"

"He told me he didn't, David."

"You believe someone who dresses like that?" Hepworth looked alarmed. "Who doesn't wash? Who obviously hasn't cleaned his teeth for a year?"

"I don't see what that's got to do with it?"

"You don't see . . .?" Hepworth stared at him in astonishment. "Why he makes a point of flouting every rule and regulation there is. He's a bad influence on the other children, Dryden. He's got to be dealt with, you know."

"He claims you're persecuting him, David."

"Me persecuting him? I should have thought it was the other way round, Dryden. You saw that disgustingly obscene note. No-one else could have written that."

"I don't think he did write it, David."

"Oh, maybe he didn't write it but he certainly had a hand in it."

"He may be a bit of a rebel, David, but I don't think he's stupid enough to do something like that."

"He's a yobbo and a hooligan, Dryden. Always grinning. I can't stand it. Sitting there in my classes grinning all the time."

"There's no law against grinning, David."

"There ought to be. He hasn't done a stroke of work. You know what I found him doing one day?"

"What?"

"Reading a book."

"Good Lord!"

"He had it open under the desk. Of course, I confiscated it. It was a public library book, three weeks overdue."

"Freud?"

"It was disgusting. All about sex, of course. I couldn't bring myself to read it. Oh, he's a menace, Dryden, an absolute menace. We can well do without his kind here."

"He seems to be very intelligent. I mean, a certain kind of intelligence."

"He's warped, Dryden. There's something seriously wrong with that boy. He needs psychiatric treatment in my opinion."

"I hoped you might settle for quits, David," Dryden sighed. "It's his word against yours. You can't prove he wrote that note."

"How much proof do you need, for Heaven's sake? One look at him is proof enough, surely?"

"It's a serious accusation, David. He could be expelled for it."

"I should think that's the least we can do."

"So, what do you want to see happen?"

"I think Pam should deal with it in the first instance and then a higher authority. I've written a full report. Everything he's done to disrupt my classes and upset the lessons over the past year."

"Such as?"

"Well, the book for instance, and grinning all the time, not doing a stroke of work, sleeping; yes, he was sound asleep one day. I woke him up, of course, and five minutes later he was asleep again. You can imagine what sort of effect that has on the others."

"They all wanted to go to sleep, I suppose?"

"Oh, very funny, Dryden. You know, I get the impression, if you don't mind my saying so, that you haven't taken this as seriously as you should. Talking to a youth like that doesn't get you anywhere, you know."

"I agree there," Dryden winced at the memory. "All right. I'll send him to Pam. You'd better see her yourself."

"I shall. Indeed, I shall."

* * * * *

Michael Kelly seemed to take it all philosophically. With a sardonic smile he left the room and still smiling reurned ten minutes later. He had stubbornly denied all charges. The case was, therefore, being referred to a Higher Authority.

CHAPTER SIXTEEN

"Who's this?" the bearded man peered at Dryden suspiciously.

"A friend of mine," Wendy explained. "He teaches at the same school. His name's Dryden. Dryden Pollock."

"Wait here." With a contemptuous glance at Dryden, the bearded man disappeared inside the house. Wendy laughed nervously.

"I should have rung him, I suppose," she said. "Security. You've got to be so careful these days."

Dryden shifted from one foot to the other. Rather foolishly he had dressed up for the occasion, in the hope that he might be able to lure Wendy out for a drink after the meeting. The bearded man re-appeared.

"Okay." He jerked his head to indicate they were to step inside, glanced quickly round the street outside, then closed the door. "You should have let me know you were bringing someone, comrade. This is a closed meeting actually."

Wendy reddened. They followed the bearded man along a shabby passageway and into a tiny kitchen, reeking of boiled cabbage. Around a small, formica-topped table sat three people, two men and a woman. They nodded gravely at Wendy and narrowed their eyes at Dryden who sat down next to her. He had been imagining some draughty church hall with rows of uncomfortable chairs and a stage, not the kitchen of a dilapidated terraced house.

"This is Dryden Pollock, comrades," Wendy murmured. "He's a friend. He was with me on Bodmin Moor. He wants to join." The others exchanged meaningful glances, the meaning of which was lost on Dryden.

"We'll see." The bearded man who had challenged them at the door said "Okay, I think we can start. Spike sends his apologies by the way. His kid's got the measles and Jenny's got her Macramé Course this evening. Now, several important matters have come up over the past few days. First of all, the setting of dates for the Army's show trial in Bodmin. According to the bourgeois press they'll be convicted of sabotage on February the fifteenth. The National Executive, as you know is organising a collection for their legal expenses. They've also asked us to send a representative. Every local branch is sending someone. Peter?"

"How much do they want? From each member—for the legal expenses?"

"That's up to you, comrade."

"We've no idea how much the legal expenses are likely to be, have we?"

"No, but there are now three hundred members of Militant all over the country."

"If everyone gave at least thirty pence," said the other woman who had the look of someone emerging from a briar thicket, "how much would that come to?"

"Ninety pounds."

"Hell, that's not much is it? That would hardly pay for Counsel's lunchtime beers."

"A pound each would be three hundred pounds, wouldn't it?"

"Two pounds, six hundred."

"Two pounds? That's a hell of a lot of money, Jason."

"Capitalist justice is expensive, comrade. We all know that."

"Six hundred pounds won't go far, comrades," Dryden heard Wendy murmur beside him. "Some way towards one person's legal fees maybe. But there are four of them, aren't there?"

"Five pounds then?"

"Still only a drop in the ocean," Wendy shook her head. "Ten or twenty might be more realistic."

"Twenty pounds?" Peter stared at Wendy aghast. "I live on that. Count me out comrades."

"I'm on the dole," said the other man who kept staring at Dryden with a look of faint amusement on his face. Dryden cursed himself for his own stupid vanity. Turning up to a revolutionary meeting in neatly pressed grey trousers and a carefully brushed black corduroy jacket was the height of idiocy. He couldn't have looked worse if he'd turned up dressed as Oscar Wilde.

"Shite!" exclaimed the woman sitting on the opposite side of the table. Jason coughed.

"I think we'll have to sleep on that one for a while, comrades. Now, about the possibility of sending someone from our branch to Cornwall for the trial. We'd like to try and settle who's going tonight, if possible, Peter."

Peter, a round-faced man wearing a bright blue Anorak, shook his head.

"I'd love to Jason but Doreen's booked us for Austria those two weeks."

"Uh, huh," the bearded man nodded sympathetically. Doreen's

Austrian bookings were clearly not to be meddled with.

"Sandra?"

"Well, Jason, I could go," Sandra frowned, "But we've got a single Parent's Conference in Loughborough on the twelfth and then on the eighteenth; the Police Powers Protest Rally in London . . ."

"Pretty hectic then?"

"Rather," Sandra smiled. "It's just that I can't see myself managing to get to Cornwall and back in between."

"I'd like to go," Wendy suddenly said. She reddened. The bearded man whom Dryden now knew to be the famous Jason, the leader of this revolutionary cell, stared at her.

"Well—comrade—that's great of you to say—but—you see—there's something of a problem about that."

"Problem? What problem?" There was a note of defiance in Wendy's voice.

"Jut that—well—you're still very new to our cause, you see. I don't mean that you're not capable or anything like that—just that—National Executive would prefer it if we sent someone more experienced."

"But aren't I experienced?" Wendy said. "I was there. I saw what the Army was doing."

"Yes, I know that, comrade, but—you've only been to one meeting so far and—well—you need to familiarise yourself with all the issues involved, you see. It's that important. Brian, what about you?"

"February the fifteenth, you said?" Brian who was on the dole smiled. "I think that's okay. What about expenses?"

Jason coughed and cleared his throat. "Bit tricky, comrade. Kitty's a bit short."

"I'm on the dole, mate, don't forget. Can't afford British Rail prices."

"Sure, yeah, I understand that, comrade. Thing is, the National Executive was sort of hoping that local branch reps would finance themselves."

Brian guffawed and shot a venomous glance at Dryden. "Finance ourselves? They must be out of their minds."

Jason shifted uneasily on his chair.

"No can do," Brian said. "I've got the time but not the lolly. What about local branch sponsorship?"

"How do you mean?"

"Well—a whip round for the fare. And expenses."

"Uh huh." Jason smiled round the circle of faces. "What do comrades think of that?"

There was a long, anxious silence.

"Do we actually have to send a rep?" Sandra began earnestly. "I mean a lot of people will be there anyway, won't they? The media'll cover it. Will it make that much difference if we don't have anybody there?"

Everyone shifted uneasily on their chairs. Dryden glanced at Wendy. She was staring hard at the edge of the table. He could feel she was near to tears.

"I suppose not really," Jason murmured. "It's quite a long way for us, isn't it?"

"You can say that again," Peter chimed in. "Fifty pounds at least, I'd reckon."

"Christ!" Sandra exclaimed. "It's amazing, isn't it? Talk about oppression of the working masses. We're just expected to walk everywhere, I suppose."

"I'm not bloody walking to Cornwall," Brian glowered at her across the table.

"I could afford it," Wendy said. "Pay my own way. I'd be quite prepared you know." The others looked at her in surprise. Wendy blushed crimson. She was clearly determined to get involved no matter what the cost.

"There's Spike of course," Jason said. "Pity he's not here tonight, in a way. He ought to have a say in this."

"Let her go, comrade," Sandra frowned. "If she wants to pay her own expenses."

"Well—" Jason began. "Well," he shrugged. "I suppose I don't see why not. Maybe we'll have a vote on it. All those in favour of comrade Wendy going to Cornwall raise their right arm." The vote was unanimous. Wendy smiled and nodded. "You'll have to be briefed fairly carefully, comrade," Jason looked at Wendy sternly. "But I suppose there's plenty of time for that. Right, make sure that goes down in the minutes, won't you Peter?"

Peter looked suddenly alarmed. His face turned bright red.

"Shit—Jason—I'm sorry—I forgot," he mumbled.

"I wondered when you were going to put pen to paper," Jason observed acidly. "You are branch secretary after all, comrade."

"Someone should have reminded me," Peter banged his forehead with the palm of his hand. "Oh hell. I left the exercise book on the sideboard at home. I'll write everything up just as soon as I get back tonight, I promise."

"This is the second time this has happened comrade," Jason said sourly. "One more time and I'm afraid we'll have to have a vote of censure."

"I won't forget again comrade, really," Peter said, chastened.

"Right, item number two on the agenda." Jason rubbed his bearded chin. "The Blackwood Hedgerow Clearance Crisis. Just as we expected the Blackwood Examiner refused to publish our letter relating to the destruction of hedgerows at Highfield Farm and the consequent threat to flora and fauna. In addition, they threatened to publish an article about us, exposing us as they so politely put it, 'as a bunch of crackpot, half-baked loonies who should be locked up'. He smiled sardonically. "I think we should see that as an encouraging sign, comrades. The bourgeois press is beginning to take us seriously. Secondly, our attempt to stop the Milborough–Tryton path being re-routed away from Derrybell Wood and under the M25 looks like meeting with the characteristic response from the vested interests in the area. The bourgeois imperialist Ramblers' Association together with their neo-Capitalist revisionist lackeys, the Society for the Protection of Wildlife, have agreed in principle to the re-routing of this path. I think our next move will be to leaflet people in the area and then press for a public meeting, probably in the Milborough Scouts' Hall. We'll have to tread carefully, however, as I don't think there's much sympathy for our aims in that district. This is where you could certainly help us Wendy and maybe your friend too, if he wants an opportunity to prove himself to the branch . . ."

"But he has proved himself," Wendy interrupted. "He was up on Bodmin Moor. He saw what was happening. It shocked him as much as it did me, didn't it Dryden?"

Dryden nodded. He decided he had taken a strong dislike to Jason.

"Okay, comrade," Jason smiled patronisingly. "I appreciate what you're trying to say but the point is that that doesn't really prove anything if you understand what I mean by that. I mean you two were hassled by the Army, sure, but you weren't there to hassle the Army back, were you? Our people were up on Roughtor waiting for them. That's the difference, you see. Our brothers and sisters are in gaol and you two are sitting here now, okay?"

Wendy bit her lip, reddened and said nothing. Jason droned on about leafleting and writing letters and lying down in front of tractors. The others yawned occasionally and every now and then glanced discreetly at their watches. Time passed and still the bearded man talked. His lips were flecked with foam. His eyes had acquired a strange, fanatical gleam. Dryden was sure he was a primary school teacher. Dryden, himself, had begun to lust for a cigarette. But unlike other revolutionaries who plotted their various attentats in a fog of cigarette smoke, Militant Ramblers planned their forays in pure, ice-cold air. Then a discussion began between Jason and Peter. It seemed to involve a difference of ideological principle. There was a vicar somewhere who was organising a campaign to save a three hundred year old oak tree from the council bulldozers. Jason was apparently opposed to Militant Ramblers' involvement in this, seeing it as a dangerous step into the arms of the bourgeois Christian establishment. Peter, on the other hand, was advocating involvement on grounds of political expediency. After all, hadn't the Bolsheviks done the same in nineteen seventeen? Hadn't they turned popular uprisings of whatever Socialist hue to their own advantage?

"Sorry," Dryden broke in and smiled sheepishly round the table. Do you mind if I smoke?"

"He was desperate for a fag. The discussion stopped. There was ominous silence.

"You smoke, do you?" Jason's eyes narrowed in suspicion.

"Yes. That is—I—" Dryden stopped. The others exchanged meaningful glances.

"I'm sorry, uh, whatever your name is again, but you can't smoke here." There was an expression of contemptuous triumph in Jason's eyes. "No Militant Rambler smokes, you see. No-one told you?"

"He hasn't read the Constitution yet, Jason," Wendy said quickly. "I haven't given it to him yet." Jason sighed. "Wendy, I think there's something you still don't quite understand about us." His tone was condescending, superior. "You see, Wendy, we're not one of your jolly little anything goes jumble sale pat on the back little old ladies' paper chase type organisations. We are a Marxist-Leninst revolutionary movement. We demand dedication and iron self-discipline. Our cause is great. The cause of the countryside. The road to its fulfilment is long and difficult. We must all show the dedication of our comrades in Cornwall. Now, you've come along to us as a result of your encounter with the Forces of Reaction over the half term break on Bodmin Moor. But don't you see, Wendy, in our terms that's not really enough. We've all been hassled by the Capitalist establishment at some time or other. Peter's had his electricity cut off three or four times for no apparent reason, Sandra's been dragged round by the hair at a demo by the thugs from the S.P.G., Brian's been arrested on suspicion of smuggling dope—you see, we're all victims of some outrage or other, all witnesses to the establishment trampling all over our civil liberties. But you do see, comrade, that the step from mere outrage at social and political injustice to the dedicated and single-minded resolve to fight for the elimination of that injustice is a giant one. Okay, so you're willing to go to Cornwall and pay your own expenses but maybe Bodmin's the only issue that means anything to you and that's not enough. There are dozens of issues just round here that are in their way just as vital. Bodmin is glamorous—a national issue, maybe, but real dedication, comrade, is the inch by inch fight down here at the grass-roots. You still have to prove to us that you're really prepared to make that commitment. Bringing a friend along isn't any use to us, you see? We can all bring our friends along, can't we? Like taking someone to a Tupperware party. The main thing is the head count. But that's not what we're all about see. It's a question of commitment and discipline. Better a handful of dedicated fighters than half a thousand fair weather friends. Lenin knew this, comrade. He knew that it was possible to bring about a real revolution with just a handful of fearless, dedicated fighters . . ."

"Didn't Lenin smoke then?" Dryden interrupted. He could feel that beside him Wendy was on the verge of bursting into tears.

"That's irrelevant, my friend," Jason smiled. "The point is that Militant Ramblers must be non-smoking. Not even herbal cigarettes. We can't start making exceptions to our constitution." Dryden stood up. "I'll wait outside," he said to Wendy. He left the kitchen, walked along the passage and out of the front door. He had just lit up and was enjoying the first few draughts when Wendy appeared.

"Is the meeting over?"

"Wendy shook her head. "They said . . . I wasn't serious . . ." She suppressed a sob. "I am serious."

"I'm sorry, Wendy," Dryden said helplessly. "It's all my fault. I shouldn't have come."

She took out her handkerchief and blew her nose loudly. "Take me home," she said quietly. "I get the impression I'm not wanted."

Dryden drove her home. He had abandoned all hope of persuading her to go for a drink. She was grieving. How he would have liked to punch that revolutionary primary school teacher on the nose, he thought bitterly. Surely, though, the meeting must have persuaded Wendy out of getting herself involved with that bunch of idiots? He glanced at her. She was staring stonily out through the windscreen. He pulled up outside her place. She had opened the door almost before the car stopped moving.

"Good night, Dryden." She leapt out of the car and closed the door. "Thanks. Good night."

He watched her mournfully as she hurried up to her front door, fumbled with her key and finally disappeared into the house. Swearing violently, he put the car into gear and drove recklessly back to Winkworth, determined to crush any hedgehog that dared venture across his path. None appeared, however, and he had to be content with squashing a tiny moth on the top of the dashboard. Let Militant bloody Ramblers put that in their pipe and smoke it, he thought viciously.

CHAPTER SEVENTEEN

Arnold Scoresby's resignation from the post of Deputy Head had been officially posted. Great Battley staff common room buzzed with excitement. There had already been signs of an indecent scramble among some of the senior staff. What caused an even greater fever, however, was the Headmaster's announcement of a number of 'new posts of responsibility'. It was the coup de grâce for Bloxham's protest movement. Once again those old spectres, greed and ambition, were abroad. Bloxham found himself utterly alone.

"This is her work," he was heard to mutter to himself rather than to anyone else, for his former supporters were already hard at work drafting their applications for one or both of the Headmaster's new jobs. The Senior Mistress glowed in triumph. 'Look at 'em now' Dryden fancied her thinking. 'So much for Bloxham's revolution. They're like wolves in for the kill, all scrambling for promotion.' Indeed, to Dryden, there seemed to be a distinct edge to the atmosphere in the common room. Knives were quietly being sharpened in corners, characters were being assassinated, eyes were darting hither and thither as fellow contenders for the prizes were carefully sized up. It had already emerged that Reg Devereaux was applying for two of the posts. He saw himself as an ideal Senior Co-ordinator of Pastoral Inter-Stellar communications or some such nonsense. Failing that, he was obviously convinced he could do full justice to the new post as Senior Adviser on Interdisciplinary Co-ordination. Or was it Interplanetary? Dryden couldn't remember. He was experiencing an overwhelming insecurity. Maurice Talbot, he knew, was applying for the post as Deputy Head. If he got that, then Maurice's job as Senior Co-ordinator of International Studies would be up for grabs which meant . . . the wheels of fortune were in motion. Prospects for the future were distinctly uncertain.

"This has completely routed Bloxham," Goldway remarked. "You've got to hand it to Basil. It's a brilliant move."

"It's blatant manipulation," Dryden grimaced in disgust. "It's tyrannical." He watched Bloxham stalking away thorugh the crowd. He was obviously incensed. Rosie was smirking. Oh, she was looking forward to the next few weeks.

"They'll all be dancing attendance on her, of course," he murmured to Goldway. "And nipping in to see Basil every few minutes on some pretext or other." Reg Devereaux, he saw, had already made a bee-line for the Senior Mistress, doubtless to begin the groundwork for his promotion. He was followed closely by Ken Tyler, the arch bore of the Science Department, who, it was well known, saw himself as a powerful contender for the Deputy Headship.

Thoroughly unnerved by this abrupt change in the political temperature of Great Battley staff common room, Dryden made his way upstairs. Wendy had looked miserable, no doubt still brooding on Jason's hurtful remarks at the Militant Ramblers' Meeting the previous evening. Maurice Talbot was in the Resources Room when Dryden entered. Talbot was dressed in an immaculate, new grey suit and exuded the confidence and dynamism of a Deputy Head designate.

"Oh—Dryden—there you are." He smiled pityingly at the bedraggled figure in front of him. "The Head's sent round a memorandum asking about our plans for International Day. I'm asking round to find out how far people have got with their planning." International Day? Dryden went cold. What on earth was that? He'd never heard of it.

"I—uh—I'm sorry Maurice but this is the first I've heard of it."

"Oh?" Talbot pretended to look surprised. "The Head's been planning this for ages. He talked about it last Spring if you remember? It was in a circular—oh—way back in March, I think. I'll find it for you if you like." Talbot reached for the filing cabinet. Dryden shrugged and grinned sheepishly. "Oh well, no matter," Talbot smiled triumphantly. "Christine and Stephen have already done quite a lot of preparation for it as it happens. Now you, as Assistant Co-ordinator of European Studies will naurally be in charge of the European section, won't you? What sort of plans did you have in mind for that, I wonder?"

"I'll think of something," Dryden murmured disconsolately.

"I beg your pardon?"

"I'll do something, of course, Maurice," Dryden smiled submissively. Talbot stood up and shuffled a pile of manilla folders on his desk.

"I'm not sure that 'something' is going to be enough, I'm afraid Dryden. The Head's naurally very eager to make this a particularly attractive and exciting day. For some time he's been feeling that the spirit of internationalism among the staff and pupils has been flagging and he's expecting us all to put heart and soul into this venture. We've got to show people we mean business with our internationalism, what with this ghastly and ridiculous war in the Falklands and Mrs. Thatcher waving a big stick round the Common Market, people are beginning to wonder if Great Battley isn't an anachronism, a relic of some bygone era of international understanding and co-operation. Commitment is the word, Dryden, Commitment and dedication."

Like two giant boulders the words rolled down a mountainside towards the Assistant Co-ordinator of European Studies, who glumly contemplated the prospect of being flattened yet again.

Dryden smiled, nodded and walked out of the Resources Room. Naturally, Talbot would play the International Day for all it was worth to him on the road to Arnold Scoresby's job, he thought bitterly.

"What's up now?" Nathan Goldway emerged from the staff toilet. "You look terrible."

"International Day," Dryden murmured. "Heard of it?"

Goldway laughed. "Yes, mate. A stroke of genius. You know my estimation of Basil goes up minute by minute. He's smashed Bloxham, got the staff all a-quiver over these ludicrous new posts of responsibility and now to finish it all off, he's setting up this little loyalty and dedication parade called International Day. The man's a born politician."

"How's the Working Party coming along by the way?"

"Fine, old chap, as far as I know."

"What do you mean, as far as you know?"

"I'm no longer on it, old man. I've been promoted."

"Promoted?"

"Working Party on Internationalism. A bit hush hush, old friend. A select committee. Chaired by Basil. There's Basil, Rosie, Maurice Talbot, me and Ken Tyler. Arnold's been left out, of course, since he's resigned."

"I never saw anything about that on the notice-board?"

No," Goldway smiled, "we were asked individually by Basil. Naturally, one couldn't refuse. Oh, my dear, it's a hoot. An absolute hoot. It's excruciatingly difficult to keep a straight face when Basil pontificates on the subject. Plans afoot to revise the curriculum, you see. And—keep this under your hat—three of its members are applying for the post of deputy head."

"Dryden took a step backwards. "You?"

"Of course. I think I'd do a wonderful job."

"Et tu Bruté?"

"Don't be stupid. I've never made any secret of my vaulting ambition. I won't get it of course. Talbot will. But I'll give him a good run for his money. Ken Tyler's out of the running, of course, though the poor sod hasn't realised it as yet. Will you be applying for Talbot's job, do you think?"

"I . . . uh . . . hadn't thought about it, actually." A slow smile spread over Goldway's face.

"I should if I were you, mate. This shake-up of Basil's will leave a lot of corpses. He's really steam-rollering now. This Bloxham business got him rattled. He's determined to put his house in order, crush all opposition."

"It's depressing," Dryden muttered. He blinked at Goldway and strode off up the corridor.

* * * * *

His European Studies class lay about the room, sleeping or reading the New Musical Express. Dryden coughed loudly as he reached the table at the front of the room and ostentatiously shuffled his notes. The class stretched, yawned and sullenly opened their books. Dryden began dictating at speed, not fast enough to provoke the inevitable cries of rage, yet just fast enough to make it something of an effort for the class to keep up with him. It was a new technique he had tested on a number of previous occasions. He had dubbed it the liturgical method of teaching. For centuries priests of all religions had used it with resounding success. Was there a book on it? he wondered idly, as he droned on about the leather industry in Upper Swabia. Writing books on teaching methods was a goldmine, though the field was fast being cluttered with pundits. There was a whole team of ex-teachers who had skilfully manoeuvred themselves out of their classrooms and onto various TV panel games via the educational publishing industry. He had a momentary vision of himself planted between two busty actresses trying to guess the last line of a dirty limerick. A team of three with one red button between them.

Soon there were only five minutes left. Stunned by the monotonous droning of his voice, the class finally dropped their pens and closed their eyes. Dryden permitted himself a gentle smile of satisfaction.

"What we got next?" he heard a sleepy voice ask a comatose figure at the back of the room.

"Uuuuuuuhh!" The figure opened its eyes. "Geography, I think."

"Geography?" The voice was incredulous. "I thought it was French."

"No, you wally, it's Tuesday, so—oh, it's History."

There was a collective groan of despair. The bell jangled violently. Dryden altered his watch for the second time that day. The class rose and dragged themselves towards the door. Through the windows, Dryden noticed a platoon of children, led by the fanatical Stephen Mott, heading away on a litter patrol, Mott directing them to sweet papers and Coca Cola cans with the aid of a long wooden pointer. Education in the Eighties, Dryden reflected. It was enough to send his old Education tutor, Professor Peabody, screaming back into the Sixties where he belonged.

CHAPTER EIGHTEEN

"It's what I've always maintained, mate," Rosie said, esconcing herself in an armchair in the staff common room. "They queue up to work here. We've had applications from all over the world."

Indeed, all the new jobs at Great Battley International School had been advertised in the national and international teaching journals. According to Rosie, hundreds of applications had been pouring in daily. Basil, Rosie and Arnold had been working overtime sifting through them. And they weren't just ordinary, run-of-the-mill people either. They were Masters of This or That, Doctors of This or That, people with strings of degrees from eminent Universities.

"You wouldn't credit what some of these blimmin' people have been doing. Mind you," Rosie chuckled, "we've had one who's worked as a gaucho in Chile, another who's been herding sheep in the mountains of Sardinia—both with doctorates. Blimmin' amazing."

"Little good it does 'em," Bernard McGraw bit into a cheese and pickle sandwich. "In the end they all want to come back here, don't they?"

"There's another one who speaks four African dialects. Fluently," Rosie went on. "He wants to come all the way from Dahomey."

"Never heard of it," Bernard grumbled. "Sounds like one of those new-fangled places. They're always inventing new places. One minute it's Rhodesia, the next it's Zimbaby or some such outlandish name. Time was, you know, when they all had proper names we could understand," he shuddered. "Winkworth's been Winkworth for a thousand years." He stared at a piece of pickle that had dropped onto the carpet at his feet. "'Cept the Romans didn't call it that. I forget what they called it now. Something unpronounceable."

"These people get stranded, of course . . ." Rosie sighed. "Rushing off to all these outlandish places to do good and poke their noses in where they're not wanted. It's all very well digging water-holes for desert nomads or teaching blimmin' Arabs to read and such like but in the end they all want a bit of money, a decent car and a house, don't they? They want their milk delivered and a proper Sunday newspaper. It's quite understandable."

"Serves 'em right," Bernard McGraw snorted. "They should never have gone in the first place. I could have told 'em that."

"There is something special about the British way of life," Rosie mused. "I mean, I'm all for internationalism, of course, I think it's a blimmin' good thing, long as it doesn't go too far. These people have got to be kept at arm's length you know or they start interfering with our way of life. Like all this business with French milk. We don't want French milk. British milk is much better. At least it doesn't taste of cardboard. We've got to make these people understand that we know what we're doing. We've been at it for centuries."

"Quite," Bernard McGraw mumbled pouring himself a cup of tea from his thermos. "Some of 'em really think they can behave any old how these days, don't they?"

Dryden took this as a veiled reference to the current behaviour of the Guatemalan Government which had declared its intention to annexe some former bit of British territory he'd never heard of. It was clear the Guatemalans were not internationalists in the Great Battley sense of the word. There had been reports of skirmishes along the border with the Queen's Own Highlanders.

"It's the rule of law they don't understand, mate," Rosie inspected her fingernails. "It's all Greek to them. They see something and they want it."

"What's all this about?" Goldway, as bright-eyed and merry as ever, appeared beside Dryden.

"World affairs," Dryden murmured. "Rosie was just saying how foreigners don't understand the Rule of Law. It's all Greek to them."

"I thought you'd invited Wendy Bashford down to the pub this lunchtime?"

"I had," Dryden said miserably, "but bloody Talbot chose to have a faculty meeting about International Day. I couldn't get out of it."

Wendy had approached him that very morning, beaming with excitement. Jason had rung her up to ask if she and 'her friend' were prepared to do some leafleting on behalf of Militant Ramblers the following Saturday. He had apologised for his rudeness to her and said that he was very upset that he had cast doubt on her commitment to their cause. But as she no doubt understood, in his capacity as leader of the local branch, he had to be very careful of infiltrators bent on passing on information to the Forces of Reaction. He had conducted a few enquiries and was now welcoming both her and her friend to the branch. Her friend was welcome to carry on smoking, too, as long as he didn't smoke during meetings. Later in the conversation it had emerged that both Brian and Sandra had dropped out of the organisation so there was now plenty of room for Wendy and Dryden. "I knew he'd see I was serious, eventually," Wendy had smiled. "You will come along to help, won't you, Dryden? I did ask Reg Devereaux, too, but he said he's too busy at present." The mention of the name Devereaux had clinched it. Dryden had agreed to go leafleting on the spot. Finally, Wendy had eagerly accepted his invitation to lunch in the 'Spotted Dog'. Now he couldn't go.

"So," Goldway frowned, "Talbot's going into action is he?"

"You'd better get a move on, Goldway," Dryden smirked. "There are people applying from all over the world."

"Oh, I know that," Goldway grinned. "It's gruesomely funny in a way. Basil's got no intention of appointing anyone new, let alone anyone who's been foolish enough to have been living in Africa or South America for the last few years."

Dryden stared at him, shocked. "But aren't they interviewing some of these people?"

"Oh yes, for appearance's sake. It looks impressive, doesn't it? But Talbot's got it all sewn up."

"But some of them are coming thousands of miles."

"Isn't it a hoot?" Goldway grinned. Dryden sat stunned. Was there no end to the chicanery people were prepared to indulge in? He tried to visualise himself winging his way towards Heathrow from the steamy confines of a jungle somewhere, fondly imagining he was eminently qualified for the post of Deputy Head at Great Battley International School. Perhaps he would believe that the very existence of such an institution in the Home Counties was an indication of the far reaching changes the old country had undergone since it joined the EEC. In fact, Dryden himself had never been abroad long enough to have the chance of wondering if dear old Blighty might have changed since he left it. It had always been as shabby, as runny-nosed, as peaky and as sullen as when he'd departed its shores but a few weeks before. He had only ever met one person who had been abroad for long enough to entertain rosy visions of old Britannia, though in an entirely different direction. This poor unfortunate, an acquaintance of Pollock mater's, had returned from a long career as a District Officer in the jungles of Borneo. He had been horrified to discover that people no longer had servants. Within a week of his arrival back in England the gentleman in question had caught a return ship to Borneo where he presumably still dwelt, gathering about his emaciated, malaria-racked frame the moth-eaten cloak of Imperial style as he lived out his tragically anachronistic retirement. In his dreadful Winkworthian way Bernard McGraw was right. 'They should never have gone in the first place.'

* * * * *

The Headmaster's International Day was rapidly becoming the biggest ordeal Dryden had yet experienced at Great Battley. The Motts were busily transforming their part in the proceedings into a display of personal power. They had written off to all sorts of places and received in the post vast cargoes of display posters, miniature dolls in national costume, travel brochures and screeds of information on such matters as rice growing in the Philippines etc. Christine had assumed responsibility for selecting the colour scheme for each room while her fanatical husband had drawn up a precise, detailed plan of how each display would be arranged. In vain Dryden had struggled to persuade, cajole and threaten his classes into preparing work for the event. His pupils had stared at him as if he was completely out of his mind. He was completely out of his mind. With anxiety. The Motts were on the march. Once again Dryden was about to be run over by a juggernaut of efficiency, precise planning and fanatical 'commitment'. Naturally he didn't stand a chance but some instinct in him drove him to desperate rearguard actions that were doomed to failure.

"The European Studies section is the problem, of course," Christine Mott remarked with a knowing glance at Maurice Talbot. "Stephen and I have been trying to think out how we might arrange that."

"I don't know what ideas Dryden has for it," Talbot smiled, glancing at Dryden, "but I'm sure he's been looking into it all very carefully."

"I . . . uh . . . thought I might . . . oh . . ." Dryden began unconvincingly. He rabbited on desperately for several minutes, explaining his plans for the European display. The others listened to him with barely concealed amusement. Christine carefully applied a thin covering of fat-free cottage cheese to a slice of Ryvita whilst her husband plunged a teaspoon into a pot of unflavoured yoghurt.

"Yes, I see," Talbot pursed his lips. "Interesting."

"It doesn't sound very exciting, Dryden, if you don't mind my saying so," Christine smiled.

"It lacks definition somehow."

"I think we've got to get across to people that our internationalism is a challenge, Dryden," Talbot sighed.

"Dynamic," Stephen Mott murmured. "Not tired."

"And not an afterthought either," Christine added. "We don't want people to get the idea that it's all just another jolly old church hall jumble sale cosy sort of venture, just another excuse to get together for a nice cup of tea and a chat about the neighbours. There's far too much of that sort of amateurism around. We must show our commitment to the ideal of internationalism, that we genuinely believe in it, that we can make our pupils believe in it."

Dryden nodded unhappily. He glanced down at the scrappy notes he had made the night before.

"The Head's inviting Simon Frobisher, you see," Talbot said.

"Our local Euro M.P., Dryden," Christine smiled. "He'll be keenly interested in your display I should imagine. He's a committed Europeanist."

"His wife's German," Stephen Mott drawled. "Frieda Frobisher. She's very keen to see the school."

Frieda Frobisher immediately assumed the proportions of a gigantic Valkyrie in Dryden's imagination. The few German women of that sort he had encountered before had utterly terrified him. They spoke in fantastically loud voices and in their eyes there was a manic gleam. They threw themselves around with that ferocious energy that seemed to be a distinctly German characteristic.

Later, on his way up to registration he met Wendy. There was a decidedly unhealthy gleam in her eyes.

"Dryden," she whispered. "You'll be there, won't you?"

"Of course."

Wendy looked round furtively. "The Stag and Hind at eleven, Jason said." He nodded. Wendy hurried away. As he walked up the stairs he fancied he heard Five Grigorescu indulging in a particularly violent brawl. Should he hide for a few minutes, wait until Pam stormed along the corridor and bellowed at them, or should he throw himself into the fray? He decided to do the latter. After all, his life recently had shown every sign of transforming itself into a vortex of futile activity.

* * * * *

It was Saturday, eleven o'clock. Jason regarded the pint of beer Dryden set down in front of him with suspicion.

"Is that Green?"

"It's Export," Dryden said. "They've run out of Green."

"Didn't they have any Blue?"

"I didn't ask I'm sorry. You should have said.

Dryden settled himself down on the bench next to Wendy and lit a cigarette. Jason waved his hand in irritation at the cloud of smoke.

"The main thing is to get round as quickly as possible. We want maximum coverage." He pointed to a map spread out on the table. "Shouldn't take any longer than three maybe four hours." Dryden groaned inwardly.

"Divide up the area between you, of course," Jason said. Wendy nodded gravely. How little she resembled a radical, Dryden thought, in her Anorak, scarf, woolly mittens, woolly slacks and black Wellingtons. She looked no different from the women he had seen in the Saloon Bar of the Stag and Hind, albeit they drove Rangerovers and owned racehorses. Jason finished his pint and stood up.

"Okay. Give us a ring tonight won't you comrade?" He smiled at Wendy, nodded curtly at Dryden and walked out to his car. There had been something in that smile that Dryden hadn't liked. Was it possible that the bearded leader of Militant Ramblers had other than strictly ideological designs on Wendy?

"We'd better get started, Dryden," Wendy stood up. "There's a lot to do." He glanced wistfully back at the Stag and Hind as they opened the little wicker gate out onto the road. How nice it might have been to while away an hour or two in the beer garden of this idyllic spot, he thought. From here the constant hum of traffic along the M25 was scarcely audible.

"We'll separate at the village green. Here you take half." Wendy handed him a sheaf of crudely printed leaflets. "See you back here in a couple of hours," she called as they parted at the common.

He trudged off glumly along a narrow lane. Presently he arrived at a row of picturesque cottages. In front of the first an elderly gentleman trimmed a rose bush. Dryden profferred a leaflet. The elderly gentleman shook his head and made a rude gesture with his secateurs. Dryden trudged on. Quite, he thought miserably. He saw himself eventually reduced to leafleting squirrels and badgers in the wood, poking pieces of paper into the hollows of trees or holes in the ground. He managed to slip up to the front doors of the last few cottages, however, without being seen and rammed a leaflet hastily into each letter opening. He came to the end of the row and stopped. A wood began. Derrybell Wood, he thought to himself. Maybe there were more houses on the other side of it. He walked on. Though it was a fine day, an icy easterly wind burrowed its way beneath his clothes. He swore silently at the birds twittering in the branches above him. He started in fright as something scuttled away in the undergrowth beside him. For them, he thought sourly, he was doing all this. For all the furry, claw-toed, goggle-eyed, voracious little creatures flapping and crawling about in Derrybell wood. What would Lenin have made of it all, he wondered. Animal Liberation. A while later the wood thinned, came to an end and he found himself walking along beside a high brick wall. Rangerover territory, he thought warily. He looked round nervously. From behind the wall a dog suddenly began barking, a throaty, vicious Hound of the Baskervilles bark. Surely, they didn't expect him to deliver leaflets round here? This was a real bastion of the Bourgeois Establishment. They probably all had private armies patrolling the grounds. He was approaching a gateway. It looked heavily fortified. He stopped and stared at it unhappily. Maybe he'd just get away with poking a leaflet between the bars and then run away.

"Who the hell are you?" The voice startled him. He was about to take to his heels when an elderly gentleman in a tweed cap suddenly appeared on the other side of the gates. In his hand he held the leash of the most vicious looking dog Dryden had ever seen. The dog lunged at the gates.

"Down, Fyodor," the man growled. "Who the hell are you, feller me lad?"

"I . . . er . . . I'm delivering leaflets," Dryden said. The man beckoned him up to the gates. The dog snarled murderously.

"What for?" Dryden passed a leaflet through the bars. The elderly gentleman frowned at it.

"Who the hell are Militant Ramblers?"

"A Marxist–Leninist organisation dedicated to the protection of the countryside," Dryden murmured.

"What rubbish!" the man snapped, then he laughed. "Oh Christ, they've got it all wrong. The path's not being changed. We put a stop to that."

"Really?"

"Weeks ago. The bloody County Council. Bunch of idiots. Path's staying right where it is."

"Are you sure?"

"'Course I'm sure you young fool. Told 'em myself. I own the bloody wood, you see."

Dryden looked at his pile of leaflets. They were out of date. So much for the bearded Jason and his campaign.

"Look, young feller, seems to me you and your organisation are barking up the wrong tree. Why don't you come in for a drink, eh? Look as if you need one."

Dryden stared at the man in astonishment.

"Come along. Fyodor won't hurt you, will you boy?" The man rattled at the gates. They creaked open. Dryden stepped through. The gates clanged shut behind him. He followed the elderly gentleman up a long curving driveway to a large, imposing house.

Kick your boots off and turn left," the elderly gentleman called back to him as they entered the building. "Nice fire in the study. I'll join you in a minute."

Dryden turned left and found himself in a large oak-panelled study. In an ornate fireplace two huge logs crackled and spat.

Presently the elderly gentleman appeared and held out his hand: "Name's Conway."

"Pollock. Dryden Pollock."

"What's your poison, Pollock?" His host swung back a section of the bookcase (which was entirely imitation) to reveal a well-stocked bar. Dryden accepted a large Scotch on the rocks. Conway gestured to an armchair by the fire.

"Only thing in this weather, eh?"

Dryden nodded. Conway frowned at him..

"You don't look like the sort of chap to get mixed up with a crackpot outfit like that, I must say."

"I'm . . . I'm helping out," Dryden reddened. "There's another one of us doing the other side of the village. A woman."

"A woman, eh?" Conway's eyes twinkled mischievously. "There'd have to be a woman mixed up in this somewhere."

Dryden stretched his toes out towards the fire. The dog snarled. Conway kicked it. The dog yelped then meekly lowered his head onto his paws and looked contrite.

"Sex, I suppose?" Conway laughed. "That's the spirit. Do anything for sex. She fancy you?"

Dryden went a deeper shade of red. There was something penetrating in the old man's eyes. Clearly, a man of experience.

"I . . . don't know. Not yet, anyway."

"Working up to it, eh? And she's one of these fanatics? Ah me, same old story. Look, you can throw that stack of rubbish in the fire for a start. It'll take more than that bunch of nincompoops to start the Revolution." The old man contemplated his Scotch. "Damn silly nonsense. Very different in our day, of course. Spain, Nazi Germany, France, Italy, Russia. Things were really jumping then. If we weren't spying for the Russians we were out blowing things up."

"Blowing things up?"

"That's correct." The old man grinned mischievously. "One of the old guard, young feller. I was an Anarchist."

"Really?"

"Oh yes. All the best people were Anarchists and Communists, my friend. We thought the millenium had arrived. I reckon I still could do a bloody good job and get away with it." He kicked the dog gently. "Fyodor here is named after an old comrade of mine. Blew himself up in Italy. One of his own bombs. Fine feller. Russian, of course. Dedicated." He took Dryden's glass and poured out another Scotch. He sat down again. As a matter of fact, I'd give anything for a real revolution, even now!"

"You're kidding?"

"Oh, don't worry about all this," the old man gestured round the room. "I'd blow it all up myself. It's all rubbish anyway. All fake. Like all the rest of it. The sellotape's just more cleverly concealed. Keeps the masses guessing, you see." The old man's eyes glittered malevolently for a second or two then softened. "'Cept I promised Sophie I wouldn't. Ah me, women. What they do to a man. She loved all this you see. Daughter of a sausage king in the Midlands. And I loved her. To distraction. Money came in handy, of course, but I would have had her preserved if I'd had my way. She made me promise not to, of course. Had herself cremated so I wouldn't get any ideas. My God." He shifted on his chair and sighed. "Fifty years ago we met. In Spain. She was driving an ambulance for the Brigade. Seems like last century. Those days intelligent people actually believed in revolution. Communists, Anarchists, Syndicalists, all clever buggers they were. And ruthless. Me too. Now, it's all idiots. We've got screaming Socialists, loony Marxists, all about as effective as the Jehovah's Witnesses and about as intelligent. Ah me, it's all dribbled away into silliness. Or brutality and mayhem. No-one believes in it any more. Just hooliganism. Proletariat's idiotised by television, police are playing blackshirt and the powers that be—well—they're only interested in pearl handled revolvers and money. All dead, believe you me. We're living in a vacuum, everything whirring and churning to no purpose. People just don't know what to do with themselves."

"Maybe there's nothing to do?" Dryden ventured. The old man

directed an intimidating look at him. Dryden thought of Wendy's mother. She had been a Communist. Conway was an Anarchist. Good Lord, if people only knew how many dangerous pensioners there were up and down the country. This old boy had actually blown things up.

"No, maybe not. I dunno. Everything's fallen flat. Disillusionment, cynicism, resignation, that's what people are all about today, young feller. I don't envy them. Masturbation, that's all that's left. Political masturbation. Least that's what I call it. Left, Right, Middle, all masturbating. Ah, give me a real revolution. I'd show 'em. Blow up a few railway stations for a kick off, then move on to the airports and then a few of those god awful banks and multi-national what have you's. What's your young woman's name, by the way?"

"Wendy."

"One of these feeble modern names, eh? Still, I expect she's got what it takes. Mind you—some of the young women of today, they've got guts. Tough, hard, like their mothers and grandmothers—well, some of them. Give them a bomb or a machine-gun and they'd know what to do with it. Another Scotch young feller?"

Dryden nodded.

An hour and a half later he tottered back down the driveway towards the gates.

"Nice chat, young feller." Conway held out his hand. "If you're ever up this way again, drop in won't you? Bring that young woman of yours, too. I'll give her the once over." Dryden heard the gates clang shut behind him. The ground moved up and down beneath his feet. He staggered away down the road towards the village green.

"Hello Dryden." Wendy looked hot and tired but in her eyes there was a gleam of satisfaction.

"Did you manage to get them all distributed, Dryden? Are you all right?"

"Yes." He tried not to slur the word. "Just a bit tired."

"I know. Come on, I think we've done enough for today. Let's get back to the car." She put her arm through his and they set off back towards the Stag and Hind.

"Wendy," he said after they had driven a mile or two. "Those leaflets are useless."

"One or two might read them," she said quietly. "It's a start."

He shook his head wincing at the incipient headache. "No, that's not what I mean. They're useless. They're wrong. The path's staying where it is. I found out."

"What do you mean?"

"I was invited up to this big house. Up past the wood. Conway his name was. An anarchist from way back. Had a dog called Fyodor. He owns Derrybell Wood. Conway I mean. He said the path was staying exactly where it was."

"I don't believe you, Dryden," Wendy said coldly. "And don't think I didn't realise you'd been drinking. I smelt it a mile off."

"Wendy, I love you," Dryden negotiated a sharp bend with some difficulty.

"Watch the road, for God's sake. You're probably way over the limit."

Dryden hiccoughed. "'Scuse me."

"You're drunk, aren't you? Look, are you sure you can get us home all right?"

"Love, love, love," Dryden sang. Wendy was silent. He glanced at her. She turned her head away and stared out of the window. Dammit, he suddenly thought violently. He'd had enough. He jammed his foot on the brake and the car lurched to a halt.

CHAPTER NINETEEN

His cassock stretched taut over his protruding stomach, the vicar strode in through the school gates. He was in the habit of arriving early on days when interviews were to take place in order to avail himself of the Headmaster's sherry. Rosie Kennedy had had her hair permed and wore her beige twin-set. She, too, disappeared into Basil's study for the sherry party. Arnold Scoresby, the outgoing deputy head, had either declined his invitation to a preliminary discussion of the various candidates' form or had not been asked. Last to arrive was the County Adviser, a dessicated individual in a funereal suit. He looked decidedly ill at ease on the premises. County Advisers preferred the safety of their featureless offices at County Hall to the rough and tumble of a school.

Half an hour later the candidates appeared, each in his best black or grey suit, two of them looking very suntanned. They were the candidates from Africa, Dryden supposed. Next to these robust individuals Maurice Talbot looked ill. He sat ramrod stiff in his new grey three-piece suit, his ashen face with its confident smile resembling the death mask of a consumptive who had just had a glimpse of the pearly gates of Paradise. Nathan Goldway was resplendent in a lightweight brown suit, which as he had confided to Dryden, offset his sallow Semitic complexion. These days Jews were perfectly welcome in all walks of life but it didn't do to look too Talmudic, did it? Hither and thither dashed Arnold Scoresby bringing everyone cups of tea, muddling everyone with everyone else and doing his best to create an atmosphere of embarrassment and confusion.

"Don't much like the look of that lot," Rosie was overheard confiding to Nerys Hughes, the power-crazed Head of Things Domestic. "Ph.D's or no Ph.D's."

"That one," Nerys nodded in the direction of one of the suntanned gentlemen, "for a start hasn't had a decent shave."

"I know," Rosie frowned. "He'll be out, of course. The Head hates stubbley chins."

"Maurice looks nice, doesn't he?"

"Yes," murmured Rosie. "Doesn't look well though, does he? Dicky heart, I reckon. Mind you, the Head's got a dicky heart and he's still going strong."

"Did he pass his driving test, by the way?"

Rosie shook her head. "No, poor dear, that's the fourth time now. He was bitterly disappointed. He wants that more than anything else in the world. He hates having to get his wife to drive him everywhere."

As the first bell of the morning rang, the interviews began. Hours would pass before the interviewing panel reached anything like a decision. The vicar would have dozed off at regular intervals. Rosie would have examined every detail of each candidate's appearance in order to pass on a full report to her cronies on the staff, the County Adviser would have hummed and hahed a dozen times while Basil would have fought endless skirmishes with the English language in his unceasing struggle to be understood.

Dryden climbed the stairs to his form room. Five Grigorescu were mostly prostrate, there having been an all night party somewhere or so he gathered. On his desk he found an official looking document from the Head of Fifth Year, informing him of Michael Kelly's imminent departure. He glanced towards the back of the room. Kelly, resplendent in leather, badges and chains, grinned at him and raised his eyebrows. Registration ended and Five Grigorescu stumbled out of the room. The majority of them seemed to be suffering from a severe hangover.

"It's official, Sir." Kelly stood on the other side of the table grinning delightedly.

"What am I supposed to do with this, Michael?"

"Sign it, Sir."

Dryden scribbled his signature at the bottom of the page and handed the document to the youth.

"I had no idea you were going. Where to by the way?"

"Kent. Boarding School. To sort me out."

"Will it—sort you out?"

"No, Sir."

"Whose idea was it?"

"My Dad's. He's a Law and Order merchant. Don't worry, I understand him completely. Mum, too. They're an open book."

"I see. And what about the business over the letter?"

"They thought it was best if I left. For Hepworth's sake. He's not a well man." The youth grinned. "But there'll be others at the new place. Fact, I bet it's swarming with them."

"That should keep you busy."

"It will. Well, cheerio, Sir."

"The best of luck, Michael. To the staff at your new school I mean," Dryden grinned.

"Thanks, Sir. I'd just like to say here and now that you're the worst form tutor I've ever come across. But—don't try to change, will you?"

"I'll try not to."

The youth raised his hand in salute and strolled out of the room. Dryden sighed, picked up his register and ambled out after him.

* * * * *

Throughout the corridors of Great Battley internationalism was on the march. The Motts were in full cry, storming about with large sheets of sugar paper, sellotape, glue and scissors. The Resources Room was cluttered with maps and posters. Some foreign embassies, however, in the mistaken belief that Great Battley was some strange new outlet for revolutionary ideas, had despatched packages of rather violent propaganda, such as posters displaying clenched fists beneath the words 'Liberation' or 'Freedom' in a dozen different languages. Though these would eventually find their way into Great Battley's litter bins, they lay round the floor of the Resources Room now, getting in everyone's way or occasionally on a sudden draught, drifting out into the corridor whence they were hastily retrieved and stuffed firmly back into dark corners.

Coming out of the Resources Room Dryden caught a glimpse of Wendy at the other end of the corridor. The memory of Saturday afternoon temporarily immobilised him. How ludicrously he had behaved, his judgment completely warped by the Anarchist's whisky. When he had jammed his foot so violently on the brake, the Viva had skidded into a bank at the side of the road.

"I love you Wendy," he had shouted. "I want to know if you love me."

"Dryden, I don't think you ought to be driving in that state. You know the law."

"Fuck the law!" he had bellowed. "Do you love me?"

Wendy had turned away to contemplate the mass of bruised foliage squashed against the window.

"I like you, I suppose," she had murmured.

"You like me." He had clung to the word. Didn't it also have four letters and begin with the letter 'l'?

"Love is a very over-used word," she had added, sphinx-like.

"Wendy, I want to go to bed with you." He had a brief sensation of horror at this utterance but he was desperate now and, therefore, entirely out of control.

"Isn't that just lust?" Wendy had giggled nervously. "Didn't they teach you the difference at Sunday school?"

"I didn't go to Sunday school," he had muttered angrily. "I had a paper round."

"I didn't either, to tell the truth. Mummy was still a Marxist then. A few years later and she couldn't have cared less. Look—Dryden—

141

things are getting a bit out of hand, don't you think? I thought you were a bit peculiar the other day, as a matter of fact."

"How perceptive of you." He had slumped over the wheel. He had had enough. The whole thing had degenerated into an emotional shambles, his emotional shambles, not Wendy's apparently. This time he had pursued a woman to the very limits of his pride. He had driven all the way down to Cornwall, just about got himself shot by the Army, spent a miserable evening at a meeting of Leftist lunatics and had now driven the Viva into a bank in the middle of the countryside after getting drunk delivering leaflets to a former Anarchist. And through all of it, every insane minute of this fruitless quest, he had been spurred on by the hope that day by day Wendy was growing fonder of him. He had finally started the car, thrown it angrily into reverse and pulled out from the bank in a series of violent jerks.

"I don't think we ought to tell Jason that the path's not being diverted," Wendy had said as they had driven up the slip road onto the motorway. "He wouldn't believe us."

"Wendy," he had said through clenched teeth, "Jason and his comrades will never be more than a bunch of loonies. I only went along to that meeting because of you. I only came along today to dish out those ridiculous leaflets because of you. I got it all wrong, I suppose, but I can't change the fact that I love you."

A long silence had ensued. Wendy had sat primly, with her hands folded on her lap, staring out at the grey chaos of houses, factories, electricity pylons, road junctions and denuded woods that passed for countryside in those parts.

"You'd better drop me at headquarters," she had said stiffly, breaking the silence. "I'll give Jason my report now, I think." A pleasure, Dryden had reflected bitterly. And so, he had driven home to Winkworth, smarting with the pain of her indifference and raging at his own helpless stupidity at having got himself emotionally involved with a fanatical 'ice-maiden.'

* * * * *

"You look terrible," Goldway confronted him at the bottom of the stairs.

"Go to hell," Dryden muttered. "Have they interviewed you yet?"

"Uh huh," Goldway laughed. "I was charm itself. The vicar only nodded off once."

"And? What are your chances?"

"Absolutely nil, old man. There's no doubt they're giving it to Talbot. I thought everyone knew that."

"Has anyone bothered to tell the two Africans?"

"Good God no," Goldway stared at him in alarm. "They'd be furious."

"It's monstrous," Dryden sighed. "Maybe I'll tell 'em."

"You won't mate. It's more than your job's worth. They'll break the place up."

"Your cynicism is measureless, Goldway."

"They've got to take their chances like everyone else, mate. They're grown men."

"But they think they're in with a chance. They've been deceived. Deliberately deceived."

"They're being interviewed. Fairly and courteously. Now run along and stop behaving as if the world was fair. Your attachment to that outmoded idea is unhealthy, old friend. Decidedly unhealthy."

* * * * *

By midday the two candidates from Africa were still sitting in the staff common room awaiting interview. They looked exhausted. Accustomed as they were to the dust, heat and flies of the African continent, they were ill prepared for the rigours of Great Battley. They had the look of men who had been lost in the Sahara for months on end. They had endured hours of monotony, high-mindedness and hypocrisy. Dryden fancied them contemplating the paradise they had so foolishly abandoned: cool beers on shady verandahs, half naked black children, colourful shanty towns. Now they found themselves in hostile alien territory, surrounded by the tribesmen of Great Battley, staring at them malevolently as they gathered for the lunchtime ritual of sandwich eating, yoghourt slurping and tea drinking.

"Whereabouts were you in Africa?" Nerys Hughes smiled at the nearest African genlteman and displayed a set of sharply pointed teeth. The man, slumped in an armchair, roused himself from his torpor."

"I . . . uh . . . a place called Wongalongo. In Nigeria."

"How fascinating," Nerys nodded appreciatively, her large earrings rattling ominously. "And what were you doing there?" Her eyes seemed to be sizing the poor man up for a post as human trophy in the Domestic Science longhouse. Her teaspoon clicked a dread rhythm against the sides of a small carton of strawberry yoghourt.

"Teaching," the man replied warily.

"Oh?" Nerys looked doubtful. "Africans?"

"Yes, all Africans."

"That must have been interesting. What did you teach them?"

"Sociology."

Nerys' spoon stopped. She stared at him. Sociology? To Africans? Beneath their brightly painted lids her eyes flickered menacingly. Sociology was dangerous. Worse than gun-running.

"What were you doing teaching them Sociology?"

The man smiled and shrugged. "They wanted to learn. In fact they were frantic to learn. Marx, Paolo Ferreire, Max Weber, Becker, Cicourel, the lot. We had trouble getting enough books."

Nerys frowned. who were these people? The names for a start sounded extremely dangerous. Dangerous foreign names.

"Marx?"

"Yes. Most of them were Marxists, I suppose, one way or another," the man went on breezily. He seemed suddenly to have relaxed, as if he believed the Cannibal Queen's interest in all this was a sudden breakthrough in communication.

"Marxists?" Bernard McGraw's mouth remained open, his chutney sandwich poised midway between his face and his lunchbox. "You mean they were Communists?"

"Oh—well—not exactly—" the African gentleman, suddenly realising his mistake, reddened slightly. "They were—uh—Christians—that is, in a manner of speaking—but Marxists in their political inspiration. Marx is very big in Africa, you know." He stared round as if looking for possible escape routes. At that moment Rosie entered the staff common room.

"Did I hear someone mention Marx?" She clumped across to an armchair next to the Cannibal Queen.

"Yes," Nerys said. A malicious smile appeared on her face. "The gentleman there was saying how he was teaching Marxism to Africans. Marx is very big in Africa apparently."

"Are you serious?" Rosie turned to the African gentleman who now seemed to be pretending he was just a part of the common room furniture. His face had turned quite red.

"I was teaching Sociology," he stammered, "not quite Marxism."

"Sociology?" Rosie looked incredulous. "But they can't even read or write can they? I mean, you were out in the bush weren't you?"

"Well—not exactly—you see—it was a college of Further Education. They were highly literate in three languages, sometimes four. English, French, Bungadungu—that was their tribal language."

"Sociology, eh?" Rosie studied him out of baleful eyes. "But you're not a sociologist, are you?"

"No, no, of course not," the man said hastily. Memories of the Old Country were crowding back into his mind. Of course, how could he have been so stupid, he was thinking. It was all very well discussing Marxism with a bunch of eager-eyed Africans out in the bush but here in Great Battley it was the worst possible breach of etiquette.

"No—I'm a History teacher actually." he said frantically. "My main subject is British History."

"I thought so," Rosie nodded triumphantly. "At least, that's what you told us in your letter of application."

"So they learn British history, too?" Bernard McGraw's chutney

144

sandwich continued its rudely interrupted journey towards his mouth. He was now greedily contemplating the apple in his lunchbox.

"Oh yes," the man smiled. Mentally, he was no doubt wiping the sweat from his brow. "It's very important out there. They love it. All the kings and queens. And the colonial period, of course. That's very important."

"Glad to hear it," Bernard McGraw said. "It's a marvellous heritage for them. Mmmm . . . this chutney's delicious. Are they—independent out there then?"

The African candidate nodded. He was visibly relieved at having successfully found the right groove.

"I bet it's a blimmin' shambles though," Rosie yawned and stretched. "I bet they wish they weren't."

"Oh, they do," the man gushed. He was warming to it all now. "They're very keen on the Royal Family, Charles and Diana. In all the newspapers."

Suddenly from outside came the sound of a wildly revving motor. People leapt to their feet in alarm.

"Don't go to the windows," Rosie bellowed. "It's the Head. He gets embarrassed."

Dryden, who all this time had been skulking morosely at the other end of the staff common room, watched the Ford Escort with its large BSM sign on the roof lurching out of the school driveway. Children scattered at its approach. If there was one thing that struck mortal fear into the hearts of all the layabout, obstreperous teenage population of Great Battley it was the sight of the Headmaster crouched behind the steering wheel of a car.

"I thought he was having lunch with the vicar?" Bernard McGraw said.

"Oh, he was," Rosie replied. "But Wednesday's his driving lesson. Interviews or no interviews."

"Do you think he'll get his licence this time round?" Nerys Hughes turned to Rosie. The African gentleman slumped back down in his armchair, relieved, no doubt, at this timely conclusion to his interrogation.

"No," Rosie shook her head. "I think he's probably past it. Last time he drove up onto the pavement so I heard," she giggled. "Poor man. He's so nervous. Oh, it's awful."

"It took me two goes to get mine," Nerys observed staring at the African gentleman as if he was now no more than part of the common room furniture. This provoked a long discussion among those around her on the intricacies of the driving test and the comparative merits of this or that driving school. The two African gentlemen quietly dozed off, reflecting, perhaps on the wisdom of a decision that had brought them thousands of miles across two continents to submit themselves to the scrutiny of a man who had failed his test four times, who had been denied his dream of a lifetime, the award of a driving licence.

CHAPTER TWENTY

In the night a strange, alarming event had taken place. A person or persons unknown had forced entry to school premises and methodically, even ruthlessly, emptied all the rubbish tins and waste-paper bins around the corridors. There was litter everywhere. To the door of the Headmaster's study a note had been pinned: 'Down with litter campaigns. Up with litter.' it read.

There was consternation. Who could have committed such an outrage? The police were summoned. They prowled about for some time, examining receptacles, peering into corners and questioning people in low, menacing tones. Bill, the caretaker, was distraught. For an hour or so he was closeted with the Headmaster in the latter's study, no doubt going over every detail of his caretakerly routine the previous evening. Some of the staff were, of course, exultant at Bill's distress. He was rude and arrogant towards his betters and, it was rumoured, charged exorbitant rates for every minute of what he was pleased to call his 'overtime'. 'Overtime' was anything Bill consented to do beyond four o'clock in the afternoon, when he usually retired to the caretaker's office to listen to the radio and play cards with the groundsmen. Now he had been caught sleeping on the job. He hadn't heard or seen a thing. He was also panic-stricken lest the finger of suspicion point at him. It was well known that Basil's fanatical campaign against litter had come to be bitterly resented by the caretaking staff who day after day had seen mountains of bulging plastic bags rising up round the school waiting for the refuse collectors who, as it happened, were into the fifth week of a prolonged and acrimonious dispute over pay. Hadn't Bill even been heard to suggest that if the bloody Headmaster was so bloody worried about bloody litter he should get the bloody staff to take the bloody rubbish home with them in the boots of their bloody cars? Rumour had it that Bill had put forward this idea to the Headmaster himself, who, always open to suggestion, even from the lower orders, had given the proposal serious consideration. But, of course, that would have caused a furore. Unions, always on the lookout for a juicy dispute to get involved in, would have stepped very smartly into that and with their extraordinary talent for escalating even the most minor disagreement, would have thrown up the barricades and painted Basil as the blackest enemy of the people since Tsar Nicholas the Second.

The finger of suspicion itself was working overtime. Rosie was heard to hint darkly at a possible conspiracy among the Sixth Form, initiated by a member of staff, as a last ditch challenge to the Headmaster's authority. This comment misfired badly. Rosie had gone too far. A staff deputation protested loudly at this insidious slander of a colleague. Rosie was ticked off. Bloxham, delighted, felt free to go around saying that the litter campaign itself had brought about the vandalism. According to him, it was a spontaneous act of sabotage by the oppressed masses, i.e. the pupils.

Indeed, children were the most likely suspects. A witch-hunt began. David Hepworth, the Head of Religious Studies, wanted to believe the evil Michael Kelly was behind it all. Saner voices tried to point out that vandalism in schools was commonplace and that Great Battley should consider itself lucky it had not been burnt down. But, as Rosie pointed out, these were no ordinary vandals who simply smashed windows and set fire to buildings. This had been a carefully planned operation, a political act in defiance of the Headmaster's campaign. Wrecking public property or burning it down was simply an expression of mindless anarchy but scattering litter that had been carefully collected and monitored over a period of weeks was the work of a cunning and calculating mind. It struck at the very heart of the most cherished notions of social responsibility.

Poor Arnold Scoresby dashed about doing his best to look as if he was tackling the affair with professional thoroughness. Secretly, perhaps, he was hoping he wouldn't actually have to do anything effective before the end of term arrived and he stepped down. Talbot, the deputy head designate, now wore a constant frown of concern. He was drawn into the high level consultations with the Head and Rosie over the litter outrage and he, too, dashed about interrogating pupils on his own criminal investigation.

With what crestfallen looks the other candidates had departed when the interviewing panel had reached its decision. Goldway, of course, had never believed that anyone other than Talbot would be appointed.

"I made an impression, mate," he said to Dryden the morning after. "That's the main thing. Basil's head over heels in love with me."

Dryden wanted to believe that the two candidates from Africa were now safely back in the sun, having sensibly decided there was no longer a place for them in the Mother Country. In fact, he was seriously considering a move to Africa himself. Naturally, his qualifications were worse than useless to Africans but he was now working on a picture of himself sitting on a shady verandah drinking gin and tonic, setting in time to the huge, orange sun behind the dusty horizon. Were the days of the English exiles, boozing themselves into oblivion, gone for ever, he wondered? Africa sounded the ideal place in which to drown his sorrows. Wendy had rejected him. Another fruitless quest for love had come to a painful and humiliating end. How could life be so cruel to one person, he brooded. That very morning he had received from her a memo in his pigeon-hole. 'Re International Day' it had begun. 'MFT saw me re Norway. Suggest I liaise DKP and SYM. WKB.' He had folded the little note up and slipped it into his breast pocket. This time it was all ending with a memo, he thought grimly. Somehow that was far worse than the cheery wave and the smile with which women usually stepped out of his life for ever. Now the memory of every moment of his hopeful pursuit of Wendy Bashford was a source of pain. He felt like Saint Sebastian hanging there as the arrows flew into him one by one. Only Saint Sebastian at least had had the comfort of a wonderful reception in Heaven when it was all over. For Dryden Pollock, however, there was only the bleak prospect of an unending loneliness, punctuated by fits of overwhelming lust.

As he made his way out of the staff common room and loped off up towards his form room, he had a vision of himself lying in a coffin, supporting on his chest a tiny, second-hand funeral wreath from Harry and Sue.

"Dryden?" He swung round. It was Wendy hurrying to catch him up. "Did you get my memo?" She was smiling, he saw, a smile of pity. He nodded wearily. Did she realise it had been an arrow straight to his heart? No, for she was frowning at him now. Suddenly he was aware of an aura of terrible cruelty around her face. He shrank from it.

"What's the matter?" She cocked her head on one side and gave him a quizzical look.

"Nothing. Nothing at all, Wendy. Yes, I did get your memo."

"And? Stephen Mott wants to know what's happening, Dryden. It's only ten days till International Day. We've still got so much to do."

"Yes, Wendy. You must be very busy at the moment," he said sarcastically. After all, it was so much better to be busy, wasn't it Wendy. It stopped one thinking about broken hearts and shattered illusions, didn't it?

"Yes. I am as a matter of fact." She had blushed at the tone of his voice. He gloated at this. Aha, she was getting the message.

"How's Militant Ramblers coming along? Have they burnt down the Houses of Parliament yet? I must say I haven't seen anything in the newspapers."

She glanced at him uneasily. "I don't know. I've dropped out." It was then he suddenly noticed that the badge had gone from the lapel of her jacket. He raised his eyebrows in surprise.

"Why's that?"

"That day we distributed the leaflets, you remember, I made you drop me off at headquarters and I . . ." she took a deep breath, ". . . I went inside to tell Jason what we'd done and . . . oh it was horrible, Dryden."

"What was horrible?"

She coloured a deep red, took another deep breath. "They were having . . . an orgy."

"What?"

"An orgy. Three of them naked on the floor. They wanted me to join in. It was awful. Jason was blind drunk. Empty bottles of Sainsbury's Spanish Red everywhere. That awful woman, Sandra, was high on something or other . . . I . . . couldn't believe it."

"Good God."

"I ran out of the house. You'd gone. Don't think I didn't know why. I had to wait hours for a bus. The number thirty one's never on time . . . It was dark by the time I got home. I rang Mummy straight away. She was in, thank God, they'd cancelled the Booklovers' Circle that evening. I cried on the phone. Cried and cried. I told Mummy everything, including what you'd said to me in the car when you were drunk . . ."

"I wasn't completely drunk, Wendy . . ." he protested, flushing.

"Everyone was drunk, Dryden. The whole world was drunk. All day. I even thought Mummy was drunk on the phone . . . I couldn't believe it . . ." He stared at her in astonishment. There were tears in her eyes. His bitterness evaporated. She was just a little girl, he thought, a poor sexy little ingénue who had suddenly discovered the world was drunk most of the time.

"What about Bodmin? What about the people in prison? Were they drunk: Were they having orgies?"

"I don't know," Wendy sighed. "But I couldn't go back to Jason and his crowd. You can't believe in an organisation that wants to defend the countryside when you see the people in it doing that sort of thing, can you? I can't. Mummy always said I was a Puritan. She used to say I'd missed the boat. I think she meant the Mayflower."

"So you're not going to Cornwall in February?" She shook her head.

"How would you like to go to Africa instead?"

"What do you mean?"

"Sit on a verandah and get drunk. With me?"

"Is that where you're going?"

He grinned. "I might. Nice climate."

She pondered this for a few seconds then shook her head. 'I don't think it would really suit me, Dryden. I'm too English. I love the countryside here."

"They're all Marxists out in Africa, so I'm told."

"Dryden, I'm not really sure I'm a Marxist, to be honest. Sometimes I think I'm really an Anglican."

"High or low?" His grin widened.

"Somewhere in between. Daddy's high. He's thinking of turning to Rome, you know. He's very keen on Malcolm Muggeridge. Dryden, I . . ." She hesitated and looked away. "I'm sorry—you know, for that business in the car. I think I was just so taken aback. It hadn't occurred to me that well—that you might feel that way. I'm very fond of you, of course, you're such a funny person in so many ways . . ." The grin vanished from Dryden's face. "Oh, Dryden, I don't mean that, I mean—oh, I mean you make everything so complicated somehow." He grinned at this. "I would never have thought you were my type at all, you see, in that way." His grin faded again. "But—well—Mummy says I'm thick about that sort of thing. She said she could see it a mile off. That day we went to Tintagel. She thought you were as moony as a calf." Dryden coloured. He'd deal with Mrs. Bashford later, he decided. Wendy smiled at him. "So I thought about it all very carefully from a number of different angles and—well—I guessed what you must have been feeling."

"Oh? And what's that?"

"That I've rejected you."

"Oh no, Wendy. Not at all. I'll admit I was contemplating suicide for a while there but then I changed my mind in favour of a slow death in Africa."

"I'm sorry, Dryden. Can we be friends again?"

"Friends?"

"Friends and we'll see what happens."

"I love you Wendy."

She put her finger to her lips and looked round furtively.

"Ssssh," she whispered. "This isn't the place. People might hear you." At that moment the bell rang and within seconds they were engulfed in a vast, jostling herd of children. "Got to go," she mouthed at him and was promptly carried away in the tide of bodies. He stayed where he was, flattened against the wall, unable to believe it wasn't all a dream, a new and ever more refined sort of nightmare.

* * * * *

For the remainder of that day nothing, but nothing could bring him down from the ethereal plane on which he was now floating. A new life was beginning, he told himself. He saw the two of them dining by candlelight, saw them browsing through brochures as they planned an exotic honeymoon. He even saw them choosing a set of tasteful shelf units at Winkworth's newly opened Habitat. It would be a soft, fuzzy, eternal dawn of a relationship, he decided, all pink sheets and delicately flowered Dollyprint wallpaper, the early morning sun illuminating their naked bodies after a night's uninterrupted sex. With the final bell of the day, he collected up his books and floated out into the corridor. Maurice Talbot was waiting for him.

"A word, Dryden." Talbot closed the door of the Resources Room discreetly behind them. The Motts were elsewhere. Dryden sat down clutching his briefcase as if it were the only thing that stopped him floating off up to the ceiling.

"International Day, Dryden." Talbot rested his elbows on the desk and placed the tips of his fingers together. "The Head's very worried about it. Frankly, some of the work he has seen so far has—well—filled him with horror. Tacky bits of cardboard and pictures cut out of old Sunday Telegraph weekend magazines. It's not quite what he had in mind." Dryden nodded dreamily. Talbot cleared his throat. "The Head has—broached the subject of promotion within this faculty, Dryden, as it happens. With the appointment of myself as the new deputy head, points for promotion will now be available, you understand. Quite what the Head has in mind, I can't say, but he is interested in promoting those members of the team who have demonstrated an outstanding commitment to the school and its ideals over the past few years. In fact, he led me to understand he would consider a promotion in the vital area of European Studies in a very favourable light. Am I making myself clear?"

"Perfectly, Maurice." Dryden nodded placidly. Basil was putting the screws on.

"This means, of course, that he will be particularly keen to see signs of commitment and dedication in that particular area."

"Of course," Talbot's voice floated across to him through a strange haze.

"Need I say more, Dryden?" Talbot smiled.

"You need not," Dryden murmured loftily. He rose and went to the door. Through the narrow strip of a window in it he suddenly caught sight of a figure ducking away into the corridor. It was Stephen Mott. As Dryden emerged, Mott was already pretending to come out of a classroom nearby. Dryden smiled at him. Mott eyed him with undisguised hatred.

"Oh there you are," Wendy called to him as he walked into the staff common room. "Someone told me you'd gone home."

He smiled at her lovingly. There and then he wanted to take her in his arms and make love to her among the armchairs.

"I was just about to go myself actually," Wendy said. "But I wanted a word about International Day." Dryden wobbled a bit on his ethereal orbit at this remark. Did she have to?

"Norway," Wendy said in a very businesslike tone.

Gravity exerted its full force on him. He sat down heavily.

"They did send me some posters," Wendy continued. "But they're not enough." She gave him an accusing look. His heart sank.

"I don't know about Norway, Wendy," he murmured absently. "What's more, I don't think I care just at the moment."

"Aren't you supposed to be responsible for the European Studies display? Wendy was looking at him as if he had just confessed to a particularly nasty murder.

"How about dinner tonight?" He stared back at her, hypnotically, concentrating his mental energy on burning a hole into the innermost recesses of Wendy's brain. But Wendy's brain was entirely preoccupied with Norway. His mental rays glanced uselessly off granite mountain blocks.

"I can't, Dryden," she said sternly. "There's too much to do."

"Then how about staying with me tonight?"

"For sex?"

"My," he grinned, "for a Puritan you don't beat around the bush do you?"

"I didn't think you were asking me to darn your socks, Dryden." She permitted herself a wan smile. "But not tonight."

"When?"

"Friday?"

Two days away. Good God!

"Friday."

"You don't smoke in bed, do you?"

"No."

"And Norway?"

"We'll discuss it over dinner. At my place."

"Promise?"

"Promise."

CHAPTER TWENTY-ONE

Humming to himself, Dryden lit the candles on the table and switched off the lights. The candles guttered fitfully in a draught and went out. There was a gale blowing outside. He checked all the windows. Where in hell was the draught coming from? He opened a door. A gust of air swept through the dining-room, lifting a pile of unpaid bills and dumping them on the table. He gathered them up hastily and stuffed them in a drawer. Maybe the wind would die down later. The dinner was warming up nicely in the oven—the wine was open—an outrageously expensive red imported—he hoped in its bottle—from France. He checked the label. No, it had not been bottled in Swindon. He glanced at his watch. In ten minutes she would be there, gracing his little terraced house with her presence. He had been careful not to dwell on what they might do as the evening wore on. With Puritans one had to be extremely careful. A fickle, moody breed, he reflected. Only a few days after her break with Militant Ramblers, Wendy had discovered a new organisation to give vent to her missionary zeal. The Friends of South America. They held meetings in the upper room of Bennington Y.M.C.A. in order to condemn a wide range of nefarious organisations and send money to guerillas fighting in the jungle.

He ran upstairs and examined himself in his wardrobe mirror. Not bad, he thought, or rather not too bad. He peered at a pimple that was developing beneath his nose. For years he had never had a pimple. Now just at this vital turning point in his life, a large one had appeared and seemed to be growing at a fantastic speed. There was always something going wrong. Washing his hair in a new type of shampoo he had been mortified to see large clumps of hair floating in the bath water. For a moment he had refused to believe it was his. He was falling to bits, he thought miserably. After a lonely youth during which he had remained physically more or less intact, his body was going to do the dirty on him just as he stood on the threshold of bliss. At this rate he would be bald in six months. Now in front of the mirror he pulled in his stomach, having overlooked that in the minutes he had been pre-occupied with his pimple and his thinning hair. The human body was a nightmare. One barely got one bit of it in line with the TV adverts before one suddenly discovered a hitherto unnoticed but monstrously disfiguring blemish elsewhere. Small wonder that folk all over the Western World spent half their lifetimes dieting, jogging, giving up this or that, devouring vast quantities of health food or playing squash until they dropped dead of exhaustion. Human beings were such imperfect creatures.

The front door bell buzzed. He glanced round the bedroom checking the vase of flowers on the dressing table, making sure all the dirty underwear and socks had been safely stowed away, and dashed downstairs to the door.

"Hullo." Wendy stepped in smartly. "Awful wind," she grimaced. She had done herself up very nicely. "Brrr, it's cold in here Dryden. If you don't mind, I think I'll keep my coat on." Damn the Gas Board, he raged. Ten days had elapsed since he had rung them about his boiler.

"Come through to the dining-room," he smiled. "The fire's on in there."

"Sherry?" He was trying to conceal his excitement. He was terribly afraid he was about to start jabbering incomprehensibly.

"Just a little one, Dryden. Don't forget I'm driving."

"How is the new car?"

"Oh, it's not new. Mummy thrashed the living daylights out of it. She really is a menace to modern technology. Still, it grinds along. Can't do anything about the black smoke though."

"I thought that was part of it. Mine's always smoking."

He sat down and tried not to stare at her body. It was the height of bad manners, he knew, to stare at people's breasts or legs or his favourite bit, their throats. Throats fascinated him. A nice throat was as much a gift as nice legs or arms or breasts. It was still a very under-rated part of the human anatomy except by certain people, of course, who usually ended up behind bars. Wendy was looking round the room.

"It's quite nice, isn't it?" she said. "Not at all scruffy."

He had slaved for an hour and a half to clean it. Had he had the money he would have had it re-decorated for the occasion.

"Do you mind if I smoke?" he said, watching the way Wendy's lips moved as she savoured the sherry. (Bristol Cream, four pounds eighty-nine.)

"It's your house, Dryden," she laughed. "You can do what you like."

His confidence was gurgling swiftly away down the plughole. What a ninny! Of course, it was his house! He lit a cigarette. Oh why, oh why did he always make such a fool of himself?

"Would you like some peanuts?" he ventured. Oh God! What a stupid thing to ask!

"No thanks," Wendy said firmly. "I don't like them. He glanced ruefully at the cupboard wherein lay a gigantic bag of peanuts (two pounds twenty-one pence). He should have bought crisps.

He smiled at the window. "It's very windy, isn't it?"

"Force nine apparently," Wendy said. "Increasing to Force Ten by midnight. I hope Mummy and Daddy's tree doesn't fall down."

"Oh, they've got a tree, have they?"

"Yes, it's very old. The neighbour's tree fell down last year. They lost everything, poor souls. They weren't insured against trees either. The insurance company wouldn't accept it as an Act of God. They said they no longer considered trees falling down under that sub-heading. Only lightning. If the tree had been struck by lightning and then fallen down that would have been an Act of God but there wasn't any lightning, you see. The tree just fell down for no particular reason. It wasn't even as windy as this. They got nothing."

"Another sherry?" Wendy shook her head.

"Shall we eat?" He leapt up suddenly and wrenched open the kitchen door. He opened the oven and took out the meal.

"Mmmm. This is excellent," Wendy said a while later. "You're a good cook, aren't you?" He smiled with pride. After his initial foolishness his confidence was slowly returning. Already he had drunk rather a lot. He ought to take it easy, he thought. There was a dangerous level of intoxication he reached when he was suddenly transformed into a loud-mouthed, vulgar and domineering lout. Over the years he had become convinced he was growing more schizophrenic.

The wind had increased in strength. The candles had blown out three times already. He had given up on them. Now the electric light flickered ominously. He saw Wendy casting anxious glances at the window.

"You're not thinking of going yet, are you?"

"No," she said quickly. "Of course not." She had been, he thought. People like Wendy had to be watched every step of the way. He poured out more wine.

"You could stay the night if you liked. There's plenty of room."

"We'll see," Wendy smiled. "I've got to get up early."

"So have I," he said quickly. "Saturdays are always busy, aren't they?"

"I've promised to do some collecting for Nicaragua." Damn the world, he thought. There seemed to be a vast conspiracy at work against him. Now it was Nicaragua. How many desirable women would be out bustling up and down the streets of England with collecting boxes for Nicaragua on the morrow? Probably thousands.

"Shall I put on some music?" he suggested hopefully. He had rushed out and bought an L.P. advertised on television. Music for making love to.

"All right."

"He got up and pretended to fish through a large record collection. "This one?" he flashed the cover at her. She shrugged and nodded. He put it on. A syrupy voice murmured something in French from the speakers. A vast orchestra that seemed to consist entirely of violins

156

began playing. Wendy yawned and looked at her watch. Grimly, he hunched over his wine. He couldn't imagine why people associated violins with love-making. There was nothing more enervating than a vast horde of violins sawing way in the background. He got up and switched off the record player.

"You haven't got any N'Djamina records, have you?" Wendy yawned. He shook his head. "African dance music. I saw them last year. They were marvellous."

"Wendy," he said helplessly. "It must have occurred to you that I'm hoping you'll stay the night."

"Yes, Dryden. I realised that."

"I love you, Wendy. I want to go to bed with you."

"I know Dryden. You keep on about it as if it were the most important thing in the world."

"It is to me."

"It' not the most important thing you know. There are things which are just as important. You're hopelessly romantic."

A violent gust of wind rattled the window panes. Somewhere outside a cat miaowed piteously. Wendy stood up. He watched her miserably. She was going. All his dreams were blowing away in the gale. His visions of a relationship, a soft, fuzzy eternal dawn of a relationship were bowling off down the street along with the dead leaves and the sheets of newspaper. He touched his pimple. It was huge. Wendy was taking off her coat. How strange, he thought. She was going home coatless. His eyes roved despairingly over her body. Against his will he began to get an erection. No matter how hopeless the prospects, that never seemed to give up. Human beings had never got used to the fact that their genitalia lived quite independent lives, waking up and stretching when everything else was settling down for the night. Wendy came round the table, her arms outstretched. He stood up, baffled.

"You've got a pimple," she said.

"I know. My hair's falling out, too."

"That music was awful," she suddenly giggled. "But the meal was nice."

"Why am I in love with a Puritan, do you think?"

"It's like Mummy says," Wendy sighed. "Opposite poles. She married a Fascist when she was at her most revolutionary. Now, Dryden, let's do this properly." She kissed him. In a daze he followed her to the door.

"On second thoughts I think I'll take my coat," she said.

"You're not wearing that in bed, are you?"

"I get cold easily."

"There is an electric blanket. Only I didn't think to put it on."

"You weren't sure I was going to stay. That's promising. Why waste electricity?"

"I sometimes wear a jumper in bed," he said as they reached the top of the stairs. He pulled back the covers.

"You haven't got an extra pillow, have you?"

"Take both of them."

"What are you going to sleep on then?"

"I don't mind."

"Where shall I put my clothes?"

"On the chair over there."

"I'll put my coat at the foot of the bed, if you don't mind."

"Okay."

"The wine was nice. Which side do you sleep on?"

"I sleep in the middle. Except when I've got company, which isn't often."

"You don't snore, do you?"

"I probably do. Do you?"

"Yes," she blushed slightly. "Just push me on my side if I start."

"I love you Wendy."

"Look at that spare tyre. You should do more exercise, you know. You're pretty unhealthy."

"I know."

"We'll have to do something about that some time. After you've stopped smoking."

With that she climbed under the covers. For a moment he reflected on the faint lavender scent of her skin before wrapping her tightly in his arms.

* * * * *

When he awoke next morning the wind was still blowing. He gazed at Wendy who was sprawled on her back, her eyes closed, but her face was earnest in sleep as it mostly was when she was awake. What did she dream about, he wondered, Nicaragua?

"Nicaragua!" he said loudly. Wendy's eyes flickered. "Norway!" he shouted. She sat bolt upright and rubbed her eyes.

"What's the time?"

"Time for you to be getting out on the streets collecting," he grinned.

"Oh, My God, is it that late?" She sprang out of bed and grabbed her clothes off the chair. After they had made love the first time she had told him all about The Friends of South America. It was a serious organisation genuinely devoted to the cause of freedom in that part of the world. After they had made love a second time, she had wanted to know what his plans for the Norway section of the International Day display were. Then she had gone to sleep. He had been quite unable to sleep for hours, his mind grappling with a strange sense of dislocation. How violently he had come inside her both times, as if he had been storing it all up for decades (which he had, if the truth be known). She had been quite wild and lascivious, confirming his suspicion that beneath the skin of a Puritan there beat the heart of a sex maniac. Just as he had eventually been about to doze off, Wendy had started snoring. As instructed, he had pushed her onto her side. She had gone on snoring for what seemed like hours. He had then pulled her onto her other side, facing him, climbed over her for some odd reason and settled down with his back pressed against hers. She had stopped snoring. In the early hours of the morning she had woken up and whispered in his ear. Still awake, he had turned over. They had made love again, this time in a rather more leisurely fashion. Then they had both dropped off to sleep.

"Do you want some breakfast?"

"I don't know whether I've got time, Dryden. I hope the car starts."

He hopped out of bed and ran downstairs in the nude. Dancing about the kitchen he suddenly noticed a large troop of people arriving to visit the neighbours. He rushed to get his dressing-gown and bumped into Wendy at the bottom of the stairs.

"I think you might have lost a bit of weight already, Dryden," she giggled then glanced at her watch. "I think I ought to go." She turned towards the front door. "Don't stand in the draught," she said, then kissed him. "I'll give you a ring." She opened the front door and disappeared.

CHAPTER TWENTY-TWO

Arnold Scoresby was busily setting up the little wooden signs that said 'Welcome' in ten different languages along the verge of the school driveway when Dryden arrived. It was a perfect day, the wintry sunlight picking out small patches of frost here and there in the grounds. To Dryden's chagrin the Motts' car was already there, parked tidily in a corner. He parked his own car, untidily, a few spaces away and climbed the stairs to the Resources Room. It was a hive of activity.

"We're almost finished, Dryden," Christine smiled, kneading a lump of blue tack at him, as he wandered about contemplating the vast areas of wall he would have to cover. Along the corridors Internationalism beamed down at him from rows of bright posters depicting funicular railways in the Alps, vineyards in France, Mediterranean resorts and luxury hotels in Rio de Janeiro.

"I took the liberty of arranging the tables in your display room, Dryden." Stephen Mott's voice intoned from somewhere behind him. "We thought it best to have something in the middle for people to circulate around."

"Thanks," Dryden murmured. He dragged out a huge pile of sugar paper and set about gluing everything to everything else. The work he had finally persuaded some of his pupils to do was uninspiring at its very best. There were crooked outlines of Europe on which the Black Sea occupied most of Germany and Scandinavia had crossed the Atlantic, there were sketches of Baroque churches that resembled Canadian grain silos, lengthy discourses on European cultural monuments that were indecipherable and various other bits and pieces that had turned up for no apparent reason, such as a huge Chinese vase and an elephant's tusk. Attached to the latter was the scribbled note: 'Please be very careful with this as it belongs to my Grandad. Will collect it at three o'clock.' He deposited the tusk and the vase in the Resources Room.

"Come and look at our room," Christine Mott summoned him from the door. It was a wonder to behold. The French Studies section was in blue whilst the German Studies section was all green. These colours corresponded to the popular notion, perpetrated by map makers, that countries of the world had a distinctive hue. Britain was red, though of course of an entirely different shade from the sinister scarlet of the Soviet Union. Stephen Mott was putting the finishing touches to his display. It was immaculate. Each piece of sugar paper had been measured down to the last fraction of an inch so that it corresponded exactly to the next piece. Dryden returned to his room, utterly dejected.

From the outset it was clear that his display would look like a dog's breakfast. No matter how hard he tried he could never match the Mott's precision. Precision was inborn, as was scruffiness. Dryden was one of the scruffiest people in all England. Anything he attempted by way of decoration could not fail to reflect his inborn chaos. Half an hour later the Motts entered the European Studies room and stared triumphantly at the blank walls. By now Dryden had succeeded in gluing bits of his clothing to his own skin and somehow had managed to attach lumps of blue tack to the soles of his shoes. Perhaps, he thought bitterly, he should seriously consider putting himself up on the wall.

"Lot of work," he murmured lamely as the Motts watched him with a gleam of intense amusement in their eyes. Oh, this would be his undoing, they silently gloated. At last, he would be revealed for the incompetent charlatan he was. Parents would be scandalised, the Headmaster would be outraged and Pollock would be the laughing stock of the school.

"That's why we got here early," Stephen Mott smirked. "We're going out to have a drink now."

"Perhaps you'd like to join us later?" Christine smiled. ""The Hen and Pig?"

"Sure." Dryden nodded. "Could be a while though."

The Motts sailed out through the door. Dryden fancied he heard them tittering as they went downstairs. He was on the verge of one of his existentialist reveries, along the lines of his life hitherto leading him inexorably to this particular moment of cruel folly. Indeed, life, he reflected in moments of despair (such as now), thrust itself upon him day by day. Other people woke up in the morning ready to master the day's events. In Dryden's case, the day's events were lined up by the bed like horribly grinning ghouls waiting for him to regain consciousness.

He toiled on with bitter determination. Wendy would soon arrive to deal with Norway. He glanced across at the neat stack of Norwegiana under a table. Their night of passionate lovemaking had led to no great change in their relationship. The Monday morning after, Wendy had approached him in the staff common room, frowning.

"I'm very worried about Norway, Dryden," she had said sternly. "We've only got three days."

"How's Nicaragua?" he had grinned at her, believing she was pulling his leg.

"We did very well," she said. "But Norway's bothering me."

She had meant what she said. Norway was bothering her. He had wanted to shout at her that he couldn't give a fuck about Norway or Nicaragua or any other goddamned place or cause she was interested in. He wanted her to tell him that she loved him, that their night in the sack meant something to her, that it had heralded the beginning of a deep and meaningful relationship. But he had simply stared at her, his eyes watering.

"Have you got a cold?" she had asked solicitously.

"No," he had whispered. "Wendy—did you—enjoy Friday night?" She had nodded, sighed and walked off. What was that supposed to mean? He had considered pursuing her angrily across the staff common room but she had disappeared into the crowd before he had reached a decision. With a sinking heart he had realised that for Wendy their night of passionate lovemaking had simply been another daily event, like popping into the supermarket for a pound of marge or posting a letter or ringing the Gas Board. It had left him high and dry. He was helpless.

Getting someone to bed once was comparatively easy these days. Getting them to bed a second time could be like trying to walk up Mount Everest backwards. The whole mythology of romance was a hollow fiction, of course. In real life people did not fling themselves into one another's arms and rut like crazed buffalo until they collapsed, sated and exhausted. Not in England, anyway. They had sex in much the same way as they switched on the TV to watch the nine o'clock news. Then they got out of bed, showered, changed and trotted off to attend to their duties. Dryden had begun to suspect that far back in his family tree some evil foreigner had sneaked in, an Italian or a Frenchman or a Jew and had implanted romantic genes that had travelled down the generations to end up in a little clump in Dryden's psyche. There, they darted about mischievously, upsetting the stolid middle-class Anglo-Saxon genes that ought to have taught him that sex was purely a utilitarian business designed either to procreate or simply to relieve testicular and/or ovular pressure.

His incessant strivings in the European Studies room had yet again come to nought. His first attempt to affix some of the display to the walls failed. For some reason the sugar paper had curled up and stubbornly refused to remain on the wall for more than a few seconds. The whole lot swooped down on him, one of the Baroque grain silos sailing majestically away across the room. He retrieved it and doggedly set about re-gluing it to its sugar paper.

"Dryden?"

He looked up. Maurice Talbot was standing in the doorway. "A word, if I may?" Dryden followed him into the Resources Room. Talbot glanced at the huge Chinese vase and the elephant's tusk with a puzzled frown.

"Has the Head had a word with you?" Talbot's eyebrows rose a fraction to indicate that this was a question of vital importance.

"No."

"I see. Well—" Talbot coughed his short dry cough. "You probably realise that there are various changes in the offing—structural changes, I mean—within the faculty."

"Yes."

"The point is, Dryden, that—should a situation arise in which—shall we say—professional rivalries come into play—then certain parties will no doubt have things to say."

"You mean Christine and Stephen?"

There was a flash of horror in Talbot's eyes at Dryden's blunt reference to personal names. He coughed. "Possibly," he murmured. His voice dropped to a near whisper. "The Head, you see, is considering a number of alternatives, Dryden. He may reach a decision very soon."

"I see," Dryden shrugged. "So? It's his decision, Maurice. Whatever." His heart nevertheless sank at the thought. He knew what Talbot was trying to tell him. The Motts were about to be promoted and he, Dryden, was being prepared for it. Well, he thought nobly, he was prepared for it. It didn't need Talbot's avuncular and patronising intervention. Dryden Pollock was man enough to take the blow full on the chin when it came. The prospect of being bossed about by the ghastly Motts was, of course, infinitely depressing. But that was the way of the world, wasn't it? Mottism was on the march nationwide. Efficiency, dedication, commitment. The new Tory vision of the cosmos. The world was in reality no more than a massive computer. Input, output, results balance the books . . . Talbot smiled at him sympathetically, the smile, Dryden thought, of a prison chaplain accompanying a condemned man to the gallows.

"I suppose we've all got our axes to grind, haven't we?" Talbot mused smugly, from within his comfortable new envelope of managerial status and power.

"To be sure, Maurice," Dryden sulked. Give Dryden Pollock an axe and you would see some action.

"Good," Talbot said briskly. "You're obviously well aware of the implications then. I won't keep you any longer, Dryden. You've clearly got a lot left to do, haven't you?" And with an ironic smile, the deputy head designate slipped out of the door. Dryden suddenly realised that Talbot had been standing within an inch of the sharp end of the elephant's tusk. He tried to visualise a gigantic, enraged rogue elephant on its other end, stomping and trumpeting its way through the corridors of Great Battley.

He wandered out and halted in the doorway to the European Studies display room. Wendy was busily hauling her stack of Norwegiana out from under its table.

"Hello?" she smiled cheerfully. "Just arrived?"

"No. I've been here for some time actually." He maintained a mildly frost edge to his voice. He was wary, oh he was as wary as a cat in a den of tigers. Play her game, that was it. Nonchalance, indifference, cheery hello's and goodbye's and 'must rush—got to catch a train' sort of behaviour. No fuss, no bother, no tacky emotions to ruffle the smooth surface of everyday toddling along through life, getting things done.

"I bought an extra packet of blue tack. Thought we'd probably need it."

"Oh, good," Dryden said briskly. "I should think we probably will. You think of everything, don't you, Wendy?"

"I try," Wendy murmured absently. "I popped into the other display room. It's super, isn't it? Christine and Stephen have done a fantastic job, haven't they?"

Christine and Stephen, he thought. Wonderful. Super. Just the two most abhorrent human beings he had ever encountered. Wendy began gluing with brisk, professional efficiency. He glued, too, turning his back on her, determined to exclude her image from his mind. Here he was gluing bits of paper to other bits of paper while a few feet away, a woman he had made love to with all the pent up emotions of past decades was quietly and methodically gluing too. Wasn't life extraordinary!

"There. How does that look?" Wendy held up a square of sugar paper upon which she had glued a photograph of the Norwegian flag.

"Lovely," he murmured through clenched teeth.

"I'll print Norway here and then beside it Norge."

"Norge? What's that?"

"Norwegian for Norway."

"Oh. And what's Nicaraguan for Nicaragua?" he asked venomously.

"I've no idea," Wendy murmured dreamily, contemplating her flag.

By twelve-thirty Dryden had managed to stick up most of his display. It looked perfectly dreadful, like a collection of tatty concert posters on the walls of a disused underground station. He glanced at Norway. The Viking queen was busily putting the finishing touches to it. She stood back.

"There. That's done. How's your bit?" She turned round and stared at Dryden's handiwork. A fleeting expression of horror passed over her face but she quickly managed a smile.

"It'll do," he grumbled to himself. "It'll have to."

He downed scissors and glue and was reaching for his jacket preparatory to making off to the 'Spotted dog' when he heard voices out on the stairs.

"But you've seen what it's like, Maurice," Stephen drawled. "It's always been the same old story."

"Yes—well Stephen—I think we must allow the Head to make his own decision in these matters."

"I think we'd all like to see the situation clarified, Maurice. It's all been too sloppy round the edges for my liking. I know Christine's never been happy with it."

"I don't think anyone's been happy with it, Stephen, least of all the Head." Dryden caught a brief glimpse of the two of them as they disappeared into the Resources Room. The door closed firmly behind them. Talbot and Mott would go on, calmly discussing his downfall. The worst of it would be their magnanimity, their concern for what poor Dryden would be feeling once the 'situation had been clarified' i.e. the Motts had been promoted. Oh poor Dryden, he could imagine Christine murmuring, we must ease the blow as best we can. They would probably invite him to dinner and sit there smiling indulgently as he grew steadily more inebriated—finally they would guide him gently to the door, they would be so concerned that he got home safely. Charity would dictate that they offered him every opportunity to salvage some small part of his self-respect. What was it called—killing with kindness? All part of wanting to believe one could single-mindedly scramble up the ladder to status and wealth without 'hurting those less fortunately endowed than ourselves.' The caring middle class. Dryden thought darkly of the end of the elephant's tusk mere inches from either Talbot's or Mott's neatly clad posterior.

"Shall we go for a drink?" Wendy was at his elbow.

"If you like."

They left the display room and started downstairs. On the landing they met Christine Mott marching determinedly upstairs.

"Hello Christine," Wendy smiled. "Your display's terrific, isn't it?"

"Yes." Christine flashed a look of pity at Dryden. "We've put a lot of work into it."

"I'll say," Wendy beamed. "It's stunning."

Christine nodded triumphantly. Dryden experienced an almost overpowering urge to push Wendy headlong down the stairs.

"Isn't it, Dryden?" Wendy glowed at him. His hands itched for her throat. Instead he took her firmly by the elbow and hurried her down ahead of him.

"They're so professional." Wendy gushed as Dryden marched her across to his car.

"So beautifully done, isn't it?" She shook her head in rapt admiration beside him as they drove out through the school gates. "They're so committed," she announced as they pulled into the car park behind the 'Spotted Dog'.

"People say husband and wife teams in schools are a disaster, don't they?" But those two are fantastic," she shouted as Dryden propelled her violently towards the door of the saloon bar.

CHAPTER TWENTY-THREE

"But why, why?" Dryden stared at her, uncomprehending, a few moments later as the two of them sat at a table in the corner of the bar with their drinks. "I feel everything for you, Wendy. I don't care about Friday night in any other way than that it was the most glorious thing that's happened to me for years."

"But Dryden, I don't really feel I know you . . ."

"What the hell do you want? A formal introduction, Wendy? We've slept together for Christ's sake."

"There you go again. Sleeping together signifies so much, doesn't it?"

"Well, doesn't it? It used to. Time was sleeping together was the end of the story not the beginning."

"I thought you wanted it to be the beginning, Dryden. You said so just a few minutes ago. You can't have it both ways."

He stared out of the window. This was impossible. Wendy felt she didn't really know him. What kind of a statement was that?

"You don't want me, is that it?" He said it almost without thinking. His heart shrank to a tiny hard nut in his chest at the horror of those words.

"No—I mean no, I don't want you—No, yes, I mean I don't don't want you." Wendy said quietly.

"You don't don't want me?"

"I don't want to put a stop to it, Dryden, if you see what I mean."

"You want me?"

She took a long time to answer.

"I want to get to know you. Both of us to get to know one another. It all takes time, Dryden. We can't rush things."

"What do you want me to do then?"

"I don't want you to do anything. Just carry on as usual."

"How in hell can I carry on as usual when I'm in love with you, Wendy?"

"You're letting yourself be dominated by the idea of love, Dryden. Real love is knowledge. Not just sex." She glanced at her watch. "I think we ought to be getting back actually."

He was intoxicated by the time they arrived back at the school. He almost drove over a row of Arnold's welcome' signs. 'Välkommen, Bienvenu, Willkommen, Bienvenido' flattened in the mud. He slammed the car door to indicate some sort of emotion though he wasn't sure which. The corridors of Great Battley were now filling with people. Wearily he went upstairs fully expecting to be greeted by a triumphant Mott announcing that the Headmaster had reached a decision. He opened the door of the Resources Room and grimly contemplated the elephant's tusk on the table. A few yards' dash and it could all be over, he thought. What a stir that would cause. Indeed, there was something appealingly original in the idea of committing suicide on an elephant's tusk. Quite in keeping with his existence in its present shape, too. He heard Christine Mott's voice out on the stairs. He pulled the door of the Resources Room shut and hastened into the Motts' display room with a vague and desperate notion of sabotage in mind but his heart instantly sank at the sight of walls covered with an immaculately presented, punctiliously composed exhibition of pupils' work in French and German Studies. He peered at samples of essays, sketches and maps, beautifully written, perfectly executed—a testament to the Motts' unflagging quest for perfection in all things. How did they do it, he thought despairingly. Any idea of sabotage was ludicrous. Rather should he be on his knees, his hands clasped, his eyes upraised in awestruck contemplation of this shining altar of professional dedication. There was a rustle in the doorway behind him. It was Christine.

"I was just admiring . . ." he stammered, reddening guiltily.

"Yes, it looks good doesn't it?" She gave him an indulgent smile. "I think the parents will be pleased."

He shrank from the triumphant gleam in her eyes.

"Dryden?" Stephen Mott's voice drawled from out in the corridor. "Dryden? Oh there you are." Mott smirked in at him. "People are pouring into your room. You'd better go in and explain your display. They've been asking me all about it and I'm afraid I can't make head or tail of it."

Dryden hurried out and took up station in the European Studies display room. People were wandering about, gazing, bemused, at the walls. Dryden withdrew to a corner. Surely they would laugh.

Nathan Goldway appeared. "Aren't they ghastly?" he whispered, smirking at the parents. "Ambitious sods. The very pillars of social advantage and the meritocracy. Still, they're the ones with the bread, aren't they?"

"We should be on our knees in front of them, Goldway," Dryden murmured bitterly. "Our fate is in their hands."

"Excuse me, are you a master here?" A large man in an immaculate safari suit was steaming towards them. Goldway fled.

"Yes," Dryden smiled obsequiously.

"My wife and I are very interested in your European Studies programme. We're both committed Europeanists. Actually I spend most of my time in Brussels these days. My business is Europe-wide, you see. I speak French, German, Spanish and Italian fluently."

My, my, Dryden thought. He had seen this type before. They were a brand new version of middle-class Englishmen, a tribe of business people who worked in 'international' concerns and prided themselves on their cosmopolitan outlook and their cultural pretensions. Their ultimate goal in life was to go to Bayreuth for the Wagner festival or to Salzburg for the Mozart festival and spend the remaining years of their allotted span telling everyone all about it. The man's wife sailed up, a beautifully dressed corpse, her skin glowing eerily with cosmetic applications, her dyed hair perfectly waved. Dryden was enveloped in a cloud of deodorant and mouthwash which was the new European style.

"Vous êtes professeur?" She leered at him. "Lehrer? Insegnante?"

"Yes," Dryden said to all three. Oh Jesus and Holy Mary she was going to speak to him in a foreign tongue or a combination thereof. She studied him out of cold, grey eyes. Clearly making up her mind which tongue to use.

"You don't do anything on Provence, do you?" The man frowned. "Or the Rheingau?"

"Not specifically, no."

"Pity. I think those are two areas of Europe I would have singled out as regions of supreme cultural interest. Still, I suppose one is spoilt for choice really. But why Norway?"

Dryden took a deep breath.

"We chose Norway because of its unique geographical features. It has a severely indented coastline."

They considered this gravely for a moment. Surely, he was pulling their leg?

"I see," the man said finally, looking Dryden up and down as if he had just caught him weeing in a public place. He walked off with his doll-like wife. A moment later they were examining sketches of Baroque grain silos with all the concentration of art critics studying Botticelli Madonnas.

The crowd circulated, moving balletically like extras in the film sequence of a grand Victory Ball after the Battle of Waterloo. Goldway was right. They were ghastly. They exuded arrogance and superiority through the very pores of their highly polished skin.

Suddenly a tall, spare figure loomed out of the crowd.

"Dryden," Talbot beamed. "I'd like you to meet the Right

Honourable Simon Frobisher and his wife Frieda."

"How do you do." Mr. Frobisher extended his hand and smiled. "Fabulous display. Fabulous school. We do admire the work you people do, you know."

"I'm German." Mrs. Frobisher bared her teeth. "My husband is the European Member of Parliament for zis area, you know." Dryden smiled and nodded.

"Splendid work. Splendid place altogether." The Right Honourable gentleman murmured.

"And you are responsible for zis?" Frau Frobisher waved her hand round the room."

"For most of it," Dryden said.

"Your European Studies programme is very interesting, may I say. Very interesting. But puzzling, too, for a German. As you know, we are very committed to ze idea of European avareness and we have tried to inculcate such an avareness in our German schools. I find ze combination of topics as revealed in zis display somevat confusing, however. Your pupils study Norway—Baroque culture and Rumania? Can you tell me why, please?"

For the next few minutes Dryden rambled on, noting with alarm that the Euro. M.P. seemed to have fallen asleep on his feet.

"Wonderful display. Superb. Excellent work," Mr. Frobisher murmured dreamily when Dryden had stopped. Frau Frobisher regarded Dryden doubtfully, her precise Teutonic intellect beaming a pure light through every one of Dryden's transparent phrases. Surely, she'd been in England long enough to accept English humbug, he thought apprehensively. The charm of an institution like Great Battley lay in its transparent absurdity. But no, Germans could never leave well enough alone, could they? They were born correctors, born to be mentors to every other tribe on the face of the earth. And they were never wrong.

"But vat have Norway, Baroque culture and Rumania in common?" Frau Frobisher persisted. "Apart from being in zis part of the world. What is the leitmotif in zis whole study programme? You understand ze word leitmotif, of course?"

"In reality, it's designed as no more than a brief glimpse of the European world beyond our shores," Dryden burbled frantically. "A bit of everything."

"You're telling me," Frau Frobisher's mouth turned down at the corners. "In Germany, I sink we would do things qvite differently. More coherence, more consequential, I think. Zis seems to me razzer amateurish, if you don't mind my saying so."

Dryden suppressed an urge to giggle at her inanely. The wretched woman was taking it all deadly seriously. He wanted to take her aside and explain to her that the secret of events of this kind in dear old Blighty was that they were not to be taken seriously. They were gestures. The British were magnificent practitioners of the art of solemn gesturing. All the while, behind the facades, people giggled nervously like schoolgirls who'd just found a used condom on the hockey pitch. That was really what this was all about. Alas, Frieda Frobisher was an upright, ramrod stiff Teutonic missionary whose piercing, frighteningly earnest intellect would never accept the glorious sham of British pretension.

"Truly inspiring. I've never seen anything like it," her husband murmured as he drifted away into the crowd. "Impressive," he mused, as his German wife steered him determinedly towards the door.

Dryden glanced across at Wendy who was enthusiastically holding forth to a collection of people in front of Norway. He could imagine her doing the same for Nicaragua on behalf of her new found organisation, The Friends of South America. Would there ever be an organisation he could join wholeheartedly, Dryden wondered mournfully. Would he ever be able to hold forth like Wendy on behalf of something or other he passionately believed in? In a strange sort of way he envied her her commitment. Committing oneself to organisations was certainly a whole lot easier than committing oneself to a person as he was finding out. If only she would glance across at him and smile. But then there was no shared secret of love to smile about, was there?

In came the Headmaster, his face drawn in a nervous smile. He nodded at people here and there and then drifted into conversation with the committed Europeanists. Beneath that slightly shabby, paunchy suit was a man, Dryden reflected, who might be far happier teaching little boys how to hold golf clubs or glue together a model aeroplane, yet here he was battling furiously with the English language in front of a pair of truly abhorent middle-class ciphers. What an extraordinary world it was. Goldway's beaky nose appeared in the doorway momentarily then vanished when it got wind of Basil's presence in the room. The committed Europeanists detached themselves from Basil who, suddenly finding himself adrift in a frightening sea of faces, now looked round frantically for a port of call. He saw Dryden.

"Hello, Dryden. How's it all going?"

"Fine, Headmaster."

"Have the Frobishers been in?"

"Yes, just a few minutes ago."

Basil gazed absently round the room, seemingly oblivious to the dreadfulness of it all. Little knots of glossily-clad people standing sharing their bewilderment at the sheer incoherence of European Studies, ranging as it did from the mountain fastness of Norway to the broad plains of Rumania.

"Splendid work, Dryden," the Headmaster suddenly beamed. "Very—as it were—thought-provoking." And with a brief, shy smile he wandered away, then suddenly discovering he was not heading for the door as he had presumably intended, he wandered back again giving Dryden another brief smile as he passed. How lonely life was at the top,

Dryden thought. Basil stopped suddenly and stared fixedly at the floor. Then he stooped, picked up a small crumpled piece of paper, the wrapping from a chocolate bar, examined it quizzically, looked round for a suitable receptacle, found none and promptly pocketed his find. Just as he was about to go through the door, he was accosted by one of the crowd. Dryden watched, amused, as Basil backed away towards the wall, looking for all the world like a prisoner of conscience who was about to have the soles of his feet belaboured with a baseball bat. The Headmaster's back encountered the edge of a large area of sugar paper displaying various minor works of art on the topic of Rumania, notably a long rambling essay on Count Dracula's castle. Over the years Count Dracula had become the focus of teaching on Rumania. Rumania was remembered as the home of Count Dracula. Basil's interlocutor moved off. Basil took a step forward. Suddenly, Dryden saw that part of the Rumanian display had detached itself from the wall and attached itself to the back of the Headmaster's jacket. Horrified, he involuntarily called out but it was too late. The Headmaster was halfway through the door before he realised. He swung round. Dryden leapt at him, catching the piece of sugar paper as the pieces of blue tack came away with it.

"Oh," Basil exclaimed. "Have you got it?"

"Yes."

"My fault. I shouldn't have leant against the wall, should I?" The Headmaster gave a sheepish grin and vanished down the stairs. Dryden returned with the sugar paper, was about to replace it when he suddenly noticed that the whole display was sagging ominously, threatening at any moment to curl outwards over the heads of the crowd like a tidal wave. Panic-stricken he rushed the length of the wall, his hands going in all directions, his palms pressing for dear life against the wall. The crowd fell back. There was a lull in the conversation. Then Wendy had crossed the room and was spreadeagled at one end of the display.

"It's all coming down, Dryden," she shrieked. Dryden closed his eyes. With a faint whoosh the laboriously blue-tacked mass of sugar paper descended. Dryden opened his eyes. The room had gone dark. He heard laughter.

"Norway's falling now," Wendy suddenly yelled. There was another gentle whoosh. More laughter. Dryden removed the large portion of the display that had fallen down over his head and surveyed the devastation.

"It's the heat, mate," a voice called. "It melts the blue tack."

The crowd was filing out of the room. Pieces of the display had attached themselves to one or two people who fought to remove them from their clothing. Within minutes the room was empty.

"Oh hell!" Dryden swore bitterly. "What a balls-up."

""It's a mess, isn't it?" Wendy shrugged. "Ruined."

"What shall we do?"

They stared helplessly at the wreckage for a minute or two. Wendy glanced at her watch.

"It's almost finishing time anyway, isn't it?" She surveyed the scene grimly. "Let's just throw it all away, shall we?"

Their eyes met. Dryden grinned. "Let's," he said. They shut the door and began gathering up the debris. A few minutes later the door opened. The Motts had heard what had happened. They marched in and stared, grinning, at the chaos of sugar paper and sellotape and blue tack strewn over the floor.

"That's why we stapled ours to the wall," Stephen drawled triumphantly. "Blue tack tends to melt in the heat."

"Sellotape's no better," Christine pursed her lips. "The Head was here when it happened, was he?"

"No." Dryden shook his head. "He'd gone."

"That was lucky." The Motts exchanged meaningful glances. "He'd have been furious. He was very complimentary when he came into us wasn't he, Christine?"

"Very," Christine nodded. "So he should be too. We put a lot of work into it."

With one last contemptuous smile at the remains of the European Studies display they turned on their heels and walked out of the room.

Dryden and Wendy began to giggle. Then they laughed. Soon they were laughing until the tears rolled down their cheeks. When, a short while later, the door opened and an agitated voice informed them that all the international posters along the corridor outside had now fallen down, they shrieked with laughter. Nathan Goldway came in and stared, astonished at the two of them standing amidst the debris, howling with laughter. Then the three of them were laughing, hopping round the room, clutching their aching sides. They laughed and laughed until they could do no more than kneel on the floor surrounded by sugar paper, blue tack, sellotape, by essays on European cultural monuments, essays on Count Dracula, on Norway's indented coastline, surrounded by phantasmagorical maps of Europe and sketches of Baroque grain silos, fully expecting that they would all die laughing.

The door opened.

"Dryden?"

A few seconds elapsed before they noticed the Headmaster standing in the doorway contemplating the scene with an embarrassed smile. Dryden leapt to his feet and snapped to attention.

"Do you think?—I know how busy you must be at this precise moment in time and I can see that there's a great deal to be done . . ." Basil glanced nervously round the room. A good part of the European Studies display was now contained in a row of bin liners bulging along one wall . . ." ". . . but could you possibly spare a few minutes for a quiet chat in my office?"

There was a moment or two of ominous silence. Dryden had gone pale.

"Of course, Headmaster." He nodded abjectly and followed Basil out of the door and down the stairs at a discreet distance. This was it, he thought grimly. Someone had told the Head all about it. Parents had been outraged. The Motts had denounced him. He had made a complete mockery of Great Battley's International Day. The Headmaster was incensed. Dryden would be stripped of his stars as Assistant Co-ordinator of European Studies and relegated to the rank of nameless private in the great army of State Education.

Basil led the way into his study and closed the door firmly behind them. He pointed to a chair. Dryden sat down. His palms were sweating. The Headmaster went to the window and drew the curtains. Then he sat down behind his desk and unplugged the gadget that worked the 'Engaged' and 'Not Engaged' lights outside the door. Dryden watched all this fearfully. The Head was intending to murder him.

"Sorry about all this, Dryden. Just a few precautions." Basil leaned over his desk. He coughed, cleared his throat and began to speak in a low monotone. "As you are no doubt aware—since it has indeed become public knowledge—a new management structure has been in the throes of evolving . . ." Dryden listened tensely, making a supreme effort to disentangle the clauses in Basil's lengthy peroration on the new management structure. Clearly, it was the introduction to the reading of a death sentence of some kind, resembling, as it did, the preamble of a High Court Judge. Basil had donned the black cap. Dryden grew more and more fearful as the Headmaster went on and on, his gaze flickering round the room, resting for an instant on Dryden's frightened face before directing itself at a chair or at the window-sill. The suspense was dreadful.

". . . and so within the contextual ramifications of these alterations in the essential structural nature of management parameters, I am prepared to institute a re-alignment in your position within the faculty." Here the Headmaster paused, reading the effect of this on Dryden's face. Utterly confused, Dryden nodded dumbly. He closed his eyes for an instant. After all, what did it matter? The Motts were right. They had put a lot of work into it. For two years they had worked assiduously towards this goal. They had dedicated themselves to promotion, given more than ample proof of their competence and commitment. They deserved to be rewarded. Dryden Pollock was a layabout, a representative of an old corrupt order. It was only right he should be demoted.

"I have already been in consultational contact with County in order to pre-arrange the appropriate re-adjustment of your remuneration . . ." Basil droned. Dryden nodded dumbly. The Headmaster leaned across the table towards him with an air of anxiety. "In the interests of staff morale, Dryden, notwithstanding that it will shortly be generally known that your position has—so to speak—been re-appraised, I would

173

ask you to exercise the utmost discretion in this matter for the foreseeable future . . ." Again, Dryden nodded dumbly. Discretion. Don't rock the boat, Pollock. Keep your demotion or rather the 're-appraisal of your position' under your hat, for your own sake and that of your colleagues. People didn't like to think it was still possible to be demoted. Promotion was the only acceptable course for anyone's career. Upwards, ever upwards.

"Well, Dryden," the Headmaster smiled shyly. "I won't keep you. I'm sure that you are aware of just how your expectations, and, of course, those of our parents who favoured us with their attendance this afternoon were more than adequately fulfilled." Basil stood up abruptly. "And I'll let you know officially just as soon as I hear from County."

Dryden got to his feet, tiredly. He nodded. He knew he should be asking a lot of angry questions, protesting, fighting for his career but he hadn't really understood a word of what Basil had been saying, and even in this moment of humiliation good manners prevented him from admitting it. His mother had always taught him it was the height of vulgarity to question openly what people in authority said, no matter how mysterious and incomprehensible. That sort of behaviour made one unpopular. The Headmaster drew back the curtains, plugged in his gadget and began dialling a number on the telephone. Dryden slipped mournfully out of the door and retreated upstairs.

"What did he say?" Wendy gazed at him anxiously.

"I don't really know," Dryden murmured, bewildered. "But I think I'm being demoted."

"Oh, Dryden," Wendy came close to him and put her hand on his arm. "I'm sorry."

"It's not your fault," he shrugged. "I deserve it, I suppose."

"You need someone to look after you," she murmured. "Don't you?"

Suddenly, from out on the stairs came the sound of furious shouting. Wendy's mouth dropped open. Maurice Talbot and Stephen Mott were having a violent argument. Bit by bit the dispute travelled upstairs. It seemed as if Talbot was trying to pour oil on very troubled waters for Stephen Mott was in a towering fury. Dryden and Wendy caught a brief glimpse of the deputy head designate backing into the Resources Room before an enraged Mott. The door slammed shut.

"What was all that about?" Wendy whispered. Her eyes were as round as saucers.

"God knows." Dryden shook his head.

"Perhaps we should go."

He nodded. They left the display room and started down the stairs. On the landing a tearful Christine Mott stared up at them. Wendy halted in astonishment.

"Christine. For Heaven's sake. What's wrong?"

Christine pointed at Dryden. "Ask him," she screamed. "Ask him, why don't you? It's disgraceful. After all we've done. All the time we've put in. And all he's ever done is sit round smoking and sneering. Oh, it's absurd. We're going to Germany." She burst into tears, turned and rushed away down the stairs. Dryden was bright red. Wendy was staring at him in alarm.

"What have you done?"

"I don't know—what she's talking about. . ." he stammered, aghast. "I've no idea."

"She's terribly upset, poor thing. It's awful," Wendy murmured.

At that moment the door of the Resources Room flew open. Stephen Mott appeared at the top of the stairs, his face contorted with rage.

"Damn you, Pollock," he shouted. "Damn your hide. In all my career I've never known anything like it. Damn you, damn you, damn you."

Talbot was at Mott's side, apparently trying to restrain him from flinging himself downstairs to seize Dryden by the throat.

"Fuck off, Pollock," Mott screamed. "Fuck off to your pub, you lazy good-for-nothing bastard."

"Stephen . . ." Talbot began helplessly.

"Fuck off!" Mott howled.

"My God" Wendy's eyes were like dinner-plates. "Dryden, what have you done?"

Dryden was transfixed. The Motts had gone berserk. Why, Why?

"Stephen, please . . ." Talbot pleaded. "Come in and let's talk about it. Please." He glanced down at Dryden, with a look of appeal, his eyes telling the latter to disappear. Dryden hurried away down the stairs. At that moment it had struck him like a bolt out of the blue. Of course. He'd been promoted.

* * * * *

Wendy caught up with him in the carpark, his mind was a whirl of bluetack, sugarpaper, Mott's violent abuse and Basil's extra-ordinary, inexplicable decision. Promotion? The word had a liturgical ring to it— like 'apostolic', like 'divinity', like 'holy communion'. Promotion! He, Dryden Pollock, was being promoted! He unlocked the door of the Viva and glanced at Wendy across its rusting blue roof. "You need someone to look after you!" her voice repeated in his mind, the phrases suddenly shouldering their way to the front past Mott's terrible imprecations and Basil's unfathomable verbiage. "Don't you?"

"Yes, you." He answered her soundlessly.

"Wendy" he heard himself say. His voice sounded feeble and plaintive. "Will you marry me?"

"Yes." She nodded, smiling. "I will."

CHAPTER TWENTY-FOUR

"Congratulations, old chap," Goldway murmured, next morning as they met in front of the staff common room notice board. Dryden looked round fearfully.

"How did you find out?"

Goldway tapped the side of his nose. "Mum's the word, I see. Fear not, Pollock, your secret's safe with me. I gather it's not a universally approved promotion."

"No," Dryden shrugged. "There were scenes."

Goldway winked. "I heard. Sounded an absolute hoot."

Dryden was incredulous. "How in hell?—Who told you, for God's sake?"

"One of the cleaning women saw Christine Mott storming into Basil's office. She told the caretaker who came and told me."

"The caretaker told you?"

"He gave me a full report."

"Goldway, is there no limit to your web of intrigue and espionage?"

"None whatsoever. Mott, you know, drove home in a towering fury and took to his bed."

"Really?" Dryden's tone was sarcastic. "You don't happen to know what his average speed for the journey was or what his temperature was at nine o'clock yesterday evening, do you?"

"No."

"You'll no doubt be getting a full report though?"

"No doubt." Goldway executed a dance step or two in front of the notice-board.

"I still don't know what to make of it all," Dryden sighed.

"It's a bit of a shock, isn't it?" Goldway murmured. "I wouldn't get up-tight about it though. So what if you're the laziest, most incompetent no-hoper that's ever graced the British teaching profession? It was Basil's decision and that's all that counts."

The previous evening Dryden had lain awake for hours in a state

177

alternating between a vicious euphoric glee at the Mott's total annihilation and a gnawing anxiety at what he perceived to be a catastrophic mistake on Basil's part.

"Not that that explains it, of course," Goldway went on. "I wouldn't have promoted you for all the tea in China."

"Thanks," Dryden grinned. "I suppose you would have promoted Mott, would you?"

"Good God no," Goldway chuckled evilly. "That'd be like appointing Oswald Moseley Ambassador to Israel, old boy. Mind you—come to think of it—no, forget I said that. No, I think, faced with the choice between a Mott and your dear self, Basil decided you were the lesser of the two evils."

The lesser of the two evils? Somehow Dryden doubted it. No, it was much simpler than that, he was sure. Basil was the sort of chap who believed that the next one on the list was the next one to promote. If the next one on the list had been a grasshopper or a tsetse fly Basil would have promptly promoted it. The Motts had been working on the teacher's pet theory. Bring Sir an apple a day and sooner or later you'll be rewarded. But Basil never noticed apples. The Motts' fanatical campaign of self-promotion had been entirely beyond the headmaster's understanding. Dear old Basil, Dryden thought. He was as straight as a die, awesomely oblivious to subordinates ingratiating themselves as any Englishman could be. God bless Basil!

Two days later Dryden's promotion to the post of Acting Co-ordinator of European Studies was posted officially. It caused something of a stir to say the least. News of the debacle of his display had spread like wildfire. People had expected him to be pilloried. Now they were told he had been promoted. There was a lot of baring of teeth as hands were extended in congratulation. Dryden remembered to be gracious at all times, however. To outsiders, of course, the difference between his old title and his new one was utterly meaningless. But within the confines of Great Battley there was a vast gulf between them. He had begun to wonder when he would feel the first twinge of hauteur.

"Congratulations, Pollock." Reg Devereaux, recently appointed Senior Adviser on Interdisciplinary something or other held out his hand.

"Thanks Reg. The same," Dryden smiled back, with some difficulty, since Devereaux's pursuit of Wendy continued unabated. He seemed totally oblivious to the fact that she was now someone else's bride-to-be. Dryden had concluded that Devereaux lived and thought without any principles whatsoever, he acted in complete accordance with whatever notion came into his head at any given moment. This had taken him quite a long way in life already. Dryden could only hope that Devereaux's incipient interest in a new young woman in the English Studies' Faculty might eventually wean him away from Wendy.

The Motts did not congratulate him. They now communicated with Dryden entirely through memos. Whenever he appeared in person they stalked off bitterly in the other direction, their eyes gleaming with an intense hatred. They would never forgive him. He had toyed with the idea of a conciliatory invitation to his grubby little terraced house for a dinner of Coca Cola and cold pizza but had decided that that would add too much insult to too much injury. They preferred to remain convinced he was some kind of Machiavellian schemer who all the while had been quietly and deviously engineering his own advancement. Maybe it was easier for them that way. After all, if they knew the truth they'd pack their bags and emigrate immediately. Nor could he really blame them, Dryden reflected. Perhaps, somewhere out there in the big wide world there was an ideal state, a sort of pristine neo-Georgian paradise, a Mott utopia where virtue was unfailingly rewarded and things ran like clockwork. Far, far away from dear old Blighty, of course.

"Well, mate, I dunno. You know what they say about husband and wife teams in the same school," Rosie frowned, by way of a comment on the announcement of Dryden's forthcoming marriage to Wendy.

"Maybe we'll both retire," Dryden grinned. "Go and grow cabbages or something."

"You'll do no such thing." Rosie feigned professional indignation. "The Head's just promoted you. You're supposed to be committed. You can't just up sticks and take off. Besides, as you well know, there are plenty of people out there waiting to step into your shoes. They queue up to work here."

Dryden grinned nervously at the word 'committed'. Alarmingly enough he had already felt moved to become a might less incompetent. Was he even now taking the first steps along the path to professional dedication? He had already found himself inspecting the files in the top draw of the cabinet up in the Resources Room. The rows of immaculate manilla folders, all carefully labelled and colour-coded, had somehow seemed less distasteful. Was it because they were now his files? He had thought of the incident of the shrivelled banana skin. Would he, too, find himself sternly reproaching a junior colleague one day for committing a similar outrage? The possibility disturbed him. The system, such as it was, certainly had its own ways of dealing with his sort, i.e. the badly educated, incompetent, guilt-ridden and disaffected middle class layabout. It promoted them.

And in time, one suspected, the disaffected themselves became the champions of the system, however much they went on sniggering about it in private.

As the term drew to a close the Headmaster's Campaign against litter gradually fizzled out, betrayed by the caretaking staff, the teaching staff and overwhelmed by the fresh tides of rubbish that swept remorselessly in from the great wide world beyond the confines of Great Battley. Once more, sweet papers had begun to accumulate in dusty little heaps around the corridors, tin cans rolled merrily along the paths in the breeze and iced lolly sticks cemented themselves to the shoe-soles of the staff and pupils alike. The lists of 'task forces', the weekly 'litter logs' and Arnold's elaborate and mostly unworkable 'flow charts' were themselves consigned to the bin. Everyone heaved a quiet, if private, sigh of relief.

At term's end there was a party. Bloxham who was leaving got horribly drunk and was seen making lewd advances to Nerys Hughes, the Head of Things Domestic. No-one actually saw her repulse them. Dryden and Wendy were showered with best wishes for the future and presented with a giant silver soup tureen and a ladle. At five o'clock on that dull, grey overcast December afternoon just as the party reached its climax of drunken hilarity, someone reported that it had just been announced from Number Ten Downing Street that Great Britain was now in an official state of war with the Central American Republic of Guatemala.

"Not again?" came a loud, drunken voice.

"Where is Guatemala?" someone enquired.

An arm flapped vaguely in a westerly direction. "Out there somewhere. North of the Falklands."

"Just a little dot on the map."

"Why are we at war with it?"

Shoulders were shrugged. Hands reached for the bottles (Tesco's Red).

"Why are we at war with this place Guatemala?" the same voice persisted. No-one would say. A fresh-faced young man eyed Dryden and Wendy's soup tureen. His face suddenly turned pale and he lunged towards the table. "Oh, migod," Wendy shrieked. A pair of hands grasped the young man by the shoulders and led him away.

"Why are we at war with Guatemala?" the voice insistent, could be heard travelling round among the crowd. No-one seemed to be taking the slightest bit of notice.

"Will someone please tell me?" the voice sounded desperate. "Please tell me. Why are we at war with Guatemala?"

CHAPTER TWENTY-FIVE

"Dryden, they're making me nervous, swerving about like that."

"It's just their idea of a laugh, Wendy. Don't worry about it. They don't mean any harm."

They had caught up with them soon after joining the motorway. There seemed to be hundreds of them, dressed in leather, some with large white swastikas emblazoned on the back of their jackets, others with skulls and crossbones, with Union Jacks, with stars or with clenched fists, a vast horde of motorcyclists sweeping up the motorway like a swarm of angry wasps. At first Dryden had slowed down, imagining they would pull ahead of him. Instead they had closed in on his decrepit Viva, forming a phalanx around it, every now and then a face visible beneath a bright blue or red helmet. One youth had brought his machine in so close to the car, his arm was mere inches from the window. Dryden had hung on to the steering wheel for dear life. One false move, he knew, and they would send him off the road. Over on the opposite side of the motorway, the traffic whizzed past unhindered, nor did the swarm of motorcyclists make any move to interfere with the traffic in the fast lane. They just rode along with Dryden's Viva in their midst, every now and then swerving back and forth dangerously in front of it.

"'If only we'd left later or earlier we might have avoided all this," Wendy muttered beside him. They had been down at Harry and Sue's for the weekend. To Dryden's sheer amazement Sue had been extraordinarily hospitable. She had cooked sumptuous meals, they had drunk excellent French wines, while the guest room, now decorated and furnished with a brand new double bed, had been warm and cosy. She had taken Wendy out shopping and chatted to her for hours, and then been the soul of charm and wit at the dinner table. She had even permitted Dryden to smoke. Naturally Wendy had been enchanted. Such hospitable, unassuming people, she had declared. Dryden had said nothing. He had guessed that the change had something to do with his getting married. Marriage was stable and respectable. In Sue's mind, it would finally make a man of him.

"How long is this going to go on for?" Wendy stared stonily out of the window. He reached over and patted her knee reassuringly.

"They won't be going to Winkworth, I shouldn't think," he said. They were doubtless on their way to the coast for the heavy metal jamboree. The police, too, were massing in their hundreds, expecting another riot.

One of the riders had moved in close. He mouthed something at Dryden and grinned. Beneath the helmet Dryden saw a pair of sharp, amused eyes watching him. The youth rubbed his forefinger against the side of his nose. Dryden frowned and shrugged.

"Dryden, look out!" Wendy suddenly shrieked. The Viva had swung to the left and was heading for the hard shoulder. He pulled at the wheel and glared out at the youth who promptly threw back his head and laughed. There was something anarchic about that laugh. In spite of himself, Dryden grinned.

"Hooligans," Wendy raged. "Perhaps someone will call the police, seeing us trapped like this."

The youth was mouthing something again. He had taken both hands off his bike and was rubbing his forefinger through a circle formed by the thumb and forefinger of his other hand. Dryden went red and grinned. The young lout pulled away and took up a position a few feet further on. They were travelling at a steady forty miles an hour and still the bikes showed no sign of releasing the Viva from their midst.

"Oh this is ridiculous," Wendy fumed. "Who are these kids?"

Dryden shrugged. "I don't know. Just kids."

"I suppose they're probaby one of these gangs that have been in the papers," Wendy said venomously. "Rioters. Hooligans."

"I guess so."

"Like that mob at Tintagel. Dryden, what about sounding the horn at them?"

"It doesn't work, Wendy, and even if it did, I don't think they'd move."

"Isn't it illegal to have a horn that doesn't work?"

"I suppose so," Dryden sighed. "The car's slowly falling to bits anyhow."

Wendy stiffened in irritation in the seat beside him. "Honestly, Dryden, sometimes I wonder how on earth you get away with it. You're so lackadaizical."

"'Cept where you're concerned, sweetheart." He grinned at her.

* * * * *

Suddenly they were gone, pulling away from them at astonishing speed. The youth who had mouthed at him, turned, grinned, waved and gunned his engine violently before streaking off into the distance. Within minutes the whole vast swarm was no more than a cluster of tiny black specks on the horizon.

"Thank God for that," Wendy sighed. "What an uncomfortable experience."

Dryden pushed the Viva up to sixty. It began to shake violently. Laughing silently to himself he dropped to forty-five. The motorcyclists had vanished. A short while later he had dropped Wendy back at her flat and drove home, feeling strangely exhilarated, as if for a moment, admidst the oppressive clutter of houses, streets, traffic and motorways, a wild, sunlit vista of untamed mountains and broad, sweeping valleys had opened up before his eyes.